"Don't worry. It'll be all right."

Donnelly's voice was filled with remorse as he lifted her gently in his arms.

The cold weakness that had swept over Carole receded quickly once he began to climb the stairs with her in the cradle of his arms. Laying her head against his chest, she said, "I'm okay."

"Sure," Donnelly agreed, continuing up the stairs and into the living room. Gently he laid her on the couch and sat next to her, holding her hand against his chest as he smoothed her hair. "Has anyone ever told you you're very beautiful when you're about to pass out?" He smiled down at her, continuing to trace the curves of her face. "You're more beautiful every time I see you. And if I weren't afraid you'd faint, I'd show you how much I've missed you."

Carole lifted her free hand to his shoulder. "Risk it," she said in a voice that was suddenly much stronger.

Dear Reader:

A writer's first book often portrays her homeland. And why not? In school we were all taught to write about what we know best. For five of Silhouette's most innovative writers, Oklahoma is more than home: Oklahoma is the blood that runs in their veins. Ada Steward, author of two Special Editions about this pioneer state, writes that Oklahoma is "a land and people still untamed beneath their veneer of civilization."

Starting with February 1986, Silhouette Special Edition is featuring the AMERICAN TRIBUTE—a tribute to America, where romance has never been so good. For six consecutive months, one out of every six Special Editions is an episode in the AMERICAN TRIBUTE, a portrait of the lives of six women, all from Oklahoma. AMERICAN TRIBUTE features some of your favorite authors—Ada Steward, Jeanne Stephens, Gena Dalton, Elaine Camp and Renee Roszel. You'll know the AMERICAN TRIBUTE by its patriotic stripe under the Silhouette Special Edition border.

AMERICAN TRIBUTE—six women, six stories.

AMERICAN TRIBUTE—one of the reasons Silhouette Special Edition is just that—special.

The Editors at Silhouette Books

AMERICAN TRIBUTE

ADA STEWARD
Misty Mornings, Magic Nights

Silhouette Special Edition

Published by Silhouette Books New York

America's Publisher of Contemporary Romance

SILHOUETTE BOOKS
300 East 42nd St., New York, N.Y. 10017

ISBN: 0-373-09319-5

First Silhouette Books printing July 1986

Printed in the U.S.A.

Where a man's dreams count for more than his parentage . . .

ADA STEWARD

creates her stories with a special magic that combines the richness of experience and history with new places and people. Mixing those elements together with a few what ifs, Ada watches the yesterdays, todays and tomorrows of her new stories come together. To her, she's not just writing fiction, but telling a story that *could* happen, if you really believe in romance.

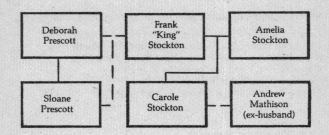

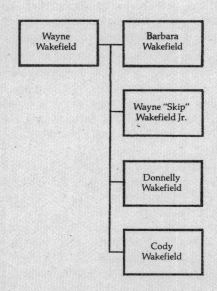

Chapter One

The steady dripping of rain against the window nudged Carole awake. Without opening her eyes, she curled deeper under her covers and listened to the peaceful sound. It was Saturday—she smiled as she remembered, relieved that this day was her own. Eagerness pushed aside the sleepy cobwebs that clouded her mind and, before she could stop them, her eyes opened, seeking the soft gray of the morning outside her bedroom window.

With a contented sigh, Carole tossed aside her covers and slipped out of bed. Her bare feet were silent on the thick carpet as she went to pull back the sheer draperies that blurred the watercolor shades of the day.

Across the rooftops of neighboring town houses, the Arkansas River wound dark and misty just below the horizon. It was a lazy morning, and Carole felt in no hurry to begin her daily jog along the riverbank. On the lawn below, dozens of small, fat birds pecked at the wet grass, their dark feathers fluffed against the rain as they fed happily on the morning's bounty.

Her hand let the curtain fall closed, then continued upward in a stretch. Reaching balled fists heavenward, Carole curled first toward one side and then toward the other, again and again. The pleasant tug of taut muscles gradually relaxed as she stretched, leaning farther with each arc. Smoothly she swung forward till her palms were flat on the floor and her back arched. The stiffness disappeared. Straightening, she released another healthy yawn just as the phone began to ring in her work area across the hall.

With a glance at the clock, Carole sighed. "Seven-thirty in the morning," she groaned, reluctant to let the world intrude so soon after waking. "Who could be calling so early?"

Passing her desk, she lifted the receiver, then curled into the corner of a pillow-strewn love seat. Next to her was a tall, narrow window that allowed the morning's muted glow to softly light the alcove. "Hello," she said, her groggy voice halfway between a sigh and a whisper.

"Carole?" a deep voice growled in her ear. "Don't tell me you weren't up yet."

She relaxed into the soft cushions with a sleepy, grudging smile. "Good morning, Daddy. I should have known it would be you." The peace of the day clung to her. Instead of the antagonism her father so often aroused in her, Carole felt only good-natured resignation and a mild curiosity. Her father wasn't one for small talk, and the chances of this being a social call were very slim.

In front of her, a fern hung suspended between the living room's vaulted ceiling and the wood railing of the loft where her cozy home office was situated. Carole stared at the lacy green fronds of the huge fern, comfortable in the solitude of her home as she waited for her father to speak again.

"You *weren't* up, were you?" he asked, prodding with his deep, smooth baritone that seemed to float across the surface of his words.

"I was up. Barely," Carole answered, smiling again in spite of herself. "And if we're having a race, I'm sure you've won."

He laughed, and Carole could hear some of the tension leave his voice. "No, your mother won. She was up hours ago. For some reason, this thing today is making her nervous. Can't figure out why. It's not like her at all. You know your mother. Nerves of steel. She'll probably feel better when you get here."

Still staring at the fern, Carole got her first, distressing impression that she had forgotten something important, and the sleepy calm that had buoyed her was jarred. "When I get there?" she repeated. Waking up for her was a long, slow process; this early in the morning her mind was barely up to half speed.

"I *knew* you would forget." King's words leaped at her accusingly. "The barbecue today, Carole," he coached, sounding very much like a father. "At the ranch."

"Barbecue?" Carole asked, aware that she sounded slow-witted, but nothing in her memory connected with what he was saying.

Carole stared harder at the fern. It blurred into an indistinct ball of green as she searched her mind for anything that would bring the conversation into focus.

"Wait," she said, frustrated that she could remember nothing. Carole placed the receiver on the cushion beside her and walked the few feet to her desk, where her appointment calendar lay open to Friday's date. She flipped the page to Saturday and found it blank.

With a deepening frown, she returned to the phone, still holding the calendar and much more awake than she had been a few minutes before. "Dad," she said quietly, "there is nothing on my calendar about any barbecue today. I don't remember Mother saying anything about it, and I certainly don't remember hearing you mention it. What is this all about?"

His laugh was a soft, self-incriminating chuckle that did little to soothe the anger beginning to pound in Carole's temples. "Well, maybe I did neglect to tell you. I thought your mother had, and she thought I had. But if you can't remember it, maybe neither of us did."

"What time does it start?" Carole asked, interrupting the casual meandering of his words. She knew her father well enough to realize that the surprises had just begun.

"Two o'clock," he answered, telling her no more than she had asked.

"And what's the occasion? And, Dad..." Her voice took on a tone of warning. "Please don't try to tell me it's just a friendly gathering."

"You're starting to wake up, aren't you?" King's second soft chuckle held admiration. "Well, sweetheart, the truth is that we're just a few days away from the primary elections. And since Donnelly Wakefield is going to win, and you've spent all your time campaigning for Susan Osburne, I figure it's about time to introduce you to the *real* governor's race. Because after that primary, things are going to start popping."

For a moment, Carole was almost blind with the rage that billowed in her. "King Stockton," she hissed in a voice tight with the strain of control, "if you weren't my father—"

"Now, darlin'," King cut in smoothly, "it's just politics. We've both got a job to do. And you're going to do yours." Beneath the soothing velvet of his voice was a firm bed of granite. His invitation was not a request; it was an order, and he would not be denied.

Silently Carole turned her head toward the window next to her. The gentle, lazy day looked suddenly as bleak and beleaguered as she felt. Rain dripped quietly past the bare panes, and the houses behind her were shrouded in a gray mist.

"Carole?"

"What should I wear?" she asked tonelessly, still staring out at the day made for solitude. "It's raining, you know. Lousy weather for a barbecue."

"It'll stop," King growled, obviously not pleased. Her lack of enthusiasm made his victory hollow. "Come casual. It'll just be a friendly little get-together. We've got a big tent pitched. Some hay spread. Maybe do a little horseback riding this evening."

Listening to the strain in her father's voice, Carole realized that her resistance was not the only thing bothering him. Narrowing her eyes, she shifted her gaze to the distant, pale peach wall of her living room, and she roamed the corridors of her mind for something she was missing.

When the answer came, she smiled softly and said, "Dad, you still aren't getting along well with Donnelly, are you?"

"We get along. We just don't agree. On *anything*."

"And you want me to be your buffer," she accused, as the thought replaced her smile with a frown. "I don't know the man, and I don't want to know him. I've told you all along, Dad, that if Susan loses the primary, I'm out of the election business."

"You're a vice president of Stockton Enterprises, Carole, and you are too valuable for this nonsense," her father said firmly. "So just get that idea out of your head. You represent the Stockton family and the Stockton business just as much as I do. And we are going to see to it that Donnelly Wakefield kicks Andrew Mathison's tail out of the governor's mansion."

King's voice had risen to a hard edge of flint; then, as quickly, it softened to a gentle plea. "It's just a barbecue, sweetheart. And your mother's counting on you. You'll enjoy it if you give yourself half a chance."

Still flinching from the impact of his earlier words, Carole sighed, knowing he was conning her and knowing she would give in to him anyway. Besides, he was right. It was only a barbecue, and the people who would be there were only people. There was nothing to be afraid of and no reason to run away. For now.

"Okay." Defeat was in her voice, defeat and a timidity that was not a normal part of her nature. In spite of her determination, the hand that held the receiver was cold and damp.

"Carole," King said gently, "it'll be all right. You'll see."

"Right." She forced a smile and took a deep, steadying breath. For once, Carole was immensely glad to have the powerful and fearless King Stockton as her father. He wasn't flawless, as a man or as a parent, but she was his daughter and he loved her. And when he promised her safety, she believed him.

"I can't guarantee you my enthusiasm, but I know how much this election means to you, Daddy, and I promise you I'll try."

"That's enough for me, sweetheart. See you at two?"

The bristling tension that had overshadowed so much of their conversation was gone, leaving only a half-sad regret in its place. If only theirs weren't such a prickly love. If only...

"Give Mom my love," Carole said softly. Her thoughts unspoken, she offered an apology that would go unsaid, just as his had.

When King had hung up, Carole sat for a few minutes in the comfort of the small loft that was her study. A minicomputer sat at the corner of her desk. A telephone linked it with the offices of Stockton Enterprises, saving her a trip downtown on weekends when restless energy or the pressure of deadlines urged her to work.

This had been one of the few days Carole had planned to devote solely to leisure, and regardless of her father's assurances, she knew that the afternoon would not be leisurely. The shrill beeping from the receiver interrupted her thoughts, and Carole stood and replaced it in its cradle as she laid her calendar back on the desk.

A tense chill ran down her back, and she paused at the landing of the U-shaped staircase to turn off the air conditioning that blasted frigid air into a morning already cool by late August standards. Downstairs, she opened the glass door that linked her second-story living room to a rough-wood balcony at the rear of her town house.

Moist fresh air curled around her, chasing away the ghosts that had briefly pressed too near. Leaving the door open, she turned and crossed the living and dining rooms to her kitchen, where a broad garden window faced toward the river.

After putting a copper teakettle on the stove to heat, Carole walked to the window and stared toward the hazy horizon. Despite the fine rain that fell steadily, she felt a rising need to bundle up in sweats and run a few miles on the well-used jogging path that followed the bank of the river. The carefully structured rhythm of her morning had been shattered, nullifying the small rituals she used to hold back a world too full of demands. The abrupt whistle of the teakettle broke the silence simultaneously with the ringing of the kitchen wall phone. Carole shut off the heat under the insistent kettle with one hand as she brought the receiver to her ear with the other.

With the receiver cradled in her shoulder, she took a teabag from a canister on the cabinet, and dropped it into a cup, then poured the steaming water over it. "Hello," she said into the receiver as she replaced the kettle and, lifting the cup of tea, started toward the dining table.

"Carole. I hope you don't mind. It was one of those mornings when I just needed to hear your voice."

Carole winced as she recognized the masculine, almost oily smoothness of the voice. She set the teacup down too roughly, and tea sloshed over the rim into the saucer. Resenting the unasked-for intrusion, she angrily clutched the receiver in her hand, as if it were responsible for the queasy reaction of her empty stomach.

"Please, baby, talk to me." His voice dropped lower in timbre, to a silky, sulky coaxing. "I've missed you."

"Andrew," she answered shortly, wanting to hang up and yet unable to, "what do you want?"

He laughed, triumphant. "I knew you'd talk to me. You're still my little Carole, aren't you, baby?" He was gloating, and Carole drew away imperceptibly from the phone. Then his tone changed to a plea. "I need you, Carole. I get so lonely without you."

Listening to the liquid flow of his words as he tried first one ploy and then another, Carole felt an old resentment at his attempts to arouse her lingering feelings of failure.

"For goodness' sake, Andrew," she snapped, "we've been divorced for almost four years." Her slowly dying guilt for a marriage that never should have happened only bothered her these days when Andrew called to aggravate the old wounds. "And our marriage was a joke long before that," she finished.

"I'm not laughing." The sly seduction in his voice brought back memories that Carole fervently wished would be allowed to die.

"Let it rest, Andrew," she said quietly. "I don't love you, and you don't love me."

"I'm tired, Carole. I'm so tired of being alone." The sincerity in his voice was so real, Carole could almost believe him if she hadn't heard it all too many times before. "This bed is too big for just me, and the nights are too long and empty without you."

"Andrew," she said softly, whispering with an anger so fierce she was sure he must feel it burning through the long-distance wires and all the way into the capitol in Oklahoma City. "You haven't spent a night alone since you went through puberty. It's been a long time since you could fool me with talk like that. What's the matter?"

Carole's voice rose abruptly as she stood with a violence that upset her teacup. An amber stream rolled across the glass top of the table and onto the floor. "Didn't you like the latest poll? Is Wakefield starting to get too close? Are you afraid I might throw my support behind him after the primary next week?"

"You wouldn't do that," he interrupted with a statement that sounded very close to an order.

"Of course I would," Carole shot back. As the dark spot spread on her silver-gray carpet, she took a damp cloth from the kitchen counter behind her and stopped to mop at the stain. "And if that's why you're calling, why don't you just say so?"

"You know it's more than that." Passion vibrated in his voice, a trained politician's voice that could slide through emotions the way a singer's could through a musical scale. "I want you back with me, Carole. As my wife. I need you."

"Is the election looking that close, Andrew?" Carole asked coolly, looking behind the mask of his words. She stopped mopping at the spot. Her arm hung limp at her side as she stood to concentrate on the verbal tug-of-war she was determined to win.

"You never used to be so hard," he said, sounding injured. "What happened to my little Carole? Baby, I know I hurt you, but can't you learn to trust me? I swear I'd never do it again."

What would have sounded like groveling in another man, sounded like self-assurance in Andrew, and it only annoyed Carole more to know that he sincerely believed she would eventually give in and remarry him. He seemed impervious to anything she said, blinded by his ego and his desperate desire for reelection.

Carole knew the truth behind his pleas, and knew that she should feel nothing but anger and resentment. And yet, she found it hard to shove aside the memories—the good as well as the bad—when he called to whisper the same old sweet lies that she had once believed were words of love. And when her anger came, the urge to strike back was strong, the urge to hurt him the way she had been hurt. But that wouldn't do anyone any good, herself least of all.

"Andrew." Carole took a deep breath. Pushing aside her confused feelings, she said calmly, "Please listen to me and believe what I say. I made a mistake when I postponed our divorce long enough for you to be elected governor four years ago. And I realize that you might find it embarrassing now to have your ex-wife campaigning for your opponent. But that's your problem."

She took another deep breath and tried to calm the rapid pounding of her pulse. But there was no way to soften her next words or the edge of determination that hardened her voice. "My problem is the embarrassment of ever having been married to you in the first place. And if I stay out of this election after the primary, it's because of *my* embarrassment, not yours."

"Carole, I know that's your father talking—not you," Andrew said understandingly. "When he switched parties after our divorce, it was like a knife through my heart. And now he's trying to get you out there in front of the whole state, supporting Donnelly Wakefield." His voice changed, twisting bitterly with the acid of his next words. "King Stockton's new golden boy."

Carole let the towel drop to the floor and sat down, listening with disbelief to the tone that came so close to hatred.

"I used to be King's golden boy," Andrew continued in a nasty whisper. "How do you look with Wakefield, Carole? He's a handsome man. Do the two of you make as striking a couple as we used to? Are you still the prize that goes with King's support?''

His voice rasped through the telephone lines, dripping with a venom that Carole found frightening. The words were still spewing out, the truth twisted and made hateful, as her thumb pushed the small white button on the receiver and ended the attack that had felt almost physical and left her cold and shaken.

A prize. That was all she had ever been to Andrew, and that's all she was to him still. She could barely remember the handsome young man who had pursued her with such poetic passion. She had never been in love before, had hardly ever dated, and he had seemed like something out of a dream. A dream that had become a distorted nightmare.

She'd been too blind to see that Andrew's roving eye continued to follow every other woman he saw, or that her own importance had remained secondary to her father's wealth and political connections.

The phone rang again and Carole jumped, surprised to find that her thumb still pressed the disconnect button. She released it to stop the ringing, then pressed it again to cut off the caller. She rose weakly on legs that trembled, and crossed the dining room to hang up the receiver. As she turned and began to climb the stairs, the phone started to ring again.

Ignoring it, Carole continued up the staircase and into the bathroom at the top of the landing. With the door shut and the shower turned on, she wasn't sure when the ringing finally ended.

As the hot sting of the water soothed her raw nerves, Carole wondered, not for the first time, if Andrew's trouble went deeper than anger and stress. When the polished veneer of the state's respected bachelor governor slipped away, what Carole saw frightened her. Lately his calls had become more frequent and more insistent.

She turned off the shower and stepped out. Wrapped in a terry-cloth robe, Carole blow-dried her straight blond hair. Her bangs fell in a fringe across her brow, and the ends of her hair tucked under in a simple pageboy at her shoulders. Finally, dressed in layers of sweat clothes, she felt calmer, safer.

Andrew was an annoyance, but he was nothing more. A voice on the telephone. It was more than two years since she had seen him face to face. If she had a real problem, it was with herself for allowing him to upset her so.

Bracing her foot against the edge of the bathroom counter, she laced her jogging shoe, then leaned into her knee, stretching out the muscles along the back of her other leg. Switching feet, she repeated the action; then, with both feet on the floor, she curled forward, legs straight, and grabbed her ankles with her hands as she pressed her nose to her knees.

Rising, she pulled the gray hood over her hair and tightened the drawstring. In the mirrored wall over the sink, she smiled at her reflection. She looked like a prizefighter going out to do road work. She hoped she didn't see anyone she knew.

Muffled by the closed door, the phone began to ring again. The smile on her face froze; from the mirror, worried golden brown eyes stared back at her. With a muffled oath, Carole turned, jerked open the door and sprinted down the stairs to the dining room landing, rounded the corner and continued down a second, L-shaped set of stairs and out the front door. Once outside, she broke into a slow jog, warming up down the sloping hill to the river.

Okay, she argued with herself as she unconsciously picked up her speed, so she was worried. So what? Andrew was part of a past she couldn't change no matter how much she wanted to. It was something she would just have to live with. And she would not go running to her father for help.

She was nobody's little girl anymore. Not King's and not Andrew's. She was her own woman. And she'd fight her own battles.

At the river she turned left and began to sprint, running hard from a distant menace that left her with no one to turn to and nowhere to hide.

Rain mixed with the sweat of exertion and rolled across Donnelly Wakefield's high brow and into his eyes. Blinking against the sting, he sucked in a deep breath and tried to ignore the faint burning in his lungs. "Great morning for running," he said, letting out his breath in a series of ragged puffs. "Glad you called me."

Smiling, the dark-haired man running beside him asked, "Do I hear a small note of sarcasm?"

"Who, me?" In answer to the laughter next to him, Donnelly slowed his pace to a lope and said, "Seriously, though, Sloan, I *am* glad you called. I don't get many chances these days to just relax with old friends."

His voice faded away for a moment, and against his will his muscles tightened, making the jogging more of a chore than a pleasure. Then he continued in a voice that seemed to hold the words away from him, "I'm going to have to do something this afternoon that I'm not looking forward to very much."

Brown eyes under dark brows watched Donnelly with a questioning frown as Sloan Prescott breathed deeply and steadily, saying nothing.

"I've been summoned for a command performance this afternoon at King Stockton's ranch," Donnelly explained, annoyed with himself for resenting the simple invitation so.

"Ouch, you have my sympathy."

"You know him?" Donnelly looked narrowly at the man who'd been one of his closest friends since they'd served together in Vietnam.

"Of him," Sloan said with a shrug, hesitating only a moment. "Just *of* him. That's about as close as I want to get."

They jogged on in silence for a while, their arms and legs pumping in a steady rhythm. The cooling rain was more of a blessing than an annoyance, and Donnelly concentrated on his breathing as his mind drifted on a relaxing plane devoid of thought. Then without warning reality intruded, jerking him back from the brief respite.

Sensing the tightening in Donnelly's stride, Sloan slowed his pace again. "This is really bothering you, isn't it, Donnelly? If it's such a headache, can't you just say no?"

Glancing toward the other man, Donnelly shook his head in silence, hating to burden a friend with a problem that still had no concrete shape. He couldn't really say why he dreaded the coming afternoon so much, or why he had agreed to go in spite of his growing sense of foreboding.

"I don't know," he said, feeling his way cautiously with his words as his pumping legs slowed their pace even more. "Sometimes I wish King Stockton had never changed party allegiance. Andrew Mathison wanted his backing, but to me, King is nothing more than a giant thorn. We disagree on everything. And now, to top it all off, I hear 'the princess' will be in attendance this afternoon.''

Sloan stopped abruptly, placing his hands on his hips, as Donnelly passed him, slowed to a walk and then came back toward him. ''You lost me on that one,'' Sloan said, leaning forward, frowning at the ground while he dragged in huge gulps of air.

''The ex-wife of our incumbent,'' Donnelly explained as Sloan fell in beside him and they began a heavy-legged walk back in the direction they had come. ''Carole Stockton, formerly Carole Mathison.'' His mouth curled around the words with distaste, and his irrational irritation grew stronger the more he talked. ''The one person I want nowhere near my campaign.''

''What have you got against her?'' Sloan asked a little brusquely.

''Nothing personal.'' Donnelly noted the subtle challenge in his friend's reaction but refused to soften his attitude. ''I just know her father. And I know he's not above dragging her, me and my entire campaign behind him down a trail of mudslinging that I want no part of.''

Donnelly's voice had risen, and his heels dug firmly into the soft earth as he stalked across the ground. ''*Damn* that man. Every time we get together it's like two rams locking horns, and this time he's invited every political reporter in the state to watch.'' Gritting his teeth, Donnelly clenched his fists at his sides. ''The closer it gets to the election, the more friction there seems to be between us. He's planning something for today, and you can bet I won't like it, whatever it is.''

Sloan placed his hand on his friend's shoulder. "Donnelly, I don't want to sound unsympathetic, but your father has been a senator most of your life. Surely you knew the kind of men you'd have to deal with when you decided to run for governor."

Turquoise eyes, furious and frustrated, glared at Sloan, and he quickly drew back his hand. Well over six feet tall, Donnelly had the tough, muscular build of a laborer, and a quick fiery temper that, combined with unwavering determination, had brought him respect from every man under his command in Vietnam.

"Okay, so you knew," Sloan said. He couldn't smother his smile as he held out his hands in innocence. "And being the idealist that you are, you thought you could run a clean campaign anyway."

"I *am* running a clean campaign," Donnelly growled, even more frustrated by Sloan's amusement. "I don't need dirt to defeat Mathison, and I'm going to prove it."

"Has it occurred to you that Carole Stockton may agree with you?" Sloan challenged in a soft and suddenly sober tone. "I don't think she's the kind of woman who would want to trade on unpleasantness any more than you would. And it *is* her life and reputation that would be paraded through the press. Not yours."

"Oh, hell, Sloan, I know that," Donnelly admitted with a tired shrug, but his nagging sense of irritation remained unchanged. "I'm just not so sure King's going to wait for our permission before he goes ahead with whatever he's planning."

Nodding in agreement, Sloan watched Donnelly from the corner of his eye. "Would you believe me if I said I know how you feel?"

"I'd believe anything you said, Sloan," Donnelly answered seriously, then winked, releasing the sense of foreboding that lately seemed to come more and more frequently. "I might not understand it, but I'd believe it."

As quickly as it had arisen, the tension between them evaporated. The rain had faded to a mist, and at an unspoken signal from Donnelly, they left the shelter of the pedestrian bridge where they had unconsciously come to a halt during their talk.

They jogged slowly away from the paved area surrounding River Parks' low-water dam and back onto the dirt path, its sodden earth squishy beneath their feet. The sweat suit Sloan wore was soaked, and he gazed enviously at the nylon T-shirt and shorts that left Donnelly unencumbered. Even with his neatly styled blond hair dripping like an unwrung mop, Donnelly looked like a poster for the all-American candidate. At each step, muscles rippled beneath bronzed skin.

In Nam, Donnelly had been a lieutenant and Sloan a corporal. Donnelly was older, a born leader who made it look so easy that everyone ended up leaning on him—everyone, that is, but Sloan. In Donnelly, Sloan had seen the older brother he had never had; but he had seen, too, a man who sacrificed too much of himself for other people. And for some strange reason never explored by either of them, Sloan had appointed himself as Donnelly's protector, confessor and best friend.

From the same hometown, strangers in a strange land, the two of them had been drawn together. And now Sloan once again found himself wanting to become the protector. The very qualities that made Donnelly an admirable man also made him a vulnerable one. He was simply a decent guy, too damned decent for the dogfight he was heading into.

"Look, old buddy, if I'm out of line, just knock me down," Sloan began slowly. "But what the hell are you doing running for governor? Forget everything I said earlier. You're a good man, Donnelly, and you have no business dealing with people like King Stockton."

"Hold on a minute, now," Donnelly protested, stopping suddenly. His legs ached from his too-abrupt halt, and he began to walk again, careful to lift his knees and stretch out with each step. "I'm no choirboy, and King's not your local crime boss. Our political views are miles apart, but he's still a fine, decent man who believes every bit as strongly in what he's doing as I do in what I'm doing."

Donnelly never believed he'd hear himself saying such things, but as he spoke he realized he was serious. Whatever the source of his antagonism toward King, it in no way lessened his admiration for the man or for his accomplishments.

"He's going to eat you alive." The cynicism in Sloan's voice offered no sympathy for Donnelly's spirited defense.

"He's not going to do anything to hurt the party or our chances for election," Donnelly insisted. Growing heated at Sloan's mocking tone, he again came to a full stop. "My differences with him are as an individual, not as a politician."

Silent laughter entered Sloan's eyes, and Donnelly slowly became aware of his own finger stabbing the air between them. His back was rigid in a square-shouldered, military stance. Embarrassed at the stylized manner that came so easily to him, Donnelly forced himself to relax as he watched a wide smile spread across Sloan's face and he heard him begin to chuckle softly.

"Too many speeches lately," Donnelly apologized. He wished he could laugh with Sloan, but his explanation was all too true. The campaign was seeping into his soul. He had begun to dream of speeches, and handshakes and a sea of faces that followed his every movement; and every night the dreams became more like nightmares.

"What does the senator think?" Sloan asked, still laughing as he turned the conversation to Donnelly's father.

Taking a deep breath, Donnelly began to walk again, grateful for Sloan's understanding of all the things he couldn't say. "That I should listen to King more. That I should wave the Wakefield family name around more." His hand circled the air in a gesture as tired as his voice sounded. "That I should drop a few more references to being a decorated war hero, and that I should have had a wife and children years ago."

They had reached the parking lot, and Donnelly stood just off the jogging path and stared at the river, dark and choppy from the gusting wind that had accompanied the rain.

"I guess you're pretty sure about the primary, then?" Sloan asked quietly.

Donnelly nodded in silent confirmation, not taking his eyes off the water. The primary had become a formality, nothing more. He would win, and then the real battle would begin.

"This is a nice town, you know?" Donnelly said, smoothly changing the subject. "After the primary I won't be around here very much. Even if I keep my apartment, Tulsa won't really be home again for a long time. I'll miss it."

Looking sideways toward Donnelly, Sloan raised an eyebrow to acknowledge his companion's maneuver. "You never answered me a while ago, Donnelly. I've seen you under fire before, gritting your teeth and doing what you had to do. I know you as well as I know myself—which isn't saying a lot—but I know you don't want to be governor. So what the hell are you doing?"

Sloan's voice had stayed soft, as gentle as the misty morning, and he watched Donnelly withdraw deeply into himself, as deeply as he had gone on the dawn of a battle.

"This is a good state, Sloan," Donnelly answered without hesitation. The emotion in his voice was quiet and strong. "It's given me a lot. And it deserves better than Mathison's giving it."

"So you've got to be the hero?" Again, the cynicism in Sloan's voice prodded Donnelly with a challenge.

A warning flame burned in the blue-green gaze that finally left the water and found Sloan. "Don't push it too hard, old friend."

Sloan glared and thrust out a firm, unwavering jaw. "You make me so damned mad sometimes, Wakefield. You've always got to be the guy in the white hat."

Donnelly didn't answer, and for a long moment they stared each other down, friends testing an old and deep trust; then Sloan blinked first. His brow crinkled in a disgusted surrender as they both relaxed and began to breathe again.

"You really think you can win?" Sloan asked at length.

"I think I've got to." Though he wouldn't admit it aloud, Donnelly recognized the truth in what Sloan had said. His friend was right, and he knew Sloan knew it.

Donnelly believed deeply in the nobility of his causes. However unwise it might be, he was a man who was willing to sacrifice for what he felt was right.

And he was aware that this quality was both his greatest virtue and his worst flaw, as a man and as a politician. Compromise didn't come easily to him. And now he sought to enter a world that demanded constant compromise and extracted a high price from those who wouldn't bend.

"Anything I can do?" Sloan's question pulled Donnelly back from his thoughts.

"Just be a friend." Donnelly laid his hand on Sloan's shoulder and squeezed lightly in an unspoken apology. "I hear they're kind of rare where I'm headed."

When he had won—if he won—Donnelly knew he was going to need all the friends he could get, and there would be few who could offer the kind of unswerving loyalty and unblinking honesty that Sloan Prescott gave.

In the days ahead, the pathway between victory and defeat would be very narrow. And, for him, there would be very little happiness in either.

Chapter Two

Unsure of what to expect at her father's "casual" barbecue, Carole stood nude from the waist up in the center of her walk-in closet, studying its contents. She knew there would be reporters there, and more than a few political leaders. Still, the ranch was her home, and to project anything less than comfortable confidence would be out of place. There would be no linen suits or high heels among the hay bales today.

Sunlight streamed in from the bedroom behind her. Once again, King had gotten his way; the afternoon would be steamy as the sun baked the morning's rain from the earth.

Straight-legged jeans molded Carole's long, lean body like a crisply starched second skin, accentuating her movements as she stepped into a pair of butternut-colored, ostrich-skin boots. A shirt the color of buckskin caught her eye, and after testing the weight of the soft cotton fabric, she slid the oversize shirt from its hanger, took a narrow brown belt from a shelf and withdrew from the closet.

Carole tossed the shirt and belt onto the foot of her bed as she passed it on the way to her dresser. In front of the huge mirror, she lifted the puff from a box of perfumed powder and spread its soft fragrance over her exposed torso, then dabbed the heavy sweetness of its matching perfume at her pulse points.

As with the ritual of her rising, Carole dressed slowly, building a wholeness layer by layer, from the inside out. She took a thin gold chain from her jewelry box; fastening it around her neck, she felt the weight of its large, clear topaz cradle in the valley between her high, firm breasts. She removed the diamonds she usually wore in her pierced ears, and replaced them with matching ovals of topaz, their sparkling amber a near match to the color of her eyes. She checked her hair again, fluffed high and away from her face. Only thin spikes of pale blond bangs touched her brow. The rest blended with the line of her hair to form a frame that curved up and out, then swept down again into a straight wedge at her shoulders.

Returning to the bed, Carole slid into the shirt, folded back its sleeves to her elbows and buttoned it only high enough to leave the topaz uncovered. Gathering in the soft, loose folds of the shirt fabric, she wrapped the long belt around her several times into a draping crisscross just beneath her waist.

Lifting her gaze to the mirror, Carole saw her reflection in varying shades of gold and brown. Except for the faded blue of jeans that hugged her like an old friend, everything blended with the blond of her hair and the amber of her eyes, enhancing and camouflaging at the same time. She was satisfied.

Downstairs, the chime of the front doorbell floated through the empty rooms, then spread like a weakened melody into her bedroom. Carole lifted her watch from the dresser as she passed and fastened the gold band to her wrist without taking her eyes from the downward curve of the stairs.

At the dining room, she checked the time, groaned and continued down to the front door. At the last landing, she turned toward the door and stopped, laughing aloud with a clear, ringing sound that carried joyously down the remaining distance.

Through the glass door below, she could see an impatient Sloan Prescott standing on her porch, clasping a large box that seemed to be sliding slowly out of his grip.

Dark eyes glared at the sound of her laughter, and he shouted, "Open this door!"

Smothering her amusement, Carole flew down the remaining steps and opened the door, pressing herself against the wall to allow Sloan to pass. He growled a thank you and trudged up the staircase. At the landing, he turned toward the dining room and called, "Where can I put this?"

"Anywhere," Carole answered, keeping a respectful distance as she followed him up. Before she reached the landing she heard a loud thud and felt the floor shake with the impact of the box.

Emerging into the dining room, Carole saw the box half blocking the kitchen doorway. Sloan stood in front of the kitchen's pass-through. His elbow was braced on the counter and he breathed in a controlled pant. "I think I'm going to hate this," he said solemnly.

"Is that it?" Carole asked, nodding toward the box.

"No. There's more."

"Well," she said cautiously, walking farther into the room, "there's an easier way to do it."

"Thank God. I was beginning to think this wasn't too great an idea." Sloan left the counter and, stepping over the box, rounded the corner into the kitchen. "By the way," he said, opening the door to the refrigerator, "you look ravishing. You wearing that to the ranch?"

Surprised, Carole stopped before entering the kitchen. "How did you know I was going to the ranch?"

Sloan took a quart of orange juice from the refrigerator and held it up, a question in his eyes. When Carole shook her head with a quick "No, thanks," he carried the juice to the cabinet and took down a glass.

"I have my sources," he said with a mischievous smile as he poured the juice, and put the bottle back in the refrigerator.

"You know," Carole said thoughtfully, stepping back to let him walk past her into the dining room, "sometimes you sound eerily like your father."

Turning his head to look at her over his shoulder, Sloan said with quiet seriousness, "Don't say that, little sister. Not even in jest."

"Sorry, but I wasn't kidding." She walked by him to the dining table and sat down. "Sometimes you're so much like Daddy, it's spooky. I don't know how anyone could grow up not knowing a man and still look and act so much like him."

Sloan pulled out a chair opposite her and sat down, staring at her with a silent, worried frown on his face. "Carole, I've got to tell you," he said quietly. "Talk like that makes me very nervous."

"When's your fight with him going to be over, Sloan? He *is* your father, and he'd give anything for a chance to act like it." They'd had the same talk before, and Carole hadn't really intended to start it again now. When she'd offered her spare bedroom while Sloan's apartment was being renovated, she'd seen it as an opportunity for them to take another small step forward in a relationship that was very new to both of them, not as an opportunity to lecture him about their father.

"My name is Prescott, not Stockton. I was born with that name and I'll die with it. A lot of my anger toward King is gone now, but there are some things that may always be there."

"I'm sorry, Sloan. I really didn't mean to start this," Carole apologized, wondering when she'd learn to let well enough alone.

"No, *I'm* sorry. I know it's a strain on everybody, but look at it this way—a few years ago we were both an only child. Now I've got a sister and you've got a brother."

He reached across the table and laid his hand over hers, squeezing with a wordless reassurance. Carole covered his hand with her other one and smiled. "It gets a little strange sometimes, doesn't it?" she asked.

"It sure does," he agreed, and then smoothly changed the subject. "You're positive it's not going to be any problem having me here for a few days?"

"No," Carole said with a shake of her head. "I've got that spare room downstairs with its own bath and entrance. It's perfect. Oh—" Remembering her interrupted train of thought from earlier, she straightened, and Sloan withdrew his hand. "You can pull your car into the garage and unload it from there. The garage entrance is just across the hall from your bedroom."

"Am I making you late?" Sloan asked. He tossed off the last of his orange juice and rose to take the glass back to the kitchen.

"No," Carole said, standing with him. "I managed to do that before you even got here." She followed him into the kitchen. "Sloan, how *did* you know about the barbecue this afternoon?"

He just laughed. "I'll introduce you to my source someday. Meanwhile, shouldn't you be running along?"

Carole shrugged and walked into the living room to pick up her purse. "I'm not really looking forward to it. It's one of those political things that Daddy thrives on, Mother endures and I hate."

Sloan patted her shoulder consolingly and walked with her toward the straight, narrow stairway at the back of the dining room that led down to the guest bedroom and the garage. "That's one of the little perks that go with being King Stockton's offspring. And you wonder why I keep my parentage a secret."

"Seriously, Sloan. Someday people will have to know. Aside from everything else, you look more like him every day."

Though Sloan was several inches shorter than King, his build had the same well-muscled strength, and his handsome features and intense nature duplicated his father's. Looking at Sloan, Carole could see the father she remembered from her childhood. Sometimes, talking to Sloan, she felt as though she were stepping back in time, sifting through the memories of misunderstanding and rejection, searching for a way to end the chain reaction that continued to haunt them all.

"Carole." At the foot of the stairs, Sloan put his hand on his half sister's shoulder, and his eyes raked hers in a silent plea for understanding. "It took me a lot of years to accept the fact that I was illegitimate, and that my father was never going to be anything more than a shadow somewhere in the background. And now that he wants to tell the world he has a son, I'm just not so sure I'm ready to play the game. His love doesn't come without a price tag, Carole. You, of all people, should know that."

Carole opened the door to the garage and stared unseeing at the Mercedes convertible her father had given her for Christmas the year before, with its specially ordered paint job in topaz to match her eyes.

"I know," she said quietly. "But it's as hard on him as it is on us. He's a man who's never learned to compromise. He's never learned to take life at anything but top speed." Turning to smile over her shoulder at Sloan, she continued in the same quiet voice, "It can be a real nuisance. But if I do nothing more in my lifetime, I only hope I can learn to live my life as bravely."

Sloan's eyes misted, and Carole could feel his pain in her heart. "That's the second time today someone's defended him to me," he said in a voice softened by emotion. "God knows I love him. I've worshiped him for as long as I can remember. Maybe I love him too much. Maybe I'm just afraid to need him, so I stay away."

"Men," Carole answered in real disgust. "You make things a whole lot more complicated than they have to be."

"Go away and let me unpack in peace," Sloan said with a frown and a gentle shove toward the step down to the garage. His smile was a little crooked, but his eyes were dry again, and the moment of unguarded honesty was past.

The heels of her boots clicked on the concrete floor of the garage; then Carole stopped, turned back and stared up at Sloan. Though his hair and eyes were darker than hers, the two of them bore more than a casual resemblance, and Carole felt a stronger kinship every day with the brother she had only recently come to know.

"You'll be okay here by yourself?"

"I just need a place to sleep," Sloan said, laughing. "Not a baby-sitter. Now, run along and do your duty."

With a final goodbye, Carole backed her car out and turned in the direction of the expressway that would take her to the ranch. She wished she could have stayed with Sloan. They had so little time together, and so many years to catch up on.

Sloan seemed to know so much more about her than she did about him; but then, her life had been an open book—or rather, newspaper—since the day she had first met the young congressional candidate who later became her father's protégé and her husband. The memory of Andrew's phone call returned with a chilling suddenness, and Carole turned down the air-conditioning that hummed through the small car.

Her tense, cold fingers stiffened on the steering wheel, and Carole longed more than ever to turn the car around and go home. King had promised her safety, but how could he protect her from the prying questions of the reporters who would be crawling over the guests like locusts over a field? How could he protect her from the watchful eyes that would measure her proximity to Donnelly Wakefield throughout the afternoon, reading meaning into every look, every gesture? How could he stop the minds that would make the same comparisons Andrew had that morning?

Surely King realized what introducing her into Donnelly Wakefield's campaign would mean. Acid churned in Carole's empty stomach at the thought. Going today was a mistake, a dreadful mistake. Unconsciously, her foot lifted from the accelerator, and she began to look for a side road where she could turn around.

Beside her, a car's horn blared angrily as the other car whizzed past, and like someone waking from a nightmare, Carole realized what she had done. Speeding up again, she turned on the radio, filling the car with the impatient sound of a heavy-metal rock band, and let the strong, raucous music seep into her.

Shaking off the anxiety that had nearly paralyzed her, Carole began to calm down. There was nothing she could do about the minds of other people, and giving in to conjured images would only make her miserable.

Her father wanted her there because he respected her abilities. She had been the wife of a congressman and, for a time, one of Washington's most successful hostesses. She had seen politics on a national level and knew the significance the state issues held for the business she helped her father run.

By the time she turned onto the two-lane road leading to the main house of Black Gold Farms, Carole knew King had been right to insist that she be there. No matter how painful it might be, hiding from old wounds would never help them heal.

As she drew near, the grounds of the ranch looked like a carnival without the rides. A huge striped tent filled the area between the two-story ranch house and the outlying stable area. On the other side of the house, row upon row of cars were parked on the already dusty sunbaked lawn. Vans with the call letters of half the TV and radio stations in the state were parked wherever they could find a space, and black electrical cables snaked everywhere, making bad footing worse.

Carole drove past the jumble of cars, people and equipment and pulled into the circular drive in front of the house's broad flagstone porch. With an eagle's eye and the moves of the collegiate lineman he had once been, King was beside the car before she could open the door.

"You're late," he growled as he helped her from the car.

"But I'm here," Carole said, grinning up at him and stretching the kinks out after her tense drive from the city.

"That beats not getting here doesn't it?" King agreed as he began to lead her toward the crowd in the distance.

"Who's here?"

"Everybody but the monkeys and the elephants. Donnelly's antsy as hell, but I can't get near him to find out what's wrong." King laughed, with a laugh that sounded more threatening than jolly. "So maybe I'm the problem."

The rumble of the gathering reached out to greet them, and the sweet, dusty scent of hay hung in the still, heavy air. Carole slowed her steps. "You may be right, you know," she said while they were still a little distance from the crowd. "The closer you get to the election, the worse things seem to get between you two."

King came to a halt, shoving his hands into the back pockets of his jeans as he stared at the polished toes of his boots. "I'm pushing too hard, I admit. But, dammit, being governor's not easy. And if he can't handle *me*, how's he going to handle that?"

"I don't think that's the problem, Dad," Carole said quietly. "And before we walk into that crowd and start saying things we're going to read in tomorrow's newspaper, I think we should get some things straight."

King lifted his gaze from the ground to the clear amber eyes of his daughter. "Like what?"

"Like the fact that you've made this campaign a personal vendetta. You're out to get Andrew no matter what. That frightens me, and I'm sure it's the source of most of your contention with Donnelly."

"Why does it frighten you?" King's concern bypassed most of Carole's words and concentrated on those that touched him as a father.

"Because I don't know how far you'll go," Carole continued in the same soft voice. "And I don't know how far you might force Andrew to go."

"I'll handle Mathison," King said stiffly. "You've got nothing to worry about."

"You're wrong," Carole insisted. "It's Donnelly's candidacy. Let him handle Andrew and *no one* will have anything to worry about."

"Including Andrew," King snapped. Taking Carole's elbow in his hand, he led her toward the striped tent that was the center of activity. As they drew near, he softened again for a moment. "I'm sorry if it upsets you, Carole. And I'm sorry if it strains my relationship with Donnelly. But I'm not leaving this one to chance. Andrew's had his day, and he won't get another one if I can help it."

Having brought Carole to the mainstream of the gathering, King left her there and disappeared with a young man bearing a clipboard and a harried expression. The trapped feeling that had Carole rooted to the spot while desperately wishing to escape was not a new one. The sense of helplessness was something she battled constantly when dealing with her father, and it left her with a strong admiration for anyone who opposed his will and won.

Deciding that this time she would be one of those who won, Carole turned to go, and found herself facing a torso with a hand-held minicamera perched on its shoulder and, beside it, a smiling black woman with a microphone.

"Ms. Stockton," the other woman said into the microphone, "does your presence here today mean that you have abandoned your well-publicized support of Susan Osburne to join Donnelly Wakefield's campaign?"

As the microphone extended toward Carole, she recognized the young woman as an interviewer from an Oklahoma City television station, who was noted for her charm as well as for her deadly questions.

"Hello, Diane," Carole said with an answering smile. "Actually, I just couldn't turn down a chance to come to one of Daddy's barbecues."

"Then you *don't* support Donnelly Wakefield's campaign?"

"I support the party," Carole answered carefully, trying not to succumb to the easy grace with which the other woman sought for answers—answers that could be damning. "And after the primary on Tuesday, I'll support the people's choice. I feel that Susan Osburne would make a fine candidate and that it's time to see a woman in office, but if Donnelly Wakefield wins the primary, he will have my support one hundred percent."

"And if Andrew Mathison is the people's choice, will he have your support?"

"Wrong party," Carole said with a teasing smile as a pain twisted through her stomach, and she stifled a wild desire to snatch away the intruding microphone and toss it across the tent. "But whoever is elected governor on the final ballot will have my full support and best wishes, as I'm sure he will those of the entire state."

"Then there's no truth to the rumors circulating that you and Governor Mathison are considering a reconciliation between now and the election?"

Stunned, Carole felt her face go blank and knew that for days she would see this moment replayed on every news show she turned to, that one unguarded instant when she had forgotten to hide the effect of the blow. Gathering herself, she didn't bother to smile when she answered quietly, "I hadn't heard that rumor. But, no, there's no truth to it."

Carole attempted to turn aside, but the camera moved with her and the microphone followed. "It's been said that the governor has stayed in frequent contact with you," the reporter persisted steadily in her soft, polite voice. "Would you care to comment on that?"

"Not really." Again Carole took a step away, searching desperately through her mind for something to say that would end this. Already, in the other woman's eyes, Carole could see another question forming.

"Aha," a deep voice said from behind the camera, "so there you are." Donnelly Wakefield stepped into the picture with her and automatically the camera shifted to include him. "There's an aide by the name of Daniel looking for you," Donnelly said to Carole as if the camera did not exist. "He's on the other side of the tent."

Donnelly's turquoise eyes, looking down on her, were kind and filled with understanding, and Carole could have kissed him for the opportunity he gave her to escape. Standing next to him, she felt protected in a way she hadn't for a long time, and suddenly all of the awful fear went away.

Carole smiled up at Donnelly and said, "Thank you," then turned to Diane and said, "There is something I would like to say. The governor and I were divorced four years ago. We will not reconcile. We do not see each other, and if we ever talk, it's only out of necessity. We are not enemies, but politically we are opponents. And I'm sure that he, as much as I, would like to have an end to the continual linking of our names."

She nodded to the camera, smiled her gratitude once again to Donnelly and said to Diane, "And now, if you'll excuse me, I have to go."

Making her way across the tent, Carole felt a giddy sense of relief. Every horrible thing she had imagined had happened, and she had survived. Donnelly's arrival had given her the time to recover from the shock of the questions she had always dreaded. Now she would see what the aide wanted, and then she would leave. One interview like that was enough for the day.

On the other side of the tent, Carole looked around helplessly at the milling crush of people and realized her search was futile. She had no idea what Daniel looked like. She had never even heard of an aide named Daniel. With that thought and a carefree shrug, she abandoned the idea of finding him.

Outside the tent door she stopped and took a deep breath. Overhead the sky was a clear, unclouded blue. From nearby she could hear the sounds of a country band and people laughing. In the distance a horse whinnied, and Carole turned away from the house and started walking toward the paddocks.

Afraid to look back, she walked quickly toward the red and white buildings where her mother bred and raised some of the best quarter horses in Oklahoma. In the brilliant warmth of the sun, as the pungent odor of horses mingled with the sweetly ripened scent of hay, Carole blossomed with a sense of vitality and well-being that she seldom allowed free rein.

In her cautious, well-ordered existence there was little room for pure joy. Daring and impulse were only words. She lived a life that was safe, and in its safety she was free from the pain and regrets that had haunted her past.

Startled by the sound of footsteps in the gravel behind her, Carole left the path and went to stand beside the paddock fence. Inside the circular white railing, a young mare trotted, mindful of the swelling girth that would bring her first foal in the spring.

The footsteps followed her, and even before she saw him Carole recognized the same rich scent of cologne she had noted when Donnelly came to her rescue earlier. Turning toward him with a smile of greeting, she said, "I couldn't find Daniel."

In the sunlight, he seemed even larger than he had standing next to her in the tent. His blond hair and the broad white flash of his smile seemed to belong under the blue ceiling of the sky. "There is no Daniel. I heard the questions she was asking you, and when I saw your face, I thought maybe you'd like an excuse to get away."

There was something at once very tender and yet terribly male about him, and Carole felt a flicker of excitement in Donnelly's presence that she had never known before. The blue-green of his eyes made the heavens seem pale and uninteresting. The full, sensuous curve of his smiling lips was compelling, and even as she felt herself being drawn to him, Carole pulled away.

"That was very kind of you," she said softly and, with an effort, turned her eyes toward the glossy brown mare.

For a long time Donnelly was silent, standing beside her without moving, and Carole could feel the pace of her heart accelerate with each moment of waiting.

"What you said was very good," he said at length. "Was it true?"

Surprised, Carole turned back automatically to face him. "What?"

He shrugged and in that movement drew closer. "I've heard the rumors, too, and they're not just idle gossip. There are people on my staff who are very good at tracing these things back to their source, and almost every one of those rumors goes straight back to Mathison's camp."

"What does that mean?" Carole asked. The same news coming from her father would have made her feel threatened. With Donnelly she continued to feel safe, protected within the calm that radiated from him like candlelight on a starless night.

"That whether you're reconciling or not, Mathison wants everyone to think you are."

The fleeting moment of joyous freedom was gone, shattered by the reality that was never far away. Once again, Carole felt like a pawn, a prize in the tug-of-war between Andrew and her father.

"Why?" Her question was a cry of pain that tore from the part of her she kept sheltered behind the fragile walls of her defenses. Raising her fist, Carole pounded the top board of the fence with a single, sharp blow and said again, softly, "Why?"

Donnelly's hand closed around her fist and stopped her before she could raise it again. Turning it over, he stared at the red skin on the side of her hand, and he shook his head slowly. "I couldn't tell you. Except you're a prize that would be very hard to let go of."

Jerking her hand from his, Carole whirled away from him. "Don't say that," she snapped as she hugged her arms and curled into herself. She longed to hide from the hurt, to shrink until she disappeared, but she couldn't ignore the man behind her.

Again, Donnelly was silent and unmoving, and again Carole's heart involuntarily raced with the waiting. The scent of his cologne enveloped her, finding its way into her protective shell, warming her in a way no touch or word could.

"I'm sorry," she said in a voice shaken and whispery. Carole uncurled slightly and took a step farther away from him.

"I don't know what I said," Donnelly answered softly, "but I'll try not to do it again."

"It's not you." With an apologetic shake of her head, Carole closed her eyes and wished herself home, safe behind the walls of her sanctuary.

"I know that." His voice was deep, calm and knowing.

Too knowing. Instead of being reassured, Carole felt threatened, as if Donnelly could see too deeply into the feelings she hid so well. Without lifting a hand, he had touched her in a way no man ever had. He made her long to turn to him and hide in the strength of his arms, to bury her head against his strong, solid shoulders and to never fear the world again.

As Donnelly's hands lightly touched her shoulders and turned her toward him, Carole squeezed her eyes shut against the sight of him and the weakness that would come with it. Fighting the image of Donnelly that lingered in her mind, she stiffened her body against the soft urging of his hands.

When his palm cupped her chin and lifted her face toward his, Carole caught her breath and fought the swift rush of her blood that leaped at his touch and surged through her in a dizzying torrent. Slowly his hand left her face and dropped to his side.

"Carole."

In Donnelly's voice was the same surprised, fierce yearning that Carole felt in herself. A tear escaped her tightly shut eyes and slid down her cheek, a tear of anger and helplessness and loss. The awakening desire between them that should have been so wonderful, so welcome, was a threat that couldn't be allowed.

With a deep, shuddering breath, Carole opened her eyes and saw in Donnelly's turquoise gaze the force of his emotions. She lifted her hand to his, still gently resting on her shoulder and savored for only an instant the feel of his flesh against hers. Then reluctantly Carole pulled his hand from her shoulder and took a shaky step back.

"I'm sorry," she said with a small, tight smile that hurt her with its falseness, "but I really have to be going now. I want to thank you again for your kindness. It was terribly nice meeting you."

Carole took no more than two steps before Donnelly's hand reached out and curled around her upper arm, jerking her to a halt.

"Just what in the hell do you think you're doing?" he demanded in a voice tight with anger. His eyes danced with a furious fire that made Carole long to embrace the madness he aroused in her. "Two seconds ago you were ready to melt in my arms. Now you say thank you very much and go walking off like nothing happened." Donnelly's words lashed at her with the sting of a whip. "I don't know what kind of game you're playing, or who you think you're playing it with, but it's not going to be *me*."

With a stiff dignity that had never failed her, even in the worst moments of her life, Carole stared coolly into the fiery turquoise of Donnelly's eyes and said, "Now that you've told me off, would you please release my arm so that I can go?"

She gave a tentative tug against his grasp, expecting to be released, and was surprised to find that his fingers only tightened in response.

"I suppose that little speech usually works?" Donnelly asked in a voice that was disconcertingly calm. "Well, it's not quite good enough to satisfy me."

Humor began to lighten the cloudy sea-blue of his eyes, and Carole felt the beginning of panic stir in her. He had come too close, too quickly. He made her think too much of old dreams that could never be anything more. Fairy tales didn't come true, and she had never seen a man who seemed more like a knight in shining armor. He made it too easy to believe, to give in to what could only be disaster. Much, much too easy.

Using the only defenses left to her, Carole arched one brow and stared into Donnelly's eyes with all the warmth of an ice cube. "Wouldn't this make a lovely picture in tomorrow's newspaper?"

Undaunted, Donnelly smiled a lazy, slowly curving smile that took his lips through all of their most appealing transformations before stopping in a broad grin;

then he shook his head. "Right after you left, they all hurried off to make their deadlines. We're perfectly safe now."

Trapped, frightened and ashamed of the weakness that left her so vulnerable to a man she barely knew, Carole twisted away from the hand that held her captive. Caught by surprise, Donnelly released her, and Carole took a quick step past him before he renewed his grip and pulled her back.

Frustrated, Carole whirled to face him and found herself much closer to Donnelly than she had been before breaking his grip. She stepped back quickly, keeping as much distance between them as she could, while she glared up at him with dark, angry eyes. "Why don't you just pull my arm off and keep it as a souvenir?" she said through clenched teeth.

With a smile, Donnelly reached out and took her other arm captive. A slight flex of his muscles drew her a step nearer. "Ah," he said with a sigh, "the kitten has claws."

The fire inside her began to smolder with something other than temper, and Carole stiffened against her desire to melt against him. Donnelly had removed the sport coat he had worn in the tent and was clad only in slim, well-worn jeans and a shirt of thin, white cotton, so delicate it was obvious he had nothing under it but the hard muscles and bronzed skin of a man who had not gone soft from a life in politics.

Tearing her eyes from the rapid rise and fall of Donnelly's broad chest, Carole ignored the pounding of her pulse in her temples and tugged once again against the hands that held her on a short rein. And once again, Donnelly tightened his grip and pulled her even nearer.

Terrified now of the silent struggle of wills that had become so much more, Carole knew she had to win soon, while the strongest part of her was still willing to fight.

"Are you aware of what you're doing?" she asked, feigning a dispassion she was far from feeling.

As he had done earlier, when Carole grew cold, Donnelly countered her directly. "Yes."

Tilting her head with a look of haughty disdain, Carole asked, "Then could you explain it to me?" her voice taking on the slicing edge of a razor. The expression on Donnelly's face did not go unnoticed.

His eyes narrowed and his jaw set with the same proud resentment that had caused him to stop Carole when she had first tried to leave. His gaze burned with silence as his hands drew her closer, inch by inch, until they were almost touching.

Defiantly, Carole glared at him. "Do you want to kiss me?" she asked icily. Relaxing the barest inch, her body filled the space that separated her from Donnelly. The challenge in Carole's eyes warmed as the tips of her breasts touched his chest, and her wayward body acknowledged the touch with an electric jolt that left her breathless.

"I'm not a little boy, Carole." Donnelly's voice was as chilled with condescension as hers had been. "And a fast game of slap and tickle behind the barn doesn't interest me."

As shocked as if she'd been slapped, Carole gasped, and Donnelly's hands slowly released her arms. Even more slowly, he stepped away from the soft pressure of her breasts, those round, scalding fists of pleasure that burned him long after they no longer touched.

"Thanks just the same," he said with a quick, wicked smile that was just a little off center, though the warm memory of her body against his continued to taunt him. "But you can keep your kisses, miss."

Carole stared at him for a long moment as a tumbling confusion of hurt, insult and vast disappointment swirled through her. In Donnelly's eyes she saw a wavering but, behind that, a stubborn refusal to bend. If he had set out to penetrate her defenses, he had certainly succeeded, and painfully so, though she would never let him see it.

With a jaunty lift of her brows and a small, crooked smile, Carole said, "Touché," then swept forward in a bow from the waist that acknowledged the victor.

Donnelly watched her, and the look of frowning sadness on his face grew heavier. "Carole," he said at length, "I *do* want to kiss you." His soft words became gravelly. "I want to very much."

Carole shrugged and blinked away the burning of tears. "It's too late." She set one foot behind her as she prepared to turn and go.

Donnelly didn't move to stop her. "I have a feeling it was too late long before I ever met you," he answered quietly.

A tear broke away from the pools gathering in her eyes and dripped down her cheek. Carole shrugged again, lost for words and infinitely grateful that Donnelly was no more than a tall, glistening shadow, hidden behind the ocean of pain that had slipped so stealthily back into her life.

"I *am* sorry," she said.

With her last reserve of strength, Carole turned and blindly made her way back up the path toward the house. Behind her, the muted grief in Donnelly's voice was the last thing she heard.

"Not as much as I am," he murmured, speaking more to himself than to her. "Not half as much as I am."

Chapter Three

The day was hot; long, burning fingers of sunlight played across Donnelly's back as he knelt on the front porch of the unfamiliar home.

"A little more to the right," he said. "This end isn't quite straight."

Tilting the wrought-iron grille for the glass door, Sloan asked, "Okay?"

"Yeah. Now hold it there while I get this corner screwed in." Perspiration gathered across Donnelly's shoulders as he strained to hold the grille against the solid wood that framed the door's glass center. Even the thin cotton of his T-shirt was too much under the high-noon glare of the sun.

"I really appreciate your help," Sloan said, uncomfortable with Donnelly's unusual silence. "I could have done this by myself, but it would have taken all day, and I wanted it to be a surprise."

"For your friend," Donnelly answered without looking up.

"Right. It's always bothered me, her living here alone with all these glass doors." Sloan shifted his position while Donnelly moved to the other bottom corner and began to tighten it.

"Sure," Donnelly said with an exaggerated drawl. "Tell you what, Sloan, when we get to the next door—" his voice drained off into a groan as the screw bit deep into the hard wood "—I'll hold and you do this part."

After giving one final twist, he stood and stretched his cramped legs, then started to work on the top corners. "By the way, do I get to meet this friend?"

Sloan stared straight ahead through the glass, to the staircase that led up to the main floor of the house. "I doubt it. She's shopping with her mother this afternoon. We should be finished long before she gets home."

Donnelly laughed, glancing quickly at Sloan and then back to his work. "Not ready to share her yet, huh?"

"It's not like that," Sloan said seriously. "She's...a friend, just a friend." His voice trailed away to a mumble.

"Sure," Donnelly said again in the same doubtful drawl. He relaxed his upstretched arms and arched his back against the stiffening of the muscles along his spine.

Sloan stepped aside and let Donnelly tighten the last screw. "I *would* like for you to meet her someday," he said quietly while Donnelly worked. "But there are some things I probably should tell you first."

"Good old Sloan," Donnelly said without turning. "Ever the man of mystery. Are you going to be around for the celebration Tuesday? You could bring your girl.''

"She's not my girl. She's—''

"Just a friend," Donnelly finished. "And you're just staying here because your apartment's being renovated." He stepped back and handed the screwdriver to Sloan with a mischievous smile. "And it just happened to be very convenient.''

Sloan took the screwdriver with a frown. "You're about as hardheaded as a mule. You know that?''

"When you have an innocent face like mine," Donnelly said with a widening smile, "people think you'll believe anything. Now where's that other door?''

With a withering look of disgust, Sloan opened the door and led the way up the stairs and across the dining room to the stairway that went down to the guest room. Behind him, Donnelly emerged into the living and dining areas and came to a halt.

From the outside, he could tell the town house was a nice one. Inside, he understood how nice. The rooms were understated, simple and elegant, furnished with warm colors and the plush textures of a butterfly's cocoon. And the scent of money hung in the air, money old enough to have long since been taken for granted.

Disturbed, Donnelly tore himself loose and followed Sloan down the stairs and across the bedroom to its private entrance. Another door of glass framed by a broad border of hardwood, it looked out onto a small patio that was enclosed on two sides by redwood fencing.

"I begin to see your point," Donnelly said quietly, looking around the cozy guest room that showed obvious signs of Sloan's occupancy. Maybe she really was just a friend, or maybe they were just very discreet. "It's all very pretty. And very vulnerable."

"Yeah." Sloan opened the door and they went onto the patio, where the second piece of wrought iron leaned against the wall. Donnelly held the grille while Sloan positioned it and began to drive the first screw into the closed door.

"About your victory party," Sloan said as he worked, "I'm afraid I can't be there. In fact, I'm leaving later today for an oil lease I've got going out toward the panhandle. I'll be there till the end of the week."

"Oh, that's all right," Donnelly answered, barely hearing him. The atmosphere of the rooms above continued to worry him. Something about them resurrected feelings that had haunted him throughout a long and sleepless night. He had made a fool of himself with Carole Stockton, handling her with all the finesse and understanding of an ox.

He'd built his career on saying and doing the right thing at the right time. But with Carole he seemed to forget everything he knew. Nothing he said came out right, and every move became a blunder.

Donnelly had felt something with her, something that was special. And he knew Carole had felt it, too, but when he took her in his arms, it was like trying to melt a glacier with his bare hands.

Hidden inside her, beneath the ice that held the world away, there was a fire burning. He couldn't see it or touch it, but he knew it was there, and it lit an answering fire in him every time he was near her. And the need to be near her was growing stronger every minute since she had left him yesterday. Donnelly had to try one more time to find the right words to say.

"Donnelly?" Sloan asked, interrupting Donnelly's thoughts. "Wake up, man, and move over. A stick of wood would be more help than you are right now."

Donnelly shifted his position, and Sloan began to work on the other corner, talking as he twisted the screwdriver. "I saw the late news last night. For a man who wanted to be as far away from a certain woman as he could get, you sure didn't waste any time going to her rescue. And on camera, yet."

"Did you see her face?" Donnelly asked, not arguing and not at all sorry.

"Yes, I saw her face," Sloan said softly. "But she's news, and there's nothing anyone can do to protect her from that. She's fair game every time she walks outside of . . . her house." He paused a minute and took a deep breath as he shifted position. "And you're not going to do anything but add to her grief and hurt yourself if you go charging in there every time someone throws a dart at her."

"You seem to know an awful lot about it," Donnelly said, his voice growing hard as a frown clamped down on his angry face.

"I'm not an idiot," Sloan snapped back at him. "And if I didn't know better, I'd say you sounded awfully close to being emotionally involved."

Donnelly smoothly shifted position as Sloan rose abruptly and reached toward the top corner on his side. "I'd say that isn't any of your business," Donnelly answered quietly.

"Well, I'd say I agree with you." Sloan's voice was stiff as he stretched to work in the third screw. "In fact, if you hadn't chosen this particular time to run for governor, I'd say it wasn't anybody's business but yours and hers. But as it is, there's a whole state watching you."

Donnelly sighed, and all the anger seeped out of him like a tire with a fast leak. "I don't know what it is, Sloan. There's just something about her. I can't get her out of my mind."

Sloan put his hand on Donnelly's shoulder and moved him out of the way, then went to work on the final corner. "All the years the two of you were in Washington," he asked gently, "you never knew her then?"

"It was impossible not to know her." Donnelly felt the sun burning into his back, felt the long hours of the sleepless night tugging at his tired shoulders. "Or not to know what Mathison was doing to her. I'd watch her from across a room, wishing I could take her away from him and knowing I couldn't even go near her."

Sloan slipped the screwdriver into his back pocket and stepped away from the finished door. "That's quite a confession, friend," he said gently. "Our Donnelly and a married woman?"

"Wouldn't that have been a pretty mess?" Donnelly agreed. "She wouldn't have listened to me anyway. She was so different then, Sloan, so innocent and fragile. No one could tell her that Mathison wasn't good enough for her. Everyone just stood back and watched her world come apart. And left her to pick up the pieces."

"She survived," Sloan said. "And if what I saw on television is any indication, she survived rather well. Are you sure it's really her you want, Donnelly? Or is she just one more crusade for the good guy in the white hat?"

"Of all the damned insolence," Donnelly said, but a grudging smile followed quickly behind his instant irritation. "That's what I keep you around for, Sloan. You ask me questions most people are too nice to even think. But at my age, son, you'd better believe I can tell the difference between a woman and a crusade."

For a minute Donnelly was quiet as his mind went back to the previous afternoon, to the soft torture of Carole's body so close to his, to the scent of her perfume that had risen like a sweet cloud with every breath she took, and to the look in her eyes that had belied every word she said.

Sloan opened the door into the guest room and, with a light tap on Donnelly's arm, said, "Excuse me, sweet dreamer, but are you ready for that beer I promised you?"

Donnelly reluctantly let go of the swelling ripple of desire his thoughts had brought, and followed Sloan into the house. "On a day like today," he said, trying to ignore the lingering sadness of loss, "I think I could take a swim in it."

The outside door closed behind them with a quiet slam, and they had gone only a few steps across the room when a sweetly feminine voice called from above, "Sloan? Is that you?"

Without warning, Donnelly was forced to tilt forward and catch himself against the wall with his outstretched hand to avoid tripping over Sloan, who had come to an abrupt halt at the doorway.

"Hey," Sloan called up the stairs as he blocked the door with his body, "when did you get home?"

"Just a few minutes ago. I called out to you, but you didn't answer."

"I was on the patio. I thought you were supposed to be shopping."

Sloan stretched out both arms and braced himself casually between the door jambs as Donnelly waited impatiently behind him.

"For some reason," the woman continued, "Dad decided to come along. Then he decided we should have lunch before we went shopping." Her voice drifted in and out as she moved around the room overhead. "Then he decided we should drive out to the lake because it was such a beautiful day. And about that time I began to realize that what he really wanted was to be alone with Mother, so I had them drop me off. I'm fixing some tea. Do you want a cup?"

Donnelly glowered menacingly, and Sloan relinquished his hold on the doorway, but as he moved into the hall, he continued to block the staircase. "Well, what we had in mind was a little colder," he answered as Donnelly pressed him from behind.

"We?" The soft voice tightened in a tone that was not altogether welcoming. "You're not alone?"

As her apartment had earlier, the woman's voice was raising pictures in Donnelly's mind and chills along his spine. He felt his impatient amusement hardening into something else as the humor of Sloan's hesitance began to fade.

"You promised me a beer," Donnelly said quietly. His hand at the small of Sloan's back urged him forward.

"I think we should talk first," Sloan answered in a hushed tone. His gaze was serious as a frown drew his brows together in a plea for patience.

"We'll talk upstairs." Whether the pounding of his heart was from anger or fear, Donnelly couldn't tell, but something had triggered that same silent alarm in the pit of his stomach that had guided him safely through two tours of combat duty. There was something at the top of the stairs that Sloan wanted to avoid, and Donnelly had no intention of letting him.

"Okay," Sloan said with a grudging shrug of his shoulders, "but when we get up there, you just remember that no matter what you think you know, you don't know anything. And then you just be quiet and let me explain."

Donnelly didn't answer. Almost shoulder to shoulder they climbed the staircase in silence, until Sloan, one step ahead of Donnelly and almost to the top, laughed softly and shook his head. "Damn," he said in a musing tone that could barely be heard, "wouldn't you just know it?"

Taking Sloan's arm in his hand, Donnelly halted him. The dark brown eyes that turned toward him were filled with a curious mingling of doubt and hope. Inside himself, Donnelly fought all of the natural instincts that told him never to give in, back down or turn aside. If he couldn't trust the man beside him, he couldn't trust anyone. He and Sloan had been through too much together to start doubting him now.

"If you'll show me the back way out of here," Donnelly said, "I'll go before we mess up something we can't fix. Whoever that lady up there is, she's your business, Sloan, and you don't owe me any explanations."

Sloan shook his head with a stubborn resignation. "No. This is something that I've got to tell somebody someday. And you've always been my choice for the first one to know." He quickly climbed the last few steps, then turned back to Donnelly with a grim smile.

His arm swept the air with a gesture of welcome. "Come on in."

Almost wishing that Sloan had taken him up on his offer, Donnelly followed him into the dining room, his gaze joining Sloan's as it turned toward the kitchen. As if all the warm blood in his body had been flushed out and replaced with ice water, Donnelly went numb.

Coming toward him from the kitchen, Carole faltered in the flawless elegance of her walk for only an instant. The teacup and saucer she carried gave one small tinkle of china against china before she regained her poise and set the tea carefully on the glass-topped dining table.

Her brown eyes were large and couldn't quite conceal the panic of a cornered animal as she looked from Donnelly to Sloan and back to Donnelly. "My," she said softly, feeling the need to speak and finding no words that were adequate.

"I'll get the beer," Sloan muttered, and went into the kitchen.

As Carole swiveled to watch Sloan pass, her eyes clinging to him as if he were her lifeline, Donnelly stared after her. Drinking in the view in stunned silence, he studied the way the orchid silk of her chemise whispered over the sleek play of her runner's muscles like wind skimming the water's surface. Stockings a deeper shade of lavender drew his eyes down her long calves, past slender ankles, to stiletto-heeled pumps of soft leather dyed to match her dress.

It was a showcase outfit, designed to catch any man's eye and, with the right body inside, hold it until he begged for mercy. And Carole's body did it justice.

The sleepless night grated on Donnelly's nerves. He was hot and tired, and the restless desire that had tormented him since his meeting with Carole the day before was nothing compared to the longing he felt as she crossed the dining room to intercept Sloan at the kitchen door.

She touched his arm and leaned nearer to whisper in his ear. In her heels, Carole was as tall as Sloan, and the easy familiarity between the two as they came back into the dining room cut through Donnelly with a pain that surprised him with its intensity.

The only thing he had felt for Carole before yesterday was a long-distance sympathy. Then, in one meeting, it was as if all the dams that held back his emotions had broken, at the worst possible time, with the worst possible girl. And none of it had mattered until he'd found out that his best friend had seen her first.

Then Sloan was in front of him, smiling apologetically and blocking out the thoughts that only went round and round. "Why don't you take a long, cool drink, and then we'll sit down and talk."

Sloan pressed the cold can into his hand and Donnelly took it, almost blind with the anger and betrayal that pounded at his temples. "Damn you," he grated out through clenched teeth. "You could have told me before you let me spill my guts to you all morning."

"Oh, hell," Sloan said, taking a step back in disgust, "are you on that again?"

A blue flame of rage burned low and cold in Donnelly's eyes. It was a flame Sloan recognized and took very seriously. "Listen, you've got it wrong, Donnelly," he explained carefully. "I swear, if you'll just listen, it's nothing like what you're thinking."

"I don't know what I'm thinking. I don't know *what* to think." Donnelly turned toward the living room, looking for a way out. Anger continued to sizzle inside of him, and he didn't know whom he was more furious with—Sloan for not telling him about Carole, or himself for caring far too much.

"Maybe I should leave," Carole said quietly, her voice fading as she spoke.

"No," Sloan said.

"Yes," Donnelly argued, turning as he spoke, to find Sloan's restraining arm around Carole's shoulders.

"Donnelly," Sloan said softly, "look. Just look. What do you see?"

What he saw was his best friend's arm around the woman Donnelly desperately and unreasonably wanted for himself, and it did nothing to abate his anger. "Let her go, Sloan. I'd rather we talked about this in private."

For a moment nobody moved. As the air between Donnelly and Sloan grew brittle with tension, Carole let out her breath with a sigh of resignation and said to Sloan, "You're going to tell him?"

Sloan closed his eyes and withdrew his arm from her shoulder. His whole body seemed to sag inward as he said, "They're words I never wanted to say aloud."

Frowning, Donnelly felt suddenly removed from the scene as he watched Sloan struggle and draw deeper into himself.

"I don't believe that, Sloan," Carole answered with a gentle smile. "I never have."

Grudgingly, Sloan opened his eyes again and looked at Donnelly, who found himself becoming more puzzled than angry. Sloan's arms hung limp at his sides as he said so quietly it was almost a whisper, "Carole is not my lover, Donnelly. She's my sister."

Ready for anything but that, Donnelly scowled. His mind leaped quickly from disbelief to a renewed burst of rage. "Tell me something I can believe, Sloan," he demanded, feeling an alarming physical urge to pound his fist into his friend's face. "If you don't want to admit your relationship, at least come up with a plausible lie. How do you expect anyone to swallow hogwash like that?"

Coming to life, Sloan shouted back at him, "Look, man, you're not making this any easier." His hands clenched into fists at his sides and his whole body became rigid as he ground out reluctantly through gritted teeth, "King Stockton is my father."

Something in Sloan's reluctance penetrated Donnelly's disbelief, and he began to see all the things that had always been there but he had never seen. The voice, the face, the way Sloan moved—it was King all over again, a little smaller and a lot younger, but King without a doubt.

And Carole—Donnelly looked from her to Sloan and back—there were the same penetrating eyes, the same stubborn set of the jaw, the same proud stance. The Stockton breeding was there for anyone to see who bothered to look.

"Well, I'll be damned," Donnelly said with a half-amused shake of his head. "How?"

"I'm sure it wasn't easy," Carole answered smoothly. "But my father is a resourceful man. Would you care to sit down?"

She indicated a long sofa that ran the length of the wall next to the balcony and curved to end at the base of the staircase. In the cool eyes that watched him, Donnelly found himself facing the woman who had so effectively held him at arm's length the previous afternoon. He couldn't help wondering what effect her father's indiscretion had had on Carole, or how long she had known of it.

With a grunt of approval, Sloan closed the distance between them and guided Donnelly toward the couch while Carole went into the kitchen. Gesturing to the end of the sofa nearest the fireplace, Sloan dropped into a chair across from Donnelly and took a giant drink of his beer.

"Which one of the million questions in your head are you going to ask first?" Sloan said.

"Who came first?" Donnelly asked in a low tone. He was having trouble reconciling an extramarital affair with King's open adoration of Carole's mother, Amelia.

"Me. By a year."

Realizing that Carole's parents might not have been married at that time, Donnelly nodded, somehow relieved. "That's good."

"Good for me," Carole said, appearing as if from nowhere. "Not so good for Sloan." She curled up in the curve of the sofa and took a sip from her teacup.

Donnelly's next question went out of his head as he turned to look at her. One leg was tucked under her, while the other was stretched out on the velvety surface of the forest-green couch, a green so dark it was almost black. She looked like a cat curled up on the floor of a tropical forest, nestling beneath a blanket of orchids.

"Come on, Donnelly," Sloan said, "this is hard for me to talk about. If you don't ask questions, I don't know where to start."

"Well," Donnelly said, tearing his thoughts away from Carole, "since everybody inside the family obviously knows, how come this is still such a dark secret?"

Instead of answering, Sloan frowned and stared at the coffee table between them.

"Somebody," Carole said, filling the silence as she pointed a finger at Sloan, "doesn't want anyone to know. He doesn't want the name. He doesn't want the money. And he doesn't want the father who would give anything to be able to acknowledge him."

Sloan's stare became a glare that left the table and moved to Carole. She smiled sweetly and said, "I offered to leave, but you stopped me."

"My mistake," Sloan answered.

"How long have you known who your father was, Sloan?" Donnelly asked quietly, beginning to realize the depth of Sloan's struggle. Whatever Carole's initial reaction might have been, Donnelly was glad to see that her acceptance of her brother now seemed total. Apparently the only thing stopping Sloan's complete recognition was Sloan himself.

"I've always known who my father was, but Carole only found out about me a few years ago, when King finally decided to open up. You see, what happened with my mother was before he was married, so there was no real reason to go on hiding my existence."

"So why do you insist on keeping it a secret?" Donnelly asked gently. He could see no real anger in Sloan, but he hesitated to push him toward any lingering feelings of bitterness.

"Self-preservation, mainly. The man is a wrecking machine when it comes to other people's lives, to which Carole is an unwilling witness."

When Carole shifted uncomfortably, Sloan looked at her sadly and said, "Sorry, sweetheart, but this is honesty time." He looked back to Donnelly and continued. "King doesn't mean any harm, but he just can't stop trying to mold the world and everyone in it according to his image. Carole is heir to the throne, and Mathison was King's hand-picked consort. And we all know how that turned out."

Carole was still, but some of the color had left her face, and Donnelly had to fight a powerful urge to pull her into his arms and stroke the pain away. Her jaw was set and her head was held high, and the look in her eyes was of cool strength. But some instinct in Donnelly could feel the fear that trembled inside her, and the thousand tiny cracks of heartbreak that had left her too fragile to touch.

She was a woman who would not easily trust; one wrong move would end forever any chance he had. Between her father's well-intentioned manipulation and Mathison's cold-blooded betrayal, Carole had already had too many lessons in men's deceit.

"He's my father, and I love him," Sloan continued quietly. "And he knows it. But I'm grown, and it's too damned late to adopt me. King can take me as a man on my own two feet, or he can leave me alone."

"And they're still at the bargaining table," Carole said. Her soft smile managed to push aside the haunting cloud that had enveloped her. "They're so much alike. If people ever saw them together, that would be the ball game." She shook her head in mock sadness, and her smile widened as Sloan turned to her with a wry laugh.

To Donnelly, he said, "She's the one good thing in all of this. I'd like to be able to spend more time with Carole, but if people saw us together, well..." He shrugged and flashed Donnelly a mischievous smile. "You know what happens. And since my sister seems to be a hot news topic, I don't want to find myself identified as her unknown escort. It could become a little embarrassing, and I think Carole's already had enough embarrassment to last more than one lifetime."

Though Sloan still smiled, the look in his eyes as he regarded Donnelly seemed to carry a message, one that he chose to deliver in Carole's presence. Any interest Donnelly had in her would eventually run the risk of becoming news, and Donnelly realized that all of the protests he had made to Sloan the previous morning were being thrown back in his face.

For Donnelly to even think of pursuing Carole romantically while he was running for governor, or during his term if he were elected, was political and emotional suicide. While it might be worth the risk for him, it would be the worst thing he could do to someone as vulnerable as Carole.

He looked into Sloan's eyes and saw the warning as clearly as if it had been written: Leave her alone. She has been through enough.

With a supreme effort of will, Donnelly stared straight ahead at Sloan and nodded his understanding. Though he could feel her only a few feet away, he did not turn for one last look at Carole. He rose, and Sloan rose with him as Donnelly said, "Well, I guess that's it. I've got a speech to make somewhere this afternoon."

Sloan's hand closed on Donnelly's shoulder as he walked with him from the room. His voice held cautious relief as he said, "Thanks. For everything."

At the front door Donnelly turned and looked hard at Sloan. "I'm not making you any promises. I understand how you feel, and I agree. But it's not going to be easy for me."

"You just met her," Sloan said. His eyes reflected the unrelenting determination of a protective older brother.

"I said I'll try." Donnelly laid each word down with a firmness that warned against further argument. "But this is the last time we're going to discuss the subject."

Angry in spite of himself, Donnelly turned and walked away. Behind him Sloan called quietly, "Don't hurt her. Please."

Donnelly kept on walking, not wanting to think of all that had just happened, not wanting to blame Sloan for the terrible sense of loss that had begun already, and blaming him just the same.

As Donnelly slid behind the wheel of the old MG that was his only memento of the luxuriously carefree days of his youth, he tried to remember where he was supposed to be that afternoon. But all his memory held was a deep and gnawing regret that he had left without speaking to Carole, without taking a final, lingering look at the woman who pushed all other thought out of his mind.

The day had only grown hotter while he was inside. The black leather of the convertible's seat burned against Donnelly's back as he started the engine and pulled slowly away from the curb, resisting the desire to look back.

He didn't want to be the one to cause her any more pain, so he would leave, and he would try to stay away. He would try, but even as Donnelly turned finally and took one last, long look behind him, he knew he wouldn't make it.

Chapter Four

The silence seemed to cave in around her, as Carole heard the front door click shut behind the two men. She rose from the couch and walked through the room that only moments before had been so filled with Donnelly's presence. His size still seemed to overpower the surroundings while the echoes of his anger laid waste the peaceful texture of her home. But with his parting Carole felt a loneliness so deep it was crushing.

From the kitchen window, she watched Donnelly jerk open the door of the faded red sports car and fold his long body into the low seat. He grew perfectly still as his hands gripped the steering wheel and he stared straight ahead. Carole waited for him to look her way, for any gesture that would wipe out the memory of his sudden, wordless departure.

Without taking his eyes from the road ahead, Donnelly slammed the car door and pulled away from the curb. Emptiness echoed around Carole as she watched him drive away without looking back.

As Donnelly neared the end of the block, Carole heard a sound behind her and turned to find Sloan watching her. "Is it my turn to get an explanation?" she asked before he had a chance to speak. Inside her, the desolate feeling of rejection grew, making her words harsh.

"I didn't think you'd be home."

"So you hadn't *planned* for us to meet?" Carole moved past him into the dining room as she spoke, and Sloan followed her.

"No."

"Good." She kept on moving, gathering up the still-full cans of beer in the living room, and stepping around Sloan on her way back to the kitchen. "I was afraid for a minute that you might be matchmaking."

"With him? No way."

Carole emptied the beer into the sink and tossed the cans into the trash. "I thought you two were friends," she said, challenging Sloan with her eyes across the distance to the dining room. Puzzled by the hostility in Sloan's answer, she wondered if Donnelly could be the kind of friend a brother would protect his sister from. "So why else would you bring him here?"

Sloan shrugged and moved back a step as he pointed to the refrigerator behind her. "Could you bring me another one of those?"

Hiding her impatience for his answer, Carole reached into the refrigerator and brought a beer with her into the dining room. After her divorce, she had spent years rebuilding a life she could be content with, and now, in one twenty-four-hour period, everything she had built seemed to be collapsing.

In spite of all Carole's efforts, Donnelly had never been far from her thoughts since she had left him the day before. That morning she had almost put him out of her mind, finally, until he had walked into her living room with her brother.

"Donnelly used to work construction," Sloan said, picking up the conversation, "so I figured he'd be a big help with the doors. Did you notice?" He popped the top on the can and looked at her with a teasing grin.

"Yes," Carole said, relenting a little as she remembered the protective grillwork on the entry door. "And thank you." Carrying a damp cloth she had brought from the kitchen, Carole went past him and stooped to wipe the black lacquered surface of the coffee table.

"You seem to know him well," she said as she worked, trying to calm her mind with movement. Long green leaves and one broad white calla lily were painted up one side of the table and into a graceful arc across the top. Carole's hand lingered thoughtfully over the golden center of the calla lily, cleaning in slow circles as she spoke. "You've never mentioned him."

"I've never seen a reason to."

There was still a stiff defensiveness about Sloan's attitude and it bothered her. The tensions that had swirled among the three of them earlier had not diminished with Donnelly's leaving. "Dad seems to think I should get to know him better," she said.

"Yeah, well, Dad's had a lot of brilliant ideas, hasn't he?"

The scathing tone of his voice drove the words into Carole with a force Sloan hadn't intended. She left the cloth on the table as she sat on the edge of the couch. "I take it you don't approve of the idea," she answered quietly, forcing a calm she didn't feel.

Whichever way she turned the past was there to greet her, and Carole was growing tired of running from something she apparently couldn't escape.

"Look," Sloan said, softening, "Donnelly's a great guy, but he's been a bachelor for almost forty years. He's married to his career."

"He doesn't have a girlfriend, then?" With studied disinterest Carole rose again, lifted the cloth in one hand and her teacup in the other and passed Sloan on her way to the kitchen.

"You asked that like you might care," Sloan said as she went by him.

"I may have to campaign for him. It would be better if he did have a girlfriend." Ignoring the hollow depression she felt at the sound of her own words, Carole set the china in the sink and hung up the cloth, then turned to smile at Sloan. "Don't you think?"

"Well, let's just put it this way," he said, still not convinced. "I've never seen him lonely."

"But there's no one special?" Carole left the kitchen and came back into the dining room, looking around for something to do with her hands.

"He's never had time for anyone special." Sloan's tone grew firmer and his eyes caught Carole's with a look of warning. "He's never let anyone *become* special. Am I getting my point across?"

"Why should you have to, Sloan?" As she grew irritated by the confusion of her own feelings, Carole's voice took on a cutting edge that carried a warning of its own. "I hardly know the man."

"Look, Carole," Sloan said apologetically, "I'm sorry I brought him here. He's like a brother to me, and a part of me wishes that, well... Anyway, I was wrong.

Things just can't always be the way you wish they could."

Something in his words touched her heart, and Carole reached out to take Sloan's hand. "That seems to be the story of our lives, doesn't it?" she asked sadly.

Her eyes looked into his with an understanding that was their bond. They each had their own special pain, their own secrets, their own way of dealing with the things they would never have and all the hopes that could never be.

Sloan's other hand took hers, and his eyes forced her not to look away while he spoke. "He's a good man, Carole. But he's not for you."

"Oh, Sloan." Carole pulled her hands from his and turned her gaze to the floor. "Do you think I don't know that? I never said he was."

"I'm not a blind man, Carole. Some things don't need words."

"And some things exist only in the imagination of others," Carole said with a quiet finality. "I think we've taken this conversation about as far as it's going."

With a sigh of resignation, Sloan took a step away from her and nodded. "You're right." He walked into the kitchen, where he poured another untouched can of beer down the drain and threw the empty away. "I'm packed. Do you need anything before I leave?"

Shaking her head, Carole said, "Not really. Will you be gone long?" Already she regretted the tension that had arisen between them.

Sloan came back into the dining room with a relaxed smile that was his peace offering. "Till the end of the week. By then my apartment should be ready."

"Aw, shucks," Carole teased.

Laughing, Sloan gave her a quick peck on the cheek and left. As she heard the garage doors close, Carole climbed the stairs to her bedroom and changed into shorts and her jogging shoes. The silence that was usually her refuge had become oppressive in its emptiness, and she hurried out of the house that was overshadowed by the sights and sounds of her memory.

Once at the river, beneath the warmth of the sun and surrounded by a menagerie of joggers, children on bicycles and couples walking their dogs, Carole felt the terrible coldness inside her begin to thaw.

For so long after Andrew she had thought that her feelings for men—any man—were dead. But then, with an ease that had left her stunned, Donnelly had aroused not only those feelings but even deeper ones. Helpless against their suddenness, Carole had felt the stirrings of emotions that had never been touched before.

And her only defense had been to turn and run away, but she hadn't been able to put the thought of him behind her. All through the night, every time she grew quiet the memories came rushing in. They filled her mind and left her barren heart aching with its loss.

In time, Carole knew, she would forget the longings that Donnelly had aroused, and the man with them. And if she couldn't forget, then she would have to learn to live with the memories of a touch, and a look, and a few careless words that had reached into her lonely soul and ignited a flame long dead.

Too quickly she began to feel isolated in the midst of the contented crowd along the riverbanks. Turning away from thoughts that were too tender to be examined in public, Carole stopped and retraced her steps toward home.

Nothing succeeded in filling the emptiness inside her for more than a few brief moments, and with nothing left to do but wait for night, she could only hope that with darkness would come peace.

Inside her house, Carole climbed the stairs to her bathroom, determined to end the depression that seemed to be growing with a life of its own. She had spent too many years learning to be happy alone to lose it all now over a few chance meetings with a man who could never be anything to her but trouble.

Maybe someday there would be room in her life for a man, but this was not the day and Donnelly would never be the man. As she stepped into a hot, pelting shower, Carole thought of Sloan's warning. Apparently she was only one of many women who had been affected by Donnelly's splendid looks and the tantalizing hint of danger in his turquoise eyes. And, as tempting a challenge as Donnelly might seem, she had already been one among many for one man, and once was more than enough for her.

Putting the thoughts behind her as she left the shower, Carole dried her hair and arranged it in a casual tumble high on her head, leaving stray tendrils around her face and down her neck to soften the look. Except for a clear gloss on her lips and a dusting of pink blush, she left her face bare, happy with the confident sparkle of the dark eyes that stared out at her from the mirror.

In the bedroom she applied perfume generously and slid into a set of ivory satin lounging pajamas. Enjoying the soft feel of the carpet on her bare feet, Carole left her shoes behind when she descended to the living room.

There, the resurgence of her fragile spirit faltered. The cold, dark stone of the fireplace caught her eye and, on either side of it, huge windows looked out on the blue sky of a day that seemed to stretch without end. Wishing it were cool enough to light a comforting fire, Carole slipped a tape of sixties' music into the stereo and went to the kitchen.

She opened a bottle of white wine, poured a glass and paused to listen as the sweet, sad sound of Buffalo Springfield began to whisper in the background. Returning to the living room, she lit the candelabras on the fireplace mantel and placed small, scented candles on the coffee table.

With a contented smile, Carole curled into the corner of the sofa, the end where Donnelly had been only a few hours earlier. As she took a slow sip of her wine and watched the flickering light of the candles compete with the still-bright sun, the doorbell rang.

Involuntarily, her smile widened and her heart began to pound with an eager and senseless hope. Placing her wineglass on the table, Carole forced herself to rise slowly, fighting the urge to run to the door. At the head of the staircase she paused, then continued past it into the kitchen.

From the window she could see a plain black sedan in her driveway, a car she had never seen before, a salesman's car. The happy beat of her heart slowed as she descended the stairs, raising her eyes only high enough to see the dark pants of a man in a navy-blue business suit waiting on the wood decking of her front porch.

Opening the door, Carole lifted her gaze unwillingly as she said, "I'm sorry, but I'm not interested in..."

Her words died in her throat when her eyes reached Donnelly's frowning face.

"Do you always open your door without looking?" he demanded. "No wonder Sloan's worried about you."

"You changed cars," she said, as if that explained her carelessness. "And clothes."

"I don't deliver speeches in blue jeans and T-shirts. As much as I might like to." He lifted his brows quizzically and smiled. "Do you mind if I come in?"

"Of course...not." Carole stepped back as he entered the small foyer, then shut the door behind him as Donnelly began to climb the stairs. When she reached the top, he was standing at the stereo, listening to the final bars of the song.

"Boy," he said with a shake of his head, "that sure brings back memories, doesn't it?" Donnelly turned to include Carole in his reminiscence and asked, "Do you mind?" Then, without waiting for her response, he rewound the cassette to the beginning of the song, and once more Buffalo Springfield began the haunting dirge that had so epitomized an era.

"Make yourself at home," Carole answered with just the faintest touch of acid in her words. Still bristling, she crossed to the coffee table and lifted her wineglass. Taking a sip, she stared through her window at the burning blue of the sky.

While she watched, it deepened to navy, so formal-looking with its tiny burgundy stripes, with broad shoulders tailored to accentuate the slope to a slender waist. Without even trying, Carole could remember every detail of Donnelly's narrow navy-and-wine tie and the pale blue shirt demanded by television cameras. She had never seen him so businesslike before, and without even trying, she seemed to know it was a look he carried well.

"You know something, woman?" Silently, Donnelly had arrived beside her. Before Carole could turn to face him, his fingers brushed hers, and he lifted the wineglass from her hand as he finished, "You have the tongue of an asp."

His eyes waited for hers above the rim of the glass while he took a sip. Handing the wine back to her, he smiled and said, "Do you think we could call a truce? And do you think I could have a glass of my own?"

"Of course," Carole answered coolly. Holding his eyes with hers across the rim, the same way he had held hers, and placing her lips where his had been, she drank from the glass.

"Of course to both?" he asked hopefully.

"We'll see." She moved past him, knowing the way the satin flowed against her skin, revealing almost more than it hid, and acutely aware of how little she wore under it. With each step she could feel Donnelly's eyes on her as he followed behind, in no hurry to catch up.

Reaching into the cabinet, Carole withdrew another wineglass and filled it from the bottle of wine still standing on the counter. Donnelly stopped next to her, so close his thigh brushed hers when he lifted the matching decanter from the cabinet shelf. He took the bottle from her hand and refilled her glass, then emptied the remaining wine into the decanter.

"Do you have a tray?" he asked.

Biting back another retort, Carole silently removed a silver tray from under the counter and handed it to him. While he arranged the decanter and glasses on the tray, she tried not to notice how domestic the scene had become.

From the first moment Donnelly had walked into her home, he had taken it from her and made a part of it his, molding the surroundings to his dimensions so naturally that Carole feared they would never again be truly hers.

"I don't suppose you cook, too," she said, unable to hold back the sarcasm when he proudly lifted the tray from the counter and stepped aside for her to walk ahead of him.

"Does this mean I get the glass, but no truce?" Donnelly answered, trailing behind her into the living room.

Carole remained silent until she had curled into the corner of the couch and leaned against the sofa's arm. "Do you always walk into a strange house and make yourself so at home?" she asked, watching Donnelly set the tray down and come around the coffee table to sit on the cushion next to her.

Without answering he lifted his wineglass and extended Carole's to her. In no hurry to end the contact, Donnelly let his fingers linger for a long moment against hers before withdrawing his hand.

"No," he said finally. His eyes were gentle on hers as he laid his arm along the back of the couch. "I feel comfortable here. There's something very warm and welcoming about your home, Carole." His fingertips lightly brushed her shoulder, and he spoke quietly. "I don't seem to be able to resist it."

Carole took a sip of the wine and felt it coat the sudden dryness of her throat. "Is that why you came back?" she asked softly. "If you were looking for Sloan, I'm afraid he had to leave."

"I know," Donnelly said carefully. "I didn't come back to see Sloan."

"Oh," Carole answered. Sunlight intensified the green tint of Donnelly's eyes and added a creamy glow to the tan of his skin. In the background, nostalgic rock stirred the instinctive yearnings of first love, wooing with a simplicity that wiped out the years of hard-learned caution.

"And I do cook," Donnelly said. His quiet smile softened the echoes of a silence that had stretched too loudly. "My brother and I are both very domestic, even though he has a wife to take care of him now."

"Your brother?"

"Cody. I thought you had met him."

Vaguely Carole remembered a younger man who had been with Donnelly at a fund-raiser several years before. "No," she said, shaking her head and trying not to feel the intimacy of Donnelly's soft tones or the deeper intimacy of his fingertips on her shoulder. "I've seen him, but I never got a chance to meet him. He's married now?"

"Yes, to an assistant D.A." Beneath a brother's pride, there was a caution in Donnelly's answer that triggered another memory in Carole.

"Oh, yes," she said slowly. "I recall my father's mentioning that."

"I'll bet he did," Donnelly answered stiffly.

"He gets a little carried away." Carole smiled, thinking of her father's indignation at the way Cody Wakefield had avoided Donnelly's campaign. He'd shown the same sort of indignation at her own support of Susan Osburne, a minor opponent who had caused barely a ripple in the immense success of Donnelly's candidacy.

"How did your speech go?" Carole asked. She stared at the flickering candle on the table in front of her while her palms cradled the tall, narrow wineglass.

"Fine, I guess. I wasn't paying a lot of attention."

"Isn't that rather dangerous at this point?" Surprised by the lack of concern in Donnelly's voice, Carole turned to look at him and, too late, realized her error.

If the delicate brush of his hand on her back and the warmth of his leg against her bare feet were disconcerting, they were nothing compared to the quiet battle of emotions that blazed into her from Donnelly's waiting eyes.

"I would have canceled if I could," he answered in an even tone that betrayed nothing.

"The primary's only two days away." Despite the tumult his gaze had stirred inside her, Carole couldn't ignore the sincerity in his voice. No politician could be so unmoved with the scent of victory so near, and yet Donnelly seemed almost to resent the effort required of him.

"The primary's won," he said, dismissing a milestone in his career with a quirk of his straight, sandy-brown brow.

"I don't understand." For the first time, Carole regretted her decision to support another candidate, a decision that had isolated her from any firsthand knowledge of Donnelly's attitudes or his motivation for running.

He might only be tired, worn down by the intensity of the last week before the primary, or he might genuinely be caught on a treadmill he would rather not be on. Either way, he was not what she had expected him to be, as a man or as a politician.

Donnelly smiled a little regretfully. "Maybe I should have taken time to change before I came over here. These clothes seem to have brought the candidate with me, and I intended to come as just a man." His hand toyed with the stray locks at the back of her neck. "Do you think we could leave the politics outside the door?" Donnelly's voice softened to a caress while his finger traced the rim of Carole's ear and continued across the line of her jaw. "Please?" he asked as his hand cupped her chin.

"All right," Carole agreed, giving up her questions and accepting his terms. Her hand shook as she pulled away from him and replaced her wineglass on the tray. Before she could straighten, Donnelly leaned forward and set his glass beside hers. "Why *did* you come?" she asked, looking into the aquamarine eyes that were only inches from hers.

"Because I couldn't stay away," he said simply.

For a moment, neither of them moved. Then Carole leaned back, growing calm, as all she had avoided seemed suddenly so near. "That doesn't leave me with a lot to say," she answered.

Donnelly swiveled to face her, bracing his hand on the back of the couch, close to her but not touching. "Did Sloan warn you away from me?" The eyes that waited for her answer were calm and totally serious.

"Yes." Carole met his gaze without flinching, but her empty hands felt lost in her lap and she wished she had the small barrier of her wineglass back again.

Donnelly's free hand closed around her cold and restless ones. "He's right, you know."

"Yes." Tentatively, her hands unfolded, silently inviting the warmth of Donnelly's clasp.

His fingers slid across the palm of her hand, then turned and intertwined with hers as his thumb slowly stroked the back of her hand. "If you tell me to go, I will."

For a moment Carole considered his offer, weighing the loneliness without him against the danger with him. Then she smiled at the irony of the thought. "But would you *stay* away?" she asked softly.

With a laughing shake of his head, Donnelly said, "No. No, I don't think I would." He watched her with a smile still gently curving his lips. "Would you want me to?"

Freeing their entwined fingers, Carole took his hand between both of hers, holding it lightly. "Therein, Mr. Wakefield, lies the dilemma." There was a sigh in her voice that contradicted her answering smile.

"Don't you ever get tired of thinking, Carole?" Donnelly sobered abruptly as he sensed her retreat. "Don't you ever get tired of being boxed up here in this safe little prison you've created for yourself?"

"That's cheap rhetoric, Donnelly. I had hoped for better from you," Carole said, withdrawing her hands as she shrank into herself.

"That was not a rhetorical question, Carole." Donnelly caught her hand in his again and held it tightly while his eyes demanded her response. "And I expect an answer. Why do you hide away here?"

"Because this is the one and only place where I am truly myself," Carole said, resenting the way he made her want to please him. "Outside these doors I'm King Stockton's daughter and Andrew Mathison's ex-wife. People don't even know my name, but they, by God, know who I *am* right down to the most intimate details of my life."

Something about the way his hand tightened on hers made her want to cry. It told her that he understood her anger and resentment, and it begged her to look at him instead of turning away. Staring straight ahead, Carole refused to look and refused to cry.

"Here I'm just Carole," she said, biting off each word to hold back the tears. "I'm just me, and nobody knows me at all. So you see, Donnelly, you're wrong. I live here, and I hide everywhere else I go."

"You know," Donnelly said quietly, "one thing I wanted to do today was avoid all the blunders I made yesterday. I don't seem to be doing a very good job of it."

Regretting her outburst almost immediately, Carole asked, "Have you considered the possibility that I'm just not easy to get along with?" With Donnelly she was awakening to feelings, both good and bad, that she had long since put behind her, and too often he became the target of the worst of those feelings.

"Well, yes, that did occur to me yesterday." Donnelly's gently teasing eyes warmed her. As his hand slid beneath the loose cuff of her sleeve to caress her arm, his voice deepened. "And I decided that, even if you are, you're worth it."

Carole closed her eyes against the powerful emotions he called up with a single touch, against the outrageous joy he offered so effortlessly.

"Where do we go from here, Carole?"

"I don't know." The patience in his voice was even worse than a demand would have been. It gently nudged her toward a decision she was terrified to face.

Donnelly lifted her hand to his lips and kissed it gently. "The next move is yours," he said in the same quiet tone.

"What do you want?" Knowing it was a mistake, Carole opened her eyes and looked at him. Outside, the sun was dimming, and candlelight glittered in Donnelly's eyes like stars reflected on a glassy sea.

"All I can get." Turning her hand over, he kissed the inside of her wrist first lightly, then with a growing, possessive intensity.

"You're mad," Carole said weakly, tired of fighting when all she wanted was to give in. "We're both mad." Her hand touched his cheek. "What are we going to do?" she asked, resigned to the fate neither one had any desire to escape.

In no hurry once he'd heard the acceptance in Carole's voice, Donnelly pulled her slowly into his arms. "We'll take it one step at a time."

Settling into the deep cushions of the couch, Donnelly cradled Carole to him. She drank in his scent, lost in the arms that surrounded her. The firm pounding of his heart against her cheek stilled her fears, and Carole's hand slipped beneath his suit jacket to feel the broad chest beneath the crisp shirtfront.

Donnelly's hand held her head to his heart, and his words rumbled in her ear. "No one's ever going to hurt you again, Carole. I swear it. I won't let anyone hurt you."

Carole's hand reached higher and caressed the muscles of Donnelly's shoulder, enjoying the strength beneath her touch. "One day at a time, Donnelly," she whispered. "For now, can we keep this our secret? At least until we've had a chance to figure out what's happening here?"

She could hear the amusement in his voice when he answered, "Do you ever stop being practical?"

"If this weekend is any example, I think I'm slipping badly," Carole said, pulling away to look at Donnelly's face. "Do we have a deal?"

"As far as I'm concerned, you're my business and nobody else's." The sound of possession was strong in his answer. "Carole, you offered me the chance to kiss you once, and I turned you down." Donnelly's hand caressed her cheek while his other arm slipped lower on her back. "I'd like to now."

His full, firm lips were parted and waiting for her answer, unmoving and silent, while her own lips separated in anticipation. Donnelly's hand tightened, pulling her face slowly nearer, until finally his mouth could reach hers.

Like the brush of a hot wind, his lips touched hers and slipped away, then returned for a light, lingering caress that sent Carole's pulse racing with its warm promise.

Donnelly's arms tightened, crushing her to him, while his mouth searched hers with a deepening hunger that left them both breathless with its suddenness. When his lips reluctantly released hers, Donnelly drew a long breath, but his hands caressed Carole's back, still unwilling to let her go. "I like this outfit," he said lightly, enjoying the feel of her heart pounding next to his.

"I have more like it," Carole answered, content to remain in his arms all night. "How late can you stay?"

"I have to catch a plane at ten." Donnelly's chin brushed the top of her head as he spoke, and her loosening pile of hair tickled the tip of his nose.

"Have you noticed it's getting dark?" Mentally Carole calculated the time and knew he would have to be leaving soon. "When will you be back?"

"Tuesday night I'll be dividing my time between watch parties here and in Oklahoma City. If you don't mind, I'd like to end the evening in the same town you're in."

"I'm going to Susan's party in Oklahoma City, but I'll be flying back to Tulsa in the company plane when it's over."

"Carole," Donnelly said softly as he lifted her chin from his chest, and his mouth once more took hers with a thirst that seemed beyond quenching.

The shrill beeping of a watch alarm ended the moment too soon. "Damn," Donnelly swore quietly as he released Carole to silence the alarm.

"Very efficient, aren't you?" Carole commented, feeling abandoned while she leaned against the corner of the couch and watched him straighten his cuffs and tie.

Donnelly slipped his arm around Carole's waist and lifted her to her feet as he stood. "I've got an hour to takeoff." He looked down at her, so much smaller in her bare feet, and wished with all he had that he could take her with him. "Do I have to pretend that I don't know you? Do I have to worry about a man answering when I call you tomorrow night? Do you want to pack a bag and go with me?"

As his arms tightened around her waist, Carole realized that Donnelly was only half teasing. The other half was very serious. "You *will* call me tomorrow?" she asked, answering all of his questions with that one.

With a sigh, Donnelly took her hand and began his exit. At the front door, he pulled her into his arms again in a final, tight hug. "I don't know what time I'll call. It may be late." He kissed the top of her head and opened the door. "Would you mind if I woke you up?" he asked, halfway out the door.

"No," Carole answered, wishing he would kiss her again and seeing in his eyes that he wouldn't. "I'll be waiting."

Chapter Five

Abandoning her restless attempt at sleep, Carole rolled over and stared at the glowing green numbers on her radio alarm. Thirty-five minutes had clicked past since the last time she looked—it was now two-thirty and deep into the middle of a brightly moonlit night. With a sigh, she looked from the clock to the silent, waiting phone beside it and wished for the hundredth time that night that such a small thing didn't mean so much.

But it did, and there seemed to be no way for Carole to stop the hope and disappointment that combined to keep her awake and miserable. Turning away, she closed her eyes and snuggled into the profusion of pillows between her and the padded headboard. Her eyes burned; her head hurt; and tomorrow was going to be a long, long day.

There were a hundred things that could have kept Donnelly from calling. With the primary only a day away, his schedule would be almost nonstop. With a weary sigh, Carole opened her eyes and stared at an arrangement of silk orchids on the nightstand. In the moonlight they were a colorless blend of light and dark. Green leaves became black; white petals glowed pearly and pale; mauve blossoms were a ghostly gray as she fought the urge to check the time again on the clock behind her.

What had he said? That he would call. No, Carole realized, thinking back to their conversation the night before. He had only said that he *might* call. They had talked in circles and had really said nothing.

Donnelly's only promise had been in his eyes, in the way his lightest touch had branded itself into her, in the way his kisses had clung as if they would never end. Any other promise existed solely in the way her heart pounded each time she thought of him, not in his words.

When the sudden ring of the telephone finally came, it was loud and insistent, not at all the happy sound Carole had been imagining. Turning too eagerly, she entangled herself in the covers that still nestled against her chin. As they wound themselves around her, she came to a halt still a foot from the edge of the bed, her extended hand inches from the ringing phone.

Struggling to extricate herself from the comforter, Carole stretched her arm inch by slow inch across the nightstand. Growing frustrated as she counted the eighth ring, she caught the edge of the receiver with her fingertips, knocking it off its cradle into the front of the nightstand, and onto the floor.

"Oh, no," Carole moaned when she finally pulled free of the covers, and she lifted the receiver from the carpet to her ear. "Hello?" she whispered, almost afraid to hear Donnelly's reply.

A long, deep laugh was his only answer; then, "I wish I could see your face." Donnelly's voice, still laughing, was achingly tender.

"You wouldn't want to," Carole answered softly, relaxing onto her elbow. "It's too red." Inside, she melted at the nearness of his voice in the dark and silent night.

"I bet it's beautiful," he argued gently. "Sorry if I woke you. When I saw how late it was, I was a little afraid to call."

"I thought maybe you had forgotten." Carole curled between her pillows and the offending comforter, cradling the receiver to her ear as if she could bring Donnelly next to her in the palm of her hand.

"No. I just got in."

His deep, soft voice caressed her as he spoke, and Carole regretted her earlier doubts.

"You must be exhausted," she said, knowing that the bone-deep ache of fatigue she felt from her hours of sleepless waiting was nothing compared to what Donnelly would be suffering.

"You make me feel better," he answered with a tired sigh. "Your voice is the best thing I've heard all day."

In the background, Carole heard a shoe hit the floor, then the rustle of clothing close to the phone. She listened in silence while her imagination flew ahead to a picture of Donnelly undressing and lying down next to her. Every move he made, every breath he took, was transmitted as clearly as if he had been in the room with her.

"Carole?"

"Yes."

He laughed, a soft, breathy laugh next to her ear, and the other shoe bounced to the floor. "Don't go to sleep on me."

"Oh, I wouldn't do that. Donnelly?"

"Yes?"

"What are you doing?"

There was a smile in his voice as he answered, "You can't tell?"

In the background, sheets were stripped back, and the bed protested feebly beneath Donnelly's weight and then was silent.

"I'm glad to see I'm not keeping you up," Carole said, and she heard his chuckle as he smiled. Then his breathing changed, and for a moment she couldn't hear anything at all.

"God, I miss you," Donnelly said suddenly.

The soft teasing was gone from his voice; in its place was a gravelly impatience that made Carole's head swim while her body responded as if with a teeth-chattering fever.

"One lousy kiss is not enough, Carole," he continued with a frustration that was close to anger.

Unprepared for the harshness that had edged into Donnelly's voice, Carole stalled for time, for a way to avoid what she still wasn't ready to face. "It was two," she answered weakly.

"One, two or two hundred," Donnelly said with determination replacing his impatience, "it's not enough. I'm a man, and you're a woman, and I want you, Carole—the way a man wants a woman. I want you so much I can't sleep at night for thinking about it."

"Donnelly." Carole got that far and no farther. She didn't want to say no, but she couldn't say yes. In spite of how she felt, there was still a wall around her heart that couldn't be breached.

Nothing but time and patience could set her free—that, and a man who cared enough to wait.

"I've done it again, haven't I?" Donnelly asked into a silence broken only by the sound of their breathing.

"It's not your fault," Carole apologized.

"Yes, it is. You didn't ask for any of this. I promised you yesterday that you wouldn't be hurt, and now here I am... Well, anyway, you obviously don't feel the same way I do."

A note of sadness and of hopeless longing vibrated in Donnelly's voice. It cried out to her, filling the darkness and shaming Carole with her own cowardice. She longed to explain, to apologize for the fears she couldn't conquer, but the salty tang of her heartbreak was too near the surface and held her silent in its grip.

"Carole, please," Donnelly groaned at the sound of her increasingly ragged breath. "Please, don't cry. I can't reach through this phone and hold you if you do, and I don't think I could stand that."

He listened for a minute to the jagged sigh that was Carole's only answer. Then he plunged ahead, putting his heart into his words, letting his voice soothe the wounds his arms couldn't reach. "Forget everything I've said, okay? I'll see you tomorrow night, and if you want to talk, we'll talk. Either way, you've seen the last of King Kong, I promise. Carole?"

Smiling through the tears that had slipped soundlessly down her cheeks, Carole said, "You know, there could come a time when I might want to see King Kong again."

"Just say the word, lady, and the mighty Kong is yours," Donnelly answered tenderly.

Relaxing, Carole held the phone as if she could caress the smooth, strong cheek of the man whose breath rose and fell with her own. "I miss you, Donnelly," she whispered.

"You have no idea how happy that makes me. I think today has been the longest, loneliest day of my life." His voice was raw with fatigue, with the force of emotions neither of them could control. "Your terms are going to be awfully hard to live by Carole."

Remembering the agony of a day spent waiting to hear his voice again, Carole couldn't contest the honesty of Donnelly's words. But if wishing could make something so, life would be a much simpler thing. Instead of arguing, she asked, "How much does becoming governor mean to you, Donnelly?"

"I don't know," he answered, considering his words without questioning her change of topic. "It used to be very important to me, but now, I just don't know anymore."

"Well, for as long as you still want to be governor," Carole said, completing the circle of her logic, "this is the only way it can be. You can't come here, and I can't go there. Maybe Sloan was right." Her voice grew sad and reflective, drawing on the protective distance between them. "Maybe we should just forget this for a while."

"Is that really what you want, Carole?"

In his tone was a gentle patience that was girded by steel. It had been there the day before when he had offered to leave if she asked. If she said yes now, Carole knew he would go.

"No," she answered, and silently cursed her weakness. Holding on to him for another few hours, or days, would only make it worse in the end for both of them.

"But I don't want to be miserable, either, wishing for things that can't be."

Taking a deep breath, Carole said the one thing they would both have preferred to ignore. "Has it occurred to you yet, Donnelly, that I could be one of the worst things that's ever happened to you?"

"I don't believe that. I *won't* believe it."

"One wrong step," she said in a voice that showed no emotion, "and Andrew will make a believer of you. We're breaking all the rules, Donnelly, and if they catch us, they'll make us pay."

"Carole, I think I'm falling in love with you. And if we have to take chances to find out what we can have together, I don't care about the risks involved. And I won't let you care, either." Donnelly's words were firm and in control. He wouldn't back away, and he wouldn't let her go without a fight. "As soon as I can get away tomorrow night, I'll be over there. Just wait for me."

Donnelly's confession left her speechless. Carole had married Andrew without feeling half as much for him as she already felt with Donnelly. But love was something she had not been willing to consider. It was too soon, and there was still far too much standing in their way. Everything was happening too suddenly.

"Carole?"

"Don't love me, Donnelly," she whispered. "Please."

"Sorry, sweetheart, but my feelings aren't negotiable." His gruff answer softened. "You can hide from yourself if you want to, but you can't make me hide with you. And you can't make me deny the way I feel."

"You hardly know me."

"But I intend to correct that. And when I do, we'll talk about this some more." His tone deepened to a lazy purr that was as physical as a touch. "In the meantime, kiss me good-night, and I'll see you tomorrow."

Carole smiled and her heart turned over at the sweet caress of his voice. "Oh, Donnelly, I do miss you," she said softly, giving up the battle she had never wanted to win.

"It's only the beginning, sweetheart. And that's a promise." Donnelly's words dissolved into a soft sound that might have been a kiss or a sigh. "Good night."

Before Carole could respond, he hung up, leaving her lonely without the sound of his voice to fill the dark, empty bed beside her.

As the others filed out of the small conference room that separated her office from her father's, Carole shuffled the loose sheets of statistics she had brought with her and slid them under the flap of her leather portfolio. Pushing her chair slowly away from the round, glass-topped table, she stood; then flipping through the pad of notes she had taken during the meeting, she turned and started toward the door.

"See anything interesting?"

Startled, Carole looked up to find King still standing in the doorway. As she drew nearer, he took her elbow in his hand and walked with her down the hall toward her office.

"Are you having any trouble with that project?" he asked quietly.

"No," Carole answered, puzzled. "Didn't the numbers look good to you? We're ahead of schedule and under cost."

King laughed, holding up a defensive hand. "I'm not criticizing, just asking. You seem preoccupied."

"Oh." Tucking the pad into her portfolio, Carole realized there would be gaps in the notes she had taken during the meeting. All through the day her mind had wandered to the past days and the coming night. As eagerness and hesitancy cartwheeled through her, Donnelly was never far from the surface of her thoughts. "Sorry," she said with a noncommittal shrug of her shoulders.

"Anything I can help with?"

Carole smiled, touched by King's concern. In spite of himself, he never seemed able to forget that one of his vice presidents was also his daughter. "As an employer, or as a father?" she teased.

"You tell me. I don't know what the problem is."

The simple request reached out to her in a way no demand could have, and Carole longed to lay her head on his shoulder and make her problems his. All of her life King had been there, her hero and protector, her nemesis and tormentor, a man larger than life whose love was as smothering as it was consoling.

"It's nothing, really," she said with a shake of her head, rejecting the impulse to give in to old habits. She looked at him as his frown deepened and he clamped his jaw shut on the urge to argue.

He was tall, the same height as Donnelly, with a breadth and muscular strength that mirrored a dominant inner spirit that bowed to no one. Lines were deep on his handsome face, and gray liberally streaked the dark brown of his hair, but the years had only polished the stone from which King Stockton had been hewn. "You know," she said softly, "some people say I get more like you as I get older."

"Then they don't know you very well," King answered, brushing an imaginary strand of hair from her cheek. "You've always been like me."

Laughing, Carole opened the door that led to her secretary's office and to her own office beyond. "They don't always mean that as a compliment, you know."

"Does that bother you?" King asked, following her.

As the door shut them away from the well-traveled hallway, Carole put her hand on his shoulder and gave her father a light kiss on the cheek. "No," she said firmly, then turned to her secretary, Sondra. "Any messages?"

With a broad smile, Sondra handed her a stack of small blue sheets, holding one back. "And then there's this one," she said, waving the single blue message just in front of her face. "From a gentleman without a name, who sounded in a hurry. He said you'd understand."

Carole could feel King moving closer behind her as Sondra looked from her to the piece of paper and back again. "I don't think he's ever called before," Sondra added.

Knowing that it could have been anyone, and knowing that it wasn't, Carole asked, "What did he say?"

"Will call first. Can't wait. Wish me luck," Sondra read from the message in her hand. "Very cryptic, don't you think?"

Almost wanting to laugh, Carole couldn't help feeling proud of Donnelly. He had told her everything she needed to know in a way that would mean nothing to anyone else. He might resent the position they were in, but nevertheless he played the game well.

Casually, Carole lifted the note from Sondra's hand and looked at it, then laid it on top of her other messages. "Maybe he'll call back."

King, a hard man to fool, growled over her shoulder, "And maybe he'll send flowers," as he followed Carole into her office.

"Was there more?" Carole asked, settling behind her desk and beginning to separate her messages into a stack that could wait and a stack for calls that should be returned immediately.

"About tonight. How soon do you think you can join us at Donnelly's victory party?"

"Well, I certainly don't intend to desert Susan at the earliest possible moment. I've supported her for two years, and I'll be there as long as she needs me tonight."

"Which shouldn't be past eight o'clock, Carole. It's going to be a short night." King sank into a tall leather chair across the desk from Carole and prepared for a fight.

"I think tomorrow will be early enough to discuss my possible support of Donnelly Wakefield. To fly from Susan's defeat to his victory tonight, I think, would be in extremely poor taste." Carole leaned forward and nervously reshuffled her messages into one stack again. She watched as King pressed his fingertips into a steeple and stared at her over the top. Determination glittered in his golden eyes, and Carole knew this was one point he was prepared to push.

"Then you do admit he's going to win," he said evenly.

"Of course he's going to win," Carole answered sharply, separating Donnelly's message from the rest and placing the others beside the phone. His, she folded into a tiny square and held in her clenched fist. "Very easily, and without my help."

"We need to get you behind him, in front of the public, as soon as possible." King leaned forward and tapped the desk with his index finger. "Andrew is running unopposed. His party won't have to stop and reorganize after the primary. Ours will, and we'll have to appear unified immediately, or Donnelly will lose ground badly in the next few weeks."

"I understand what you're saying, but I've never had any indication that Donnelly even wants my support."

"Damn it all, Carole," King exploded. His open hand hit the desk as he rose to his feet, and he stalked halfway across the office, then turned and stalked back. "Donnelly's his own worst enemy with all of his ideals and gentlemanly rules. You have visibility, Carole, and whether he likes it or not, Donnelly needs you."

"You want to bring the snake out of his hole by putting me up there in front of the whole state. You think Andrew doesn't know that? You think he's not waiting for it?"

"So what if he is? What can he do?" King's voice rose to match hers as he planted his hands in the middle of her desk and leaned over it, almost nose to nose with Carole.

Glowering into eyes so like hers, where the fires burned more gold and less red but certainly no more fiercely, Carole answered, "You may not be afraid to find out, but I am. And it's my life we're talking about. *I'm* the one with the visibility."

With a heavy sigh, King withdrew and sat down again. "What are you really afraid of, Carole?" he asked quietly.

Sensing a change in tactics, Carole refused to be lulled by the all-too-obvious note of fatherly concern in King's voice. "Look, Dad, I appreciate your concern, but I will not be manipulated into a position I don't want to be in. If and when I choose to campaign for Donnelly Wakefield, it will be in my own time and on my own terms. And, not meaning any disrespect, but the whys and wherefores are my business."

"Well," King said, rising from the chair, "okay." With a shrug of resignation, he started toward the door, then stopped with his hand on the doorknob. "I'll still have a car at the airport for you tonight." Watching her as he opened the door, he continued, "You can have it take you anywhere you like. You know where we'll be."

Adrenaline was coursing through Carole's veins with nowhere to go, and she felt strangely let down by King's sudden withdrawal. "That's it?" she asked. "No more argument?"

The deep grooves of a suppressed smile lined King's cheeks. "Would it do me any good?"

Afraid to let down her guard, Carole answered slowly, "No."

"Then have a good night, and give Susan my regards." With a wink, he pulled the door shut behind him and was gone, leaving Carole as exasperated as she was relieved.

A tickle of worry lingered as she unfolded Donnelly's message and reread it. The words warmed her but did nothing to dispel the worry. Everything she had said to her father came back to her, along with the warning she had given Donnelly the night before.

Like children playing an elaborate game of hide-and-seek, they would search for ways to meet away from the prying eyes of others. But it was a dangerous game they were playing—the princess in her ivory tower, the handsome knight who risked all, and the dragon who lay waiting.

With a shudder, Carole pulled herself back from the dark fantasy and answered the buzzing intercom. "Yes, Sondra?"

"It's almost five-thirty. You're running late if you're going to change before the plane takes off. And do you need anything else before I go home?"

"Oh, my Lord," Carole cried, scooping the papers off her desk and into a drawer. She slipped Donnelly's message inside her purse and hurried out of her office. "I'm gone," she said as she passed Sondra's desk. "See you tomorrow."

At home, she showered and applied makeup suitable for television cameras and unflattering flashbulbs. With the speed gained from years of practice, she released her hair from the chignon she had worn to the office and restyled it into a look of casual chic that could withstand a hectic night with no time out for touch-ups.

In the bedroom, she hurriedly slipped into a slim white linen skirt, a navy sweater vest and navy flats and, tossing an unlined white linen jacket over her shoulders, ran down the stairs and out the door just as the car pulled up to take her to the airport.

"Great timing, Thomas," Carole said, relieved to see that she recognized the driver as she settled into the back seat.

"It's going to be a busy night, Miss Stockton," the older man said, easing into the traffic on the road to the small airport where the company plane was hangared. "I just dropped your father at the reception. Then, after I get you to the airport, I've got to go back to the ranch for your mother. Later tonight I've got to meet you

again, and pick up Mr. Wakefield when he comes in."
Thomas expelled a weary breath. "Your daddy's going
to have me a busy man tonight."

"I didn't know you'd be driving for Mr. Wakefield,
too," Carole said, hoping her heart wouldn't continue
to thump wildly every time she heard his name.

"Him and anybody else your daddy can think up,"
he said, accelerating as he turned onto the airport ac-
cess road. "There's big doings tonight. Almost as ex-
citing as the old days."

The old days. Carole barely heard Thomas's goodbye when she left the car and entered the airplane. No,
it was nothing like the old days, not for her. Then, she
had loved the excitement. On the arm of the first boy-
friend she had ever had, there had been no shadows to
mar the glitter of the moment.

Andrew had wooed her as if nothing else mattered,
as if his candidacy for Congress were nothing more than
a party he had thrown in her honor. And soon, on the
arm of her new fiancé, Carole was happily embracing
the attention of the press.

Before the campaign had ever ended, Andrew had
become her husband, and his victory was something she
had shared in proudly. It was only then that the shadows began to close in, growing heavier and heavier, until all the light was gone.

Somewhere deep inside of her, Carole could feel the
excitement longing to break free again. The thrill of a
challenge met and matched was still there, the joy of a
victory that could be won and rewon by anyone who
dared to become a hero.

But the fear inside of her was stronger. When a hero
fell, the world was there to watch. In this election there

would be only one winner: Andrew or Donnelly. One hero would stand while the other fell—and the icy whisper of her fear told Carole she would be the one to decide.

Chapter Six

The late-August evening was hot and wind-whipped as Carole exited the taxi. Though the sun was low, its light burned with a midday brilliance as she paused on the sidewalk to take a deep breath. An elegantly dressed couple hurried past, casting a shuttered glance her way, and Carole drew her jacket protectively about her.

Lifting her head, she entered the hotel lobby, where more couples milled, greeting each other with the ready laughter and excited spurts of conversation that mark election day euphoria. Heads turned with her passing, and a wave of silence followed her progress across the lobby and up the staircase to the meeting rooms above.

As she approached the Oklahoma Room, where Susan Osburne's contingent awaited the election results, Carole noticed a blue-jean-clad youth shove the last of an hors d'oeuvre into his mouth and, in a continuous movement, pull a snapshot from his shirt pocket. After glancing from the picture to her and back to the picture, he hesitated only a moment before hurrying away to the bank of pay phones a short distance down the hall.

Watching him dial as he slipped the picture back into his pocket and stole another glance at her from the corner of his eyes, Carole wanted to turn and run back out of the hotel. Instead, she pulled open the door to the meeting room and entered with a muttered, "Damn it."

Next to a potted palm just inside the door, a young woman stood clutching a steno pad to the front of her dark green double-knit suit jacket. When Carole stalked through the door, the young woman's eyes widened; then she slipped from behind the palm, past Carole and out the door.

"Carole."

Turning toward the voice while she wondered how many others had been posted to watch for her arrival, Carole was relieved to find Susan Osburne reaching to take her hand.

"I'm so glad you're here," Susan said in a reedy voice that had aided little in a televised campaign demanding charisma more than content.

"I got tied up at the office," Carole apologized, holding the other woman's hand a little tighter as she noted Susan's strained smile. "I'm sorry I'm so late. How's it going?"

Across the room a forty-five-inch television screen showed the earliest of the returns. "With only one percent in, you wouldn't even know I was in the race," Susan said with a forced cheerfulness. "But the night's young." Her voice dropped. "Did you see those reporters?"

Carole nodded, wishing away the churning stomach that made it hard for her to concentrate on anything else. "I was hoping it was my imagination."

"All they've done is eat, and wait for you to get here so they could call in. I guess the camera crews are on their way by now."

A shading of bitterness bled through Susan's words, and Carole winced inwardly, knowing it made no difference how uncomfortable she was with such publicity. Her support had done little to improve Susan's chances for election, but her presence had done a lot to draw attention away from the candidate, who should have been the main attraction. Even in defeat, the primary news interest seemed to lie in Carole's next move rather than in Susan's.

A hail of cheers and applause interrupted her thoughts as the first votes for Susan appeared on the televised tote board. Even though she was a distant third among the candidates, the supporters present were in a party mood, secure in their faith that they couldn't lose.

"Everyone seems to be enthusiastic," Carole said. Despite her anxiety she couldn't help smiling at the infectious excitement that crackled like electricity in the air.

"This is my town," Susan agreed. "If the rest of the state knew me the way these people do, I might have won this thing."

"The night's not over yet." Wishing she could believe her own words, Carole tried to help her friend hold on to the magic just a little longer.

"No," Susan said with a shake of her head. "You and I both know better than that. This night was over months ago. I'm only glad that if I have to lose, I can lose to a man I respect." Touching Carole's arm, she leaned closer. On her face was a sad smile that fought with itself. "You'll love my concession speech. I think it's the best of the campaign."

"Have you decided when you'll give it?" Carole asked quietly, discarding the pretense of confidence.

"Soon, I think. There's no need to drag this out all night." Straightening her back, Susan smiled again, a little more surely. "Then we can lick our wounds and get on with the business of beating that damned Mathison."

Carole felt the name drive into her as if she had been kicked in the stomach. Other people divorced and put the memory behind them, but she had never been able to do that. Every time Andrew's name was mentioned in public, a guilty silence came over the gathering and all eyes turned to her, watching.

And their guilt became her guilt. Guilt for having known him, for having helped put him in power, for having left him and, by doing so, making everyone else feel so uncomfortable.

"Oh, Carole, I'm so sorry," Susan apologized with a worried grimace. "I shouldn't have said that."

"Of course you should have, Susan." Carole's voice was sharper than usual as her impatience with them both showed through. "Any minute now there's going to be a roomful of reporters here, all trying to get me to say that same thing."

"Well, why don't you?" Susan encouraged, happy to be relieved of her guilt. "Everyone knows what he did. There's no sense in your being so...so *decent* about it."

"You're wrong, Susan. Very few people know why I really divorced him, and I'd just as soon keep it that way." Looking into the candidate's unconvinced hazel eyes, Carole said, "You've been around politics long enough to know what happens once the press gets hold of a sexual indiscretion. With Andrew's track record, I'd become his poor little wife Carole, and *he'd* become a living legend.''

Susan was preparing to argue, but suddenly she laughed in amused sympathy. ''You're right. Andrew might never be elected to office again, but they'd keep dredging up his exploits until the end of time.''

Another roar of applause and cheers went up in the background as the televised returns were updated. ''Oh, my,'' Susan groaned as her gaze quickly scanned the giant screen. ''With only four percent of the returns in, I'm holding steady with a whopping eight percent of the vote.'' She sighed and lifted her shoulders in a shrug of grim irony. ''Another half hour of this and it's over. Oh, well,'' she said with another sigh, ''I think Donnelly would be a good governor, even if he is a bit inexperienced. And I think he's got a good chance of winning. The best thing I can do tonight is make sure I don't do anything to hurt those chances.''

''Can I quote you on that, Mrs. Osburne?''

Turning toward the sound of the familiar voice, Carole and Susan found themselves facing a minicam and the pretty bronze face of Diane Michaelson, a microphone in her hand.

''If you'll wait until I've had a chance to concede first,'' Susan answered smoothly.

''I'll be happy to,'' Diane replied.

''And I'll leave you two alone,'' Carole said, taking a step away and eager to be gone.

''Don't go too far,'' Diane called with a smile as Carole began to move away.

Blending into the crowd, sheltered from the eye of the camera, Carole watched the happy, excited faces of the people around her. On the television, the tally of precincts reporting in had risen to ten percent, and Susan's percentage of the vote had dropped to six. With Fred Gulley, their party's third candidate, drawing only eighteen percent, Donnelly was already a clear, though undeclared, winner.

The gleam of victory began to dim in the eyes around her. Forced smiles stretched tightly across the faces of those who had poured their hearts, time and money into a dream that was staggering to its knees while they watched helplessly.

Outside, unseen by those partying around her, the sun shone brightly, refusing to acknowledge the night that had already begun. Somewhere, she knew, King was watching the results and smiling as the clock neared eight.

A mutter from the crowd caught her attention, and Carole lifted her gaze to the television, to see a slightly blurred image of Andrew speaking with convincing gravity from the forty-five-inch screen.

His words were lost in the babble of the crowd, and Carole marveled at the soundless play of emotions across his handsome face. With a curve of his mouth or a crook of his brow, he portrayed humor and sincerity in a ceaseless flow. His darkly golden hair was a sleek, perfectly waved cap, and his pale blue eyes were charmingly guileless, yet wise.

He had never played his part better, and watching him, Carole had never detested him more. As easily as Andrew had deceived her, he was deceiving an entire state, wooing them with sweet, empty lies and preparing to desert them without remorse when he no longer needed to keep them happy.

In a transition that went unheard, the scene on the giant television screen left Andrew to pick up again with Donnelly in a hotel convention room across town. The crowd behind him was younger and less restrained than the one with Andrew had been, and Donnelly's smile was wider and less practiced.

For an instant, the screen went blank, then was filled again with new results. Twenty percent of the precincts statewide were reporting in, and Donnelly's edge had increased to eighty percent.

As the picture shifted again to Donnelly, the crowd around Carole joined in the cheers that came from the television, and she could feel the loyalties beginning their inevitable shift. Though she couldn't hear the interviewer's question, Donnelly's answer was a lift of his brows, a quick, broad smile and a firm shake of his head.

A stern frown grew while he listened to the next question. Carole smiled, recognizing the granite-hard thrust of his jaw, the flash of impatience that struck sparks in Donnelly's turquoise eyes as he answered.

With his blond good looks and photogenic eyes, some had compared Donnelly to the Andrew who had campaigned as the underdog only four years earlier. But to Carole, and for those who had the wisdom to see, his contrast with Andrew was deep and striking. In Donnelly, great strength was combined with genuine humility, creating great kindness. And the confidence that could have become arrogance was tempered by an integrity that would never allow Donnelly to put his own well-being first.

Over the noise around her, Carole couldn't hear a word that came from the television, but she didn't have to hear the exchange to know what the reporter had attempted, or what Donnelly's reply had been. With eighty percent of the vote, any candidate would be excused a prediction of victory, and any interviewer would have been surprised by the reaction of stubborn, even angry, refusal that Donnelly had given.

Carole was beginning to realize that, regardless of what had motivated him to seek office, Donnelly operated by his own rules, and no victory was important enough for him to compromise his own code of ethics. For him, he would be the winner only when all the votes were in or when both opponents had conceded, and not before.

As Carole saw the hard edge of tension ease from the set of Donnelly's jaw, she moved closer to the television, hoping to hear his voice. Slowly he began to smile again, and a bittersweet longing to be near him burned in her. The deepest, loneliest part of her was warmed by the gentle strength that shone in his eyes while he patiently fielded the remaining questions.

Too soon the picture changed again and the coverage returned to the studio for an update of the results, leaving Carole lonely for the comfort of Donnelly's presence. A growing number of precincts were in, and as areas outside of Oklahoma City added more and more to the tally, Donnelly's lead became overwhelming.

Again without warning, the picture shifted, and Susan's drawn yet bravely smiling face appeared on the screen. In the shocked silence that fell over the crowd, an announcer's voice quietly said, ''Coming to you now from where she has gathered with her supporters in Oklahoma City is Susan Osburne. Behind from the beginning of the returns, she has now asked to make an announcement. Many believe it will be her concession speech. Are you ready, Diane?''

From a position directly in front of the podium, Diane appeared briefly on the screen. ''Thank you, John,'' she answered in a hushed, reverential tone usually reserved for golf tournaments and funerals. ''I believe Mrs. Osburne is about ready to begin. With us also in the audience is Carole Stockton, whom many of you will remember as the former Mrs. Andrew Mathison. If you'll stay with us at the end of Mrs. Osburne's statement, Carole has promised us an exclusive interview.''

With a warm smile, Diane dismissed the camera and returned the audio to Susan Osburne, whose frail voice would have been a whisper without the microphone in front of her. ''I would like to begin by thanking all those who gave me their hearts as well as their help. Without them, we would never have come this far.''

Around her, like the rasping of dry grass in the wind, Carole could hear the beginning sounds of mourning for what could have been. Men stared straight ahead with tear-filled eyes; women wept without shame or reserve; and she herself could hardly hear Susan's words for the roar of fury that pounded through her with each pulse beat.

Trapped by Diane's clever maneuvering, Carole was left with no graceful way out and no chance to refuse the interview she had never granted.

''...no way I can repay the debt for the long hours, the hard work and the loyalty you have given to me,'' Susan continued. Though tears glistened in her eyes, she held her head high and her voice had grown stronger. ''This campaign has been a labor of love, of sharing and dedication. And we haven't lost.''

The camera panned the crowd and as a roaring cheer went up, the television screen showed smiling faces with trails of tears on their cheeks. Victorious arms were lifted into the air, and when the camera returned to the podium, Susan was gazing with love and unchecked tears at the crowd below her.

"We've shared a lot," she began again, in a voice that was untouched by the emotion on her face. "And we're going to continue to work for victory, together. With our hearts, and our voices and our efforts, we will continue. But it won't be for Susan Osburne. For me, the race is finished."

Though she had seen it so many times before, Carole would never grow used to the awful bitterness of loss after so many years of hope and sacrifice. She could hear it in the whispered sorrow of Susan's last words. She could see it in the faces around her as they clung fiercely to a dream that was lost. She could feel it in the cold chills that crept along her back, in the stinging sadness that filled her chest and throat, as she watched Susan's battle for dignity in the face of overwhelming grief.

When the protests of the crowd had quieted, Susan continued, "For Donnelly Wakefield, the race has just begun. And with him now must go our hopes, our dreams and our support. We have only one opponent, and that's Andrew Mathison. If we don't join forces now—tonight—and begin to pull together, we will ultimately defeat ourselves."

Lifting a hand to quiet the sporadic clapping that punctuated her sentences, Susan continued in a more subdued voice. "At this time, I would like to offer my official concession to Donnelly Wakefield, and to pledge to him my full support and fervent prayers from this day forward. His victory is a victory for us all."

Over the cheers and applause that rose to a deafening pitch, Susan lifted a champagne glass and waited for the quiet that slowly drifted over the room again. "To a good fight," she shouted over the impatient rumbles of the gathering. "To Donnelly Wakefield, my candidate and yours. On to November!"

With wild roar of agreement, the crowd joined the toast and quiet was gone. Victory wore a new face. In barely two short months, glory would again wait in breathless excitement before a tote board, ready to reward, to celebrate, to make dreams come true. The party had begun again.

As corks popped around Carole and laughter replaced tears on the faces of the gathering, cold chills continued to dance along her spine. She watched Susan slip away from the podium and out of the room, her exit unnoticed by the camera crew, who had disappeared, or by the crowd, who were happy to save sorrow for another day.

Her duty done, Carole was eager to escape. As she wound her way through the mob, she checked her watch. It was barely eight-thirty. With any luck she could be safely home by ten o'clock, and Donnelly should be free soon after that.

The thought brought a smile to her face, and Carole felt her cheeks flush with warmth. In four short and fragmented days, Donnelly had grown from a nuisance to the best thing in her life. The soft depths of his voice, the subtle strength of his touch, the unspoken hunger in his eyes, all formed a memory with textures as real as the man himself.

A secret, eager happiness hid away in her heart as Carole impatiently pushed the door open and entered the broad hallway that connected the hotel's meeting rooms. Before she could react to the two cameras blocking the way to the lobby, a hand touched her arm and guided her into position.

"Good. I was about to send someone after you. We're going live any second now," Diane said calmly. "Watch for the red light on the camera in front of you."

"I have to catch a plane," Carole protested, wondering if she could flee before the station switched to them.

"I'll make it short and painless." Diane's words had a clipped, detached quality as she listened intently for the signal in her headset. Then, as if someone had flipped a switch, she came alive. Her eyes sparkled, her smile was soft and her voice melodious as she said, "I'm here with Carole Stockton outside the room where Susan Osburne has just given a moving speech conceding the election to Donnelly Wakefield."

Turning to Carole, she said, "We've just received word that Fred Gulley will be making an announcement shortly after nine o'clock." She smiled encouragingly into Carole's eyes and continued in a soft, friendly voice, "It would appear that Donnelly Wakefield has easily won the night. The last time we spoke, Carole, you told me that if Mr. Wakefield won your party's election, he would receive your full support. Does this mean you'll be campaigning for him?"

Like the black head of a serpent, the microphone was extended toward her, and Carole involuntarily flinched. "We really haven't had a chance to discuss that," she said cautiously, cursing herself inwardly for once again being caught by surprise. "I've never been much of a public speaker. I prefer to keep to the background as much as possible."

"And yet in your support of Mrs. Osburne, your presence was always felt. Do you intend to be as visibly supportive of Donnelly Wakefield, if not vocally so?"

Stiffening her spine as she fought to keep the ice from her voice, Carole answered, "As I stated, that's as much Mr. Wakefield's decision as it is mine. I believe he has a very different campaign style from Susan's, and I wouldn't presume to make decisions for him. And now if you'll excuse me, I have to catch a plane. I'm due back in Tulsa."

"Thank you, Carole," Diane said, undaunted. "We'll talk again when you've had a chance to meet with Mr. Wakefield. I know we'll all be looking forward to hearing about your place in his campaign." Swinging back to face the camera, she concluded, "And we'll all be looking forward to seeing you on the campaign trail again. I think I speak for the entire state when I say your absence since your divorce from Andrew Mathison has been deeply felt. Welcome back to Oklahoma politics, Carole Stockton. We've missed you."

The red eye of the camera darkened, Diane handed the mike to the sound man and Carole walked slowly away, feeling very much as though she had just been mugged and wishing she weren't too old to cry.

Soft music rose from the living room. Spiraling up the staircase and curling over the half wall of the loft, it found its way, like a distantly remembered melody, into the bedroom.

Standing in front of the mirror of her dresser, Carole fastened a single-stranded pearl choker around her neck, leaving its diamond-studded clasp visible at the side of her throat. Her hair was pinned up in a soft, loose crown. Stray curls drifted free to float like a pale cloud around her face.

Far away, thunder rumbled, promising an eventual end to the heavy quiet of the night. Carole looked toward the window and, seeing nothing through the sheer curtains and the blackness beyond, turned back to the mirror and nervously retucked her silvery pink camisole top into the waistband of its matching silk pants.

Unsoothed by the music, her heart beat a quick, unsteady rhythm in answer to the darkly pagan drumrolls of thunder. Slipping the slim golden watch onto her wrist, Carole checked the time. It was eleven-fifteen, and her nerves were growing taut with the waiting.

Fred Gulley's concession had come during her flight home. At ten forty-five, after her bath and the ten o'clock news, Carole had watched Donnelly, with King beside him, in a replay of his victory speech. In a live interview afterward, Donnelly was still at the hotel, presiding over a jubilant victory celebration that looked as if it could go on all night.

Still on the dresser was a dazzling diamond-and-pearl earring to match the one she already wore. On the bed behind her was a loose knee-length coat to complete her outfit. Downstairs on the coffee table, a bottle of champagne was on ice.

Once Donnelly's call had come, she would put on the waiting earring. When the doorbell rang, she would slip into the pink silk jacket. When they reached the living room, he would open the champagne and their night would begin.

Outside, the wind rose, moaning and nudging at the windows. Inside, the air conditioner came to life, struggling to overcome the heat and humidity that seemed destined to drag into September. Checking her watch again, Carole saw that it was eleven twenty-five and she had just passed ten minutes standing in the middle of her bedroom staring into space.

Too tired and distracted to work, she slowly descended the stairs, careful not to hook the slender heels of her sandals in the thick pile of the carpet. In the living room, she turned on the television and settled into the center curve of the sofa.

Though the governor's race was over for the night, a few major posts were still undecided, and election returns continued to dominate the late-night programming. As she relaxed, the long day and night caught up with her, and Carole slipped into the soft, dark womb of sleep.

Minutes or hours later—she didn't know which—the ringing of the telephone penetrated the thick cloud that covered her mind. Slowly, Carole felt her way to the telephone, shielding her eyes from the bright light of the dining room.

Her hand closed over the receiver and slid it from its hook. Grateful for the ensuing silence, Carole lifted the receiver to her ear. "Hello there," she said in deep, sleepy tones as she smiled at the unseen caller. "What time it it?"

"Eleven-forty," the wrong voice answered. "Did I wake you up?"

Almost sick with dread, Carole shivered and came instantly awake. "Who is this?" she demanded, praying that she was wrong. Not now. Not tonight. Not when all she wanted was finally to forget the past and be happy again, the way any woman had a right to be.

"You know who this is, Carole. Don't tell me you weren't expecting my call?" Andrew sounded almost genuinely surprised. He let silence hang between them for a moment, then began again in the softly coaxing voice that the public never heard and Carole knew too well. "Say the word, and I can be there in half an hour."

"No," Carole snapped. She took several steps backward, then turned and began to pace, stretching the long cord behind her.

"That's not the word," Andrew said with patient good humor.

"It's the only word I have for you," she answered stiffly.

"Carole." Andrew made her name a sensuous caress. "I remember the good days. I know the kind of woman you really are. I made you happy once. If you'll let me, I can do it again."

"Oh, Andrew," Carole cried, wondering if there were any words that could make him give up. "Why can't you understand? I don't love you anymore."

"I understand more than you know, Carole." His voice rose with a harsh and demanding edge. "I understand you're the kind of woman who needs a man. And I swear to you, that man's going to be me."

"Never," Carole shouted, whirling to face the wall phone as if she could see the man behind the voice.

"Then it will be no one," Andrew shouted back at her. "Believe what I say, Carole. I'll destroy any other man who thinks he can have you."

Hardly believing what she'd heard, Carole tried to plead with the man she had once thought she knew. "If the press knew about these phone calls, Andrew, it would ruin you."

In a voice that continued to rise, swelling with a note that was close to hysteria, he argued, "I'm a man fighting for the woman he loves."

"Don't insult my intelligence, you piece of garbage!" Carole cried, shaking, as inside of her, all the years of hurt and hiding and resentment came unsprung in a giant tangle of anger and desperation. She wanted to be free of him. She *had* to be free of him.

"You're a man fighting for reelection and nothing more," she shouted. There were no tears in her, no sorrow, just a white-hot rage that refused to be quiet any longer. "I've never been anything to you but something to use, and that's all I am now."

As she stopped for breath, Andrew said quietly, "If that's the way you feel about it, Carole, why don't you just hang up?"

"For the same reason I wouldn't turn my back on a mad dog," Carole hissed between gritted teeth.

"I didn't know you had so much anger in you still," he continued in the same quiet voice. "Why haven't you said anything before?"

"Because you haven't threatened me before."

"I haven't threatened you *now*, Carole," Andrew denied in the same calm tone an adult would use to placate an unreasonable child, and Carole was reminded of how dangerously convincing he could be in public.

"Are you practicing your denial in case I say anything about it later?" Carole asked, masking her anger with acid sweetness. "I don't want to roll in the dirt with you, Andrew. And I know that's where any public fight with you would end. So don't worry. I don't plan to say or do anything you don't force me into. But don't ever threaten me again."

Andrew laughed. "I used to wonder how the daughter of King Stockton could have stayed so sweet and innocent. I see you're finally outgrowing it."

"I wouldn't give King all the credit if I were you, Andrew," Carole said with an icy clarity.

He laughed again, a short, gentle laugh that seemed to turn inward. When he spoke, Andrew's words were slow and a little sad. "You probably won't believe me, but to set the record straight, it's not just the election, Carole. I don't need to tell you how many women I've had. But none of them have been able to make me forget you. Letting you walk out on me was the worst mistake I've ever made."

"No," Carole corrected quietly, "the worst mistake you ever made was giving me a reason to leave you in the first place. That's why I could never support your campaign, Andrew, and it's the reason I could never love you again. I don't trust you; I don't respect you; and I don't think you're fit to run this state."

"And yet," he said softly, "you won't attack me publicly. I saw your interview last Saturday, and the one tonight. I was proud of you, Carole. You gave me hope I might still have a chance with you."

"That wasn't sentiment, Andrew. It was good sense. I'm tired of being reminded that I was once married to you. And there's no way to campaign for Donnelly without inviting too many comparisons."

"Donnelly?" The short question gave new meaning to the name, and Carole flinched at the quickness of Andrew's instincts. "I saw him come to your rescue, but I told myself there was no way you would be foolish enough to become involved with him. Is it possible I was wrong?"

"My private life is none of your business."

"Then you're not seeing him?"

"My private life is none of your business," Carole repeated in a calm, strong voice that did not betray the hard pounding of her heart.

Andrew expelled his breath in a relieved sigh. "If you *were* seeing him, you'd deny it," he said slyly.

"I don't owe you any explanations, Andrew."

"No, of course you don't. But don't betray me, Carole. Please, for both our sakes, just don't betray me."

"Is that a threat?" she asked in a calm, tight voice.

"A reality. I owe you that much."

The gentle whisper of his words did nothing to diminish their deadly power. She was feeling trapped by Andrew; she could sense him circling, searching for a weak point in her defenses. "What would you do?" she demanded in a quiet tone, sounding almost as if he held a loaded pistol to her head.

"I still want you, Carole, and there's nothing you can say that will stop me from trying to get you back. But you can hurt me, and we both know it." Through the long-distance wires his words stroked her like a physical touch, and Carole shivered from the coldness of his voice. "I won't let you hurt me, Carole. I won't even let you try. And now, good night, my love. I'll call you again soon."

With a click the line went dead, and Carole stood frozen to the spot, wishing she could cry, wishing she could scream, wishing she could bring him back and make him stop. Fury and desperation throbbed inside her. The pain in her heart seemed to swell, filling her chest and pushing into her throat, pounding with a fierce beat that threatened to shut out everything else.

Then she moved, taking a step forward, and all of the frozen fury came to life. "No," she cried, throwing the receiver across the room, "I won't *let* you!" With a crash, the instrument hit the wall and ricocheted into the corner. "I'll stop you," Carole continued to shout, lifting her gaze to the phone on the wall, as if it still held her connected to Andrew.

Quieting, she closed her eyes and took a deep, steadying breath. "I don't know how," Carole whispered, more to herself than to the lingering threat of Andrew, "but I *will* stop you."

Simultaneously, the chime of the doorbell and the pounding of a fist on the door below penetrated the storm of emotion inside her. Physically drained, she moved toward the door on shaky legs, unable to hurry as Donnelly's voice rose over the pounding of his fist.

"Carole!"

Slowly, Carole descended the staircase. In the light of the porch, she saw Donnelly sag with relief and step back to wait until she reached him. With his tie tugged loose, his dark jacket unbuttoned and askew and his face lined with fatigue and worry, Carole thought he had never looked more handsome.

Once again the sense of safety in his presence came over her, but she knew it was a luxury she could never allow herself. Whatever else Donnelly might be to her, he could never be her refuge.

Until after the election, *she* must be the protector, and Andrew's threats must remain a secret she would never share.

Chapter Seven

Carole turned the lock, then stepped back as Donnelly pushed the door aside and stalked into the tiny foyer. Wrapping his arms around her, he pulled her against his chest and held her tightly, their pounding hearts the only sounds in the quiet night.

Then Donnelly gripped Carole's shoulders between fingers of steel and held her away from him. "I heard you scream," he said, glaring down at her with a worried frown.

Unable to look into his eyes, Carole stared at the black-and-white contrast of his shirt and tie, and the rapid rise and fall of his chest beneath. "I dropped something," she explained with a negating shake of her head.

"That's not what it sounded like to me." His fingers tightened, digging into her bare skin, as he forced her shoulders back and her head up. "Are you alone?" he demanded, searching her face with fierce eyes.

Twisting away from the pain of his hands, Carole nodded, and Donnelly's fingers moved lower on her arms. "You were talking to someone," he insisted, refusing to release her.

Carole watched the throbbing pulse at the side of his throat. She wanted to tell him, to bury her face against the warmth of his neck and pour out her heart. She wanted to feel Donnelly's strong arms surround her with his protection.

She searched for something to say, something that would satisfy him, and instead heard Andrew's threats return to spin inside her head in a dizzying confusion. *I'll destroy any man...Donnelly...don't betray me....*

Her body felt numb, as if it were a part of someone else who stood to the side, watching. The firm, lush outline of Donnelly's lips blurred, and Carole reached for the solid support of his shoulder as her trembling legs began to give way. To her ears, her voice was no more than a distant buzz as she whispered, "Donnelly."

"Oh, my God, sweetheart." His soft words were filled with remorse as he lifted her gently into his arms. "Don't worry. It'll be all right."

The cold weakness that had swept over Carole receded quickly once Donnelly began to climb the stairs with her in the cradle of his arms. Laying her head against his chest, she said, "I'm okay."

"Sure," Donnelly agreed, ignoring her as he continued up the stairs and into the living room. Gently, he laid her full-length on the couch and sat on the edge next to her, holding her hand against his chest as he smoothed her hair from her eyes.

"Has anyone ever told you you're very beautiful when you're about to pass out?" He smiled down at her, continuing to trace the curves of her face where no errant hair lingered. "Do you feel better?"

Carole returned his smile, listening to the sound of his voice through the ringing in her ears. "Fine."

"You sound like a newborn kitten, and you're still a deathly white."

Wrinkling her nose, Carole teased weakly. "That doesn't sound very attractive. And I worked so hard."

"You're beautiful." Donnelly leaned nearer, drawing his finger across her jaw and down the side of her neck to the narrow camisole strap across her shoulder. "You're more beautiful every time I see you. And if I weren't afraid you'd faint, I'd show you how much I've missed you."

Carole lifted her free hand to his shoulder. "Risk it," she said in a voice that was suddenly much stronger.

Gently Donnelly pressed his lips to hers in a slow savoring of flesh on flesh. The dry, firm warmth of his mouth on hers jolted Carole in a way she hadn't expected. Here was no tentative boy seeking permission.

Donnelly's hands slid under her shoulders and lifted Carole into his arms as his lips parted on hers, moving deeper, drawing her with him into the soul of the kiss where thought was suspended and only feeling remained. Crushing her to him with a low moan, Donnelly pressed his kiss harder as her lips parted to invite his search. Breathless from the spin of her emotions, Carole gasped for air while Donnelly's lips moved over hers in a series of light pecks and then drew away.

When her eyes opened, she found his smiling eyes watching her from only a few inches away. "You've got your color back,'' Donnelly teased as he slowly slid his hands from beneath her.

Like a cannonball landing in her living room, a jagged streak of lightning struck the earth outside with a nerve-shattering explosion. As Carole jumped, curling against the arm Donnelly kept protectively at her side, a low moan of wind rattled at the balcony door. ''You don't have to fly anywhere tonight, do you?'' she asked apprehensively.

Donnelly shook his head and laughed gently. ''I may be a hard worker, but I'm not crazy. Planes the size of mine don't fly in weather like this.''

Carole smiled, happy to have him with her a little longer. ''By the way, I forgot to congratulate you. So... congratulations.''

Donnelly returned her shy smile and kissed the tip of her nose. ''Thanks. Sorry I was so late. I didn't expect to have so many people there tonight.'' Noticing the champagne for the first time, he said, ''Hey, what's that?''

''For you.'' Uncomfortable suddenly, Carole slid to a sitting position with her back against the arm of the sofa. All of her careful preparations were out of sync, thrown off by Andrew's unexpected and unwanted phone call.

Upstairs, her left earring was still on the dresser. Her jacket still lay across the bed. And the champagne was too much and too late. As Donnelly lifted the bottle from the ice bucket, Carole stopped his hand with hers. ''I know you've already had more toasts tonight than any man should be expected to endure,'' she said softly. ''We can save it for another time.''

Wrapping a towel around the dripping bottle, Donnelly brought it out of the bucket. His eyes watched

Carole's face as he said, "I haven't had a toast with you yet, and that's the one I've waited for all night."

"If you'll pop the cork," Carole answered quietly, a relieved smile slowly lighting her face, "I'll get the glasses."

Donnelly set down the champagne and helped her rise. "Don't be long." He let her fingers slip through his with obvious reluctance.

In the kitchen Carole took a pair of tulip-shaped champagne glasses from the cabinet and listened to the contented beat of her heart. At the sound of the cork's muffled pop, she shoved the cabinet door closed with the side of her hand.

Inside her, the anxiety stirred by Andrew's phone call still reverberated, but at the thought of Donnelly's nearness a slow, peaceful smile etched its way across her lips and into her turbulent soul. She had missed him, and now that he was here, she began to realize just how *much* she had missed him.

Carole turned to find Donnelly standing in the dining room. The champagne bottle dangled at his side, its neck clutched in his fist. The instant rush of happiness Carole felt at the sight of him faded as quickly as it came. But the hard pounding of her heart remained when she saw that his eyes were fixed not on her, but on the wall beside her.

Following Donnelly's unwavering gaze as she entered the dining room, Carole turned and saw the receiver of the telephone still lying on the floor in the corner. Above it, at eye level, a long, dark scar was visible on the silver-and-apricot-striped wallpaper.

"I guess that's why I kept getting a busy signal," Donnelly said without looking away from the silent phone.

"You called?" Carole asked, moving past him into the living room and away from the reminder of something she would rather forget.

Donnelly turned and followed her. "Once from the hotel and once from my car on the way here," he said stiffly. "It looks like there was a small war in there. You want to tell me about it?"

Carole took advantage of a long, rumbling freight train of thunder to curl herself into a protective knot in the corner of the couch. When Donnelly sat beside her, prompting her with an insistent stare, she shrugged and kept her eyes on the twisting tree limbs at the side of the balcony. "I told you I dropped something."

"Dropped something," he repeated with a sigh. Donnelly held on to his irritation an instant longer, then reluctantly smiled. "Well, please don't ever drop anything in my direction, lady," he said lightly. "I think it could be deadly."

With an amused shake of his head and a quickly fading smile, Donnelly seemed willing to let the subject rest. From the corners of her eyes, Carole watched him turn away and pour the champagne.

Outside, the first drops of rain began to pelt at the windows, and Carole relaxed, grateful for the storm that held them captive. Away from the world and the reality that would return with the dawn, she could pretend that there was no past and no future, no price to be paid, no retribution waiting, only one magic, eternal night filled with happiness and love.

With a contented sigh, Carole took the glass Donnelly handed her, and the pretending died as she looked into his eyes.

In a voice that was quiet and laden with a sadness he made no attempt to hide, Donnelly asked, "When are you going to trust me, Carole? Tell me it's none of my business. Tell me to go to hell. But don't lie to me.''

Trapped between the uncompromising honesty Donnelly demanded and her own need to end the disappointment she saw when he looked at her, Carole began haltingly, not realizing what she was about to say until it was out. "Andrew still calls."

Donnelly said nothing as his gaze froze on her face and his eyes grew hard. With a nervous gesture, he jerked the knot in his tie loose, leaving the two ends to hang crookedly down the front of his shirt. "How often?" he asked finally.

Afraid of what she had done, not even knowing why she had done it but determined to go on, Carole said slowly, "For a long time, it wasn't very often. But lately..." Her voice died away and she took a sip of the champagne, grateful for its cool bite. "Lately," she began again, "it's more."

"How much more?"

The cold, angry look in Donnelly's eyes began to frighten her more than the memory of Andrew's phone calls, and Carole wished she could take back her words and lock them away inside her again. She was tired, and as the tension in her stomach turned to nausea, she realized she hadn't eaten all day. "Twice this week."

Carole stared into the pale gold of her champagne while she drained the glass, then watched the dancing bubbles as Donnelly refilled it. "What does he say?" he asked in a voice that sounded strained.

Lifting her gaze finally to meet Donnelly's, Carole saw a struggle for control that matched her own. Gone was the bright Indian turquoise of his eyes. In its place was a dark and stormy green, like an ocean surge driven before a hurricane.

"What does he say?" he asked again through lips that barely moved.

Carole closed her eyes, lifted her glass and took a long drink. "I shouldn't have told you," she said while Andrew's threats echoed in her thoughts. She would give anything to be able to wipe them out of her mind; and to repeat them to anyone, especially Donnelly, was more than she could bear.

"Carole, I heard you," Donnelly said quietly. "I heard the phone hit the wall. I heard your shouts. I heard the panic in your voice."

His words reached out to her, pleading, urging, as strong as if he had touched her, and Carole waited to feel the warm reassurance of his hand. But it didn't come. Desolate in her aloneness, she opened her eyes and found her glass full again.

"I can't tell you," she said, and knew that she should never have said anything. Andrew was her mistake and her burden. She had already endangered Donnelly enough just by letting him be near her. To repeat the implied threats and twisted sentiment of Andrew's calls could do nothing but harm to everyone involved, and there was no way to pretend that Donnelly was no longer involved.

"Damn it, Carole!" Donnelly exploded. Slamming his glass down on the coffee table, he stood and paced to the other end of the couch. With his hands on his hips and his jacket flared behind him, he threw back his head and stared silently toward the dining room ceiling.

Futilely wishing she could begin the evening over again, Carole looked away from the somber image of Donnelly's back and watched a small pool of spilled liquid form on the coffee table at the base of his glass.

Foaming champagne still rocked within the glass, climbing the side in undulating waves, each one ending a little farther from the top than the one before.

Releasing a loud sigh, Donnelly turned around, took off his jacket and folded it neatly over the end of the couch. With the look of a man who had made up his mind, he walked back to Carole, took her folded knees between his hands and stretched her legs out behind him as he sat down beside her.

His hip felt warm and intimate against her thigh as Donnelly put one hand on the couch beside Carole's waist and one hand on the back of the couch at her shoulder. "Now," he said, leaning near enough to have kissed her with no effort, "I want to know what that bastard said. And I want to know now."

Tiny ripples of frustration and resentment rose in Carole, then were washed away by the larger waves of longing and desire that swept through her as Donnelly came nearer still.

"I'm not your father," he said in a low, steady voice that throbbed with tension. "I'm not Andrew. I'm not any man you've ever known before, and I'm tired of having to fight what they've done to you." Without touching her, he seemed to surround her with the intensity of his emotion. "What did he say!"

Startled by Donnelly's shout, Carole said, "He—" Her dry throat closed over the word and shut it off with a squeak. As she stared helplessly into the blue-green depths of Donnelly's eyes, his hand guided her glass to her lips and he waited for her to drink.

"Now say it," he insisted, pressing his advantage while he still held it.

"He still wants to marry me." Feeling a headache beginning, Carole closed her eyes and drained her glass.

Donnelly took the empty glass from her hand and asked, "And what did you say?"

"What do you think I said? I said no," Carole replied sullenly, opening her eyes to see that he had refilled her glass.

"Do you still love him?" Donnelly demanded immediately, refusing to allow Carole enough time to regain her composure.

Jerking upright in anger, she cried, "No!" and found herself chest to chest and eye to eye with Donnelly. In an instant, her anger was gone.

His free hand caressed her cheek, then slid to the nape of her neck to hold her immobile. "Do you love *me*?" he whispered against her lips. As her mouth opened for his kiss, Donnelly waited. "Do you?" he asked again, and his lips brushed hers as he spoke.

Unwilling to form an answer, for him or for herself, Carole pressed closer. Her mouth moved impatiently on his, and she took the kiss Donnelly withheld, hungry for the taste of his lips. For a long, tantalizing moment he resisted, holding his mouth stiff against hers. Then his hand cupped the back of her neck, and he crushed her to him with a fierce passion that had been held too long in check.

For one wild, eternal instant their lips were welded, as if in that touch they could satisfy the empty aching of their hearts. In Carole, a fire burned that she had never felt before, flaring with a heat she had never dreamed of. If she could have stopped time in that kiss, she would gladly have lingered there forever. But with an angry cry Donnelly tore away.

"Stop it!" he lashed out in a voice laced with pain. Releasing her abruptly, he shoved Carole's champagne glass back into her hands and turned away. Unable to look at her, he braced his elbow against his knee, cradling his forehead in the palm of his hand.

"Donnelly?" Carole asked. She touched his shoulder with a hand that shook.

Ignoring her hand and her entreaty, he demanded, "What's wrong with you, Carole?" He spat out each word as if it pained him. "You'd give me your body, but hold back you heart?"

Donnelly lifted his head and stared at her through slitted eyes, studying her as though he had never seen her before and never wanted to see her again. "You're willing to make love to me, but you can't tell me what's going on inside your mind?" He drew in a deep, shaky breath and his voice fell to a whisper. "Well, I won't settle for that kind of love, Carole. You know," he said slowly, "I almost feel sorry for Andrew. Is this what you did with him, Carole? Did he finally turn to other women just for a little human warmth?"

Stunned, Carole felt a searing pain as his words went through her. Then she drew back her hand and slapped his agonized face with all the strength she had. "Get out!" she cried in a voice that quivered with the same kind of rage she had felt when she hurled the phone.

Rising with a proud, stubborn anger that matched her own, Donnelly rounded the coffee table, hooked his finger under the collar of his jacket as he passed the end of the couch, and disappeared around the corner of the staircase.

In the mirrored wall behind the dining table, Carole watched his straight, stiff back quickly descend the stairs and turn out of sight. He never once looked back.

Closing her eyes, Carole swallowed a sob and downed the last of the champagne in her glass. It wasn't true.

She hadn't made Andrew the way he was. And the feelings she had for Donnelly were anything but cold.

None of what he'd said was true, but she couldn't tell him. It was better to let Donnelly walk out of her life believing a lie than to tell him the truth about Andrew's calls. And maybe in a way he was right. Maybe she was still too afraid of her own frailty to risk the kind of emotions that Donnelly aroused in her.

Opening her eyes with a resigned sigh, Carole felt her stomach do a somersault at the sight of Donnelly glowering at her from across the coffee table. With his finger still hooked beneath the collar, he slammed his jacket back onto the end of the couch.

"Hell, no, I'm not leaving," he said, and jammed his fists onto his hips. "This is the most emotion I've gotten out of you since I met you. So let's get back to some of those questions you still haven't answered."

On his tanned cheek, Carole could see the pink imprint of her hand, and the remainder of her anger faded. But she still couldn't give Donnelly the answers he insisted on having. Relieved and immeasurably happy to have him back, she stalled.

"I have a headache," she said and, with a wan wave of her hand, asked, "Could you get me an aspirin from the kitchen counter?"

Still ready for a fight, Donnelly looked perplexed. His eyes narrowed while he regarded her with more than a little suspicion; then he shrugged. "Sure."

He turned toward the kitchen, and Carole watched his progress in the mirrored wall of the dining room. Detouring at the kitchen doorway, Donnelly lifted the receiver from the floor and paused to listen before replacing it on the telephone hook and continuing into the darkened kitchen.

"It's just inside, in the corner," Carole called out. Fluctuating between anxiety and ecstasy, she lifted the champagne to refill her glass and was surprised to see that the bottle was only half full.

Without Donnelly's distracting presence, she became aware of the stuffy warmth of the room. As she contemplated opening the door to the balcony, the high, monotonous whine of the wind slowly penetrated the cottony barrier that had numbed her senses. Hurled by the storm's fury, raindrops landed like missiles against the windowpanes.

"Top mine off too, would you?" Nodding toward the champagne bottle Carole still held in her hand, Donnelly appeared beside her and extended his palm with two aspirin in its center. With a smile, she complied as he sat beside her.

"Will two be enough?" he asked, concerned. "Is there anything else I can do? I never get headaches. I feel kind of helpless."

Carole took the tablets from his hand and downed them with another half glass of champagne. "It comes and goes," she answered, crinkling her nose at the bitter aftertaste. "I get headaches sometimes in weather like this."

As if to emphasize her words, a lightning bolt flashed with the brilliance of daylight. Startled by the simultaneous crack of thunder, Carole shuddered. Chills replaced the flushed warmth she had felt only minutes before, and, seeing her shiver, Donnelly ran his hand along her arm in a firm, soothing caress.

"You were going to let me leave in weather like this?" he teased with a half smile, while his hand lingeringly stroked the satiny smoothness of her skin. "I might have been blown into the Land of Oz on the way to my car, and *then* who would be our next governor?"

Amazed by his sudden shift of mood, Carole nonetheless felt herself carried with him, warmed and reassured by the light in his eyes. "We never did have that toast," she said, lifting her glass to his. "I really am proud of you, Donnelly. Sincerely." With a bell-like chime, her glass touched his. "To your victory."

His eyes held hers as Donnelly remained unmoving. "There's only one victory I'm really interested in," he said seriously. "And I'm beginning to think that tonight won't be the night. So let's dedicate this drink to understanding, because that's what I really want, Carole. I just want to understand."

Halfway between them, in an undeclared no-man's-land, their glasses remained rim to rim, and Carole apprehensively watched Donnelly's expression undergo another change. "Understand what?" she asked.

"You. You're a challenge and a reward. And I want you, Carole. But I want you happy and whole, and I'm willing to wait. For a while."

Feeling backed into a corner by Donnelly's relentless demands, and tired of trying to defend herself to him, Carole tapped her glass against his and lifted her champagne in a salute. If he wanted honesty, she would give it to him. But if he wanted her heart on a platter, he would find that it was not so easily given.

"Then let's drink to it, Mr. Wakefield," Carole said with a cold flame of anger in her voice. "Let's drink to your slim chance of being the one man who's going to rescue me from my hopelessly pitiful state."

Donnelly caught her hand before Carole could bring the glass to her lips. "That's not what I meant, and you know it." In spite of his words, his voice sounded apologetic.

"Do I?" Carole challenged. "I didn't invite you into my life, Donnelly. And I don't need your righteous sermonizing on what's wrong with me—not from a man who's running for an office he doesn't even want. And don't tell me that's not true, because I've watched you. You couldn't care less if you're elected."

Carole could see that for the first time she had landed a blow that hit home, and as she watched the color leave Donnelly's face, she didn't feel very good about the victory. "I'm sorry," she said quietly. "I shouldn't have said that."

"No." Donnelly shook his head, refusing her apology. "You're not entirely right. But you're close."

"But I'm so sorry," Carole insisted, feeling responsible as she watched the fight leave his spirit. The golden light that always glowed from him seemed to dim, and she would have given anything to be able to take back her words.

Sensing her distress, Donnelly took Carole's hand in his and smiled reassuringly. "Come on, slugger, don't look so upset just because you scored a hit. I shouldn't ask you to be open with me if I'm not willing to take as good as I give."

"It's not that I don't want to be honest with you, Donnelly," Carole said hesitantly.

"I know." He nodded, looking less stricken as they began to talk quietly. "It's just that some things are hard to talk about." Lowering his head and watching her through his lashes, Donnelly said with difficulty, "What I was really upset about was that ... Well, the way you protect him, Carole, sometimes it's like ..."

His voice drifted away and, frowning, Donnelly clamped his jaws together with a bulldog finality. Waiting impatiently for his silence to end, Carole demanded, "What?"

Donnelly's frown deepened and so did the silence. The muscles in his jaw twitched as his gaze lost focus and he seemed to be staring through her. When Carole thought he would never answer, he finally said, "It's sometimes hard to believe that you don't still care about Andrew. A woman isn't usually so sensitive about a man who means nothing to her."

His eyes refocused and he calmly watched her. While Donnelly waited for a reaction, Carole for the first time began to see her reluctance through his eyes.

"A simple denial doesn't go very far, does it?" she asked.

"Your phone's broken and there's a hole in your wall."

"Oh," Carole said, surprised and a little upset that her brief tantrum had done real damage. "I thought I'd just scratched the wallpaper."

Donnelly shook his head slowly and almost smiled at her pink blush of embarrassment. "No. There's definitely a hole." His eyes sobered. "There was a lot of emotion behind that."

"Yes," Carole admitted, remembering the anger behind her outburst. "But it wasn't love."

"You said he wants you back. What else does he want?" Donnelly prodded gently, carefully gauging the level of her restrained tension, afraid it could easily erupt again into a violent reaction that would do nothing but hurt them both.

"He wants me as far away from you as possible," Carole said evenly, seeing no harm in admitting such an obvious fact.

"Me?" Donnelly asked. "Me personally?"

"You're the only person who could beat him. And Andrew's smart enough to know that my support could be political dynamite. He and my father still think a lot alike. Andrew is as convinced as King is that whoever ends up with my support will end up as governor. And if it can't be him, Andrew is determined that it won't be anybody else."

"You've campaigned for Susan Osburne for two years. He hasn't said anything about that?"

"She was a lost cause from the beginning. He knew it, and he knew I knew it. And," Carole added softly, "she wasn't a man."

"Then he *is* afraid that I might be more than just political competition," Donnelly concluded, not bothering to make it a question. As he watched the answer on Carole's face, he saw more than just affirmation. "My God, Carole, you're not afraid of him?"

Cursing inwardly, Carole closed her eyes and fought the tears that welled up inside her like a cold chill. Without saying a word, she had told Donnelly everything she had sworn to keep hidden, and now all she wanted was to curl up in his arms and cry with relief.

Rigid with anger at her own weakness, Carole struggled with the emotions that longed to break free. Refusing to allow her feelings to surface, she battled the storm inside her until, inch by inch, it abated. Her control restored, Carole opened her eyes to find Donnelly watching her closely.

"You are, aren't you?" he asked, quietly returning to his question. "That's what all this has been about, hasn't it? You don't love Andrew. You're terrified of him."

As the realization struck him, Donnelly squeezed his eyes closed in a frown that grew increasingly fierce. The hand that held his champagne glass began to shake, and a single tear escaped his tightly shut eyes to roll across his cheek. With a voice terrible in its calm, he whispered, "I'll kill him. So help me God, I'll kill him."

Stunned by the force of his reaction, and more afraid for Donnelly than she had ever been for herself, Carole caught his shoulder and turned him to face her. "No," she cried. "You can't do anything. We can't either of us do anything. That's what he's waiting for."

"You should have told me, Carole." Shame was mixed with the grief and anger on Donnelly's face. "I feel like such a fool. The things I said to you tonight. I wanted to make you angry, to shake you up." He turned his head and looked away, unable to meet her eyes. "I should never have said those things."

Carole touched his arm and said softly, "They worked."

"That's no excuse."

"It's good enough for now. Donnelly," she said, eager to move the conversation in another direction, "what I've told you tonight, no one else knows. And I don't want anyone else to know."

"This is nobody else's business," he answered grimly. His eyes were dry now and as coldly grim as his voice. "But I'm not going to stand here and do nothing, either."

Donnelly's words slowed as his thoughts played leapfrog across the coming weeks. "Unfortunately, my schedule's already set, so I can't get back here for a couple of weeks. Carole, do you suppose he'll be calling again soon?''

Her thoughts more concerned with Donnelly's long absence than by what he might be planning for Andrew, Carole shook her head. "Not unless something happens to set him off again. He saw that television interview on Saturday. And tonight, of course, with the primary and all." She shrugged and let her sentence trail away.

"Of course," Donnelly repeated bitterly, then continued, "Just how threatening does he get? And don't tell me he's not threatening, because I can't believe you're a woman who scares easily."

"It's nothing overt," Carole explained, growing nervous as she remembered the calls. "He's just so determined to get me back. And he's never quite said that no one else can have me if he can't, but it's there in his voice. He sounds so..." She hesitated over the word, then said it. "So desperate."

Donnelly nodded with a cold smile. "Okay then, we'll just see." Lost in his thoughts, Donnelly barely looked at Carole as he spoke and made no move to touch her. "I know a man who can get me the equipment, and the rest will be easy."

The tension on his face relaxed once the decision was made, and Donnelly's hand lightly stroked her bare arm just above the wrist. "When I get back, Carole, we're going to bug your phone. It'll activate before you answer, and if it's not Andrew, you'll be able to shut the recorder off manually."

"You mean we're going to record Andrew's calls?" In spite of her misgivings, Carole smiled, overjoyed at the thought of being able to hold a tape of Andrew's own words as a weapon against him. "Isn't that illegal?"

"Technically, yes," Donnelly agreed. "But what's he going to do? Unless he forces us to call his hand, Andrew will never know the tapes exist. That's important, Carole." Looking sternly into her smiling face, he stressed, "Andrew can't know what you're doing, and you can't keep the tapes here. Do you have a safety-deposit box where they'll be secure?"

She nodded that she did; then, feeling the anxiety that glittered in Donnelly's eyes like an aquamarine flame, Carole grew serious. "You don't think he'd do anything, do you?"

"Don't you?" Donnelly countered. "Why have you been afraid of him?"

"Well, I never thought he'd do anything *physical*," Carole protested. "He's the governor of our state, Donnelly. He can't walk from one room to the next without an entourage at his heels."

"He has money, and he has power. I thought I was just being paranoid before, but now I don't know."

"What are you talking about?"

"Lately, I could almost swear somebody's been tailing me."

"That's impossible," Carole argued, shocked by the thought.

"Is it?" Donnelly asked quietly. "You know the man better than I do. Is it?"

"No," Carole answered slowly, remembering her own fears that grew stronger every time she talked to Andrew. He was a man on the edge of panic, a man who recognized no rules but survival, and he would do anything he had to do to win. "No," she said again, growing surer the longer she thought of it. "It isn't at all."

Chapter Eight

Outside, the fury of the storm intensified. On the television, an empty screen crackled with the static of a station that no longer transmitted. Through a buzz of fatigue and champagne Carole absently wondered how long ago "The Star-Spangled Banner" had signaled the channel's sign-off.

"You must be exhausted," Donnelly said, breaking the silence of their thoughts as he gently traced the curve of her jaw.

Carole caught his hand and held it to her cheek. "You're the one with the rough schedule."

"I get paid to be a maniac. I'm a politician." He lifted her wrist and studied the delicate face of her watch, then gave a mournful shake of his head. "Two in the morning already. My plane leaves at nine-thirty, and I won't be back for weeks. I think I may cry."

"You should sleep," Carole said, stroking the back of his hand with her fingertips. Concerned with the aching tiredness of Donnelly's voice, and wondering what the next two weeks would be like without him, she felt a little like crying herself.

"No." He lifted her hand and kissed it, then absently rubbed the stubble of a day-old beard against the soft skin of her wrist. "I don't want to lose a minute of the time I have left with you."

"How long can you stay?" Almost too tired to think, Carole still marveled at how comfortable she felt with a man she barely knew. Just as hers were, his family and his background were common knowledge. A father who had spent the better part of his life in politics, lately as a member of the U.S. Senate. A beloved older brother who had died in a tragic accident while still in college, leaving the position of successor to his father to the unwilling Donnelly. A solid, happy family life with a mother and a younger brother. And a successful career as a contractor that Donnelly had finally, reluctantly, abandoned to become his father's aide and heir.

But of the man himself, the Donnelly who sat with her now in the half light of her living room, she knew next to nothing. Yet in her heart it seemed that she had always known him, and always would. The rest would come in time.

"I should leave before daylight," he answered slowly, reluctant to let reality intrude. "Just in case I'm not imagining things and there really is someone out there."

"That wouldn't make any difference now, would it? I mean, your car's parked just outside."

He shook his head. "No, it's not. I left it a block and a half away and stayed in the shadows on my way back here." In spite of the seriousness of their conversation,

Donnelly smiled. "My jungle training seems to be coming in handy for something."

Beguiled by the mischief in his eyes and the hour of the night, Carole laughed with him and added, "I hate to remind you of this, but my front porch wasn't very dark."

"Oh, yeah." Donnelly frowned as he remembered the scene at Carole's front door. Then he shrugged. "If you'll remember, I'm not the one who wants to keep this thing between us a secret. I'm more than willing to admit that I've become thoroughly enchanted by the ex-Mrs. Mathison and am pursuing her with all possible haste." Donnelly's smile grew wider as Carole's frown grew heavier.

"That's not very funny, Donnelly."

"I agree," he answered softly. "And I'm not kidding. Governor or not, I'd take Andrew Mathison apart limb from limb before I'd let him keep me away from you."

"More of your jungle training?" Carole asked stiffly. "Because if it is, it won't work here. Whether we like it or not, Andrew is the governor. And if he didn't want us to, neither one of us could get within twenty feet of him without being arrested."

"It'd be worth it for one good shot at him." Donnelly doubled his fist menacingly, and as Carole looked into the anger and stubborn pride in his eyes, she saw all of the reasons she should never have told him about Andrew.

To her it was one more battle in an old war, but to Donnelly it was fresh and new and filled with meanings that had no place in his life right now.

"You can't fight him, Donnelly, not physically." Carole uncurled his clenched fist and held it between her hands, squeezing tightly. "You have an election to win, and you can't do that if you let Andrew turn it into a personal war. Save your anger until after you've beaten him in November."

The muscles at the side of Donnelly's jaw stood out, and the antagonism in his eyes was unremitting. "I can't do that if he puts you in the middle, Carole. I know this is what you were afraid would happen, and I'm sorry. But if he brings you into it, Andrew's going to find out just how personal I can get."

"And if it costs you the election?" Carole demanded. "There's more than just us involved here. There are a whole lot of people out there who are counting on you."

As she spoke, Carole watched Donnelly retreat inside himself, shielding his thoughts with the same withdrawn, combative look he had hidden behind each time she questioned his dedication to the election.

"Tell me something, Donnelly," she asked slowly, "would you really care if you lost?"

For a long time he stared at the television, its quietly irritating static filling the room. "Yes," he said finally, "I'd care."

"But you don't sound very excited about it." Carole searched Donnelly's face for any enthusiasm and found none. He looked so earnest, so determined, as if his candidacy were a duty that held no pleasure. "You know," she said softly, "if you don't really want the job, those are going to be four very long years if you win."

He nodded, still staring at the television screen. "I've thought about that. But I do want the job. I want it very badly. It's the rest of it that I don't want—the people like your father who'll expect favors, the society sycophants who'll want invitations to the mansion, and all the others who'll be waiting for handouts because their third cousin was married to the brother-in-law of somebody who stuffed envelopes for my campaign.''

Unable to stop herself, Carole laughed at the pained look on Donnelly's face that grew fiercer the longer he talked. As he turned his scowl on her, she asked, "It's just a wild guess, but has some of that already started after your victory tonight?"

"Both of our fathers are of the opinion that I should be 'more realistic and more accommodating,'" Donnelly said, stressing the words as he quoted them.

"King may respect you for being an idealist, Donnelly, but he'll never understand you and he'll never stop trying to change you. And that is the unfortunate reality."

"And you?" He lifted Carole's hand, folding it across his and kissing the rounded crest of her knuckles as he watched her through lowered lashes. "How do you feel about it? What are you going to do if I'm elected, Carole? Do I lose you?"

Though he asked the question quietly, Carole could feel the tension building in him. Once more he seemed to be pushing for a decision she wasn't ready to make. She asked hopefully, "Couldn't we just go on the way we are?"

"No," Donnelly said emphatically. "I'm forty years old, Carole, and you make me feel like I'm in high school and in love with a girl whose parents won't let her date. I'm too damned old to be taking cold showers every night."

Carole smiled at his glowering indignity, and at the memory of her own frustrated attempts at sleep while thoughts of Donnelly intruded with greater force each night.

"You seem to find this a lot more amusing than I do," Donnelly said impatiently.

"Not really," she said, trying not to giggle. "I just hadn't thought of it that way." She cradled his face in her hands. "I'm open for suggestions."

"You know what I want." The look on his face chased her giggles away and left butterflies in their place.

"I'm here," Carole said in a voice that trembled from the yearning he aroused in her. "All you have to do is reach out and touch me."

"Oh, Carole," Donnelly groaned. His hand covered hers as his face twisted with a look of agony, and he buried his lips in the hollow of her palm. "God, how I wish I could."

Waiting for the move he didn't make, Carole slowly realized that Donnelly had rejected her invitation. Hurt and confused by his reaction, she froze. After years of hiding behind the barriers around her heart, she had finally offered Donnelly a way inside, and he had refused her. Pulling her hand away, Carole swung her legs from behind him and put her feet on the floor.

"It's late," she said, rising unsteadily. "I'll get you a blanket and pillow, and you can sleep on the couch."

"Carole." Rising, Donnelly caught her wrist and pulled her to him. "Wait."

Stepping an arm's length away from him, Carole said, "I don't know what you want, Donnelly. And obviously you don't either. So why don't you just let me go and maybe we can salvage what little there is left of this night."

"Damn it, Carole." He reached out as he stepped toward her and pulled her into his arms. "Don't make me do this," he whispered as his lips caressed the delicate shell of her ear, then moved down to the soft underside of her jaw.

"You're tired." His voice was a murmur as his mouth traced the curve of her neck. "You're upset." His kiss lingered on the pulse that beat wildly in the hollow of her throat.

Raising his mouth slowly, Donnelly caught the side of her chin in a playful nip that did nothing to slow the rush of blood that left Carole dizzy and pliant in his arms. "You've had practically a whole bottle of champagne," he said with a tender smile that crumpled into a look of pleading, "and I'm trying desperately to be a gentleman about this."

His eyes were deep blue swirls of desire as his arms tightened and he crushed his body against hers. "Oh, to hell with it."

Every nerve in Carole's body was alive to the throbbing demand of the embrace as Donnelly's mouth ground against hers in a release of needs that had been too long denied. Unchained, the passion that had sparked from the moment of their first meeting was ignited in a searing explosion that left them both breathless and clinging to each other with shivering weakness.

Donnelly pulled his lips from hers and rested his forehead against Carole's while he breathed in short, unsteady gasps. Almost unconsciously, his mouth touched her cheek in short, soft pecks. "Stop me now," he whispered, "or don't stop me at all."

Beneath her hands Carole could feel the barely reined tension of his muscles, the wild beat of his pulse that fanned the flames in her to a heat she had never known, and she knew she couldn't stop now, and wouldn't if she could. In a silent answer her arms tightened around Donnelly, and she reveled in the instant response of his body.

"Carole." With a low moan, Donnelly held her against him while his breathing accelerated. "Oh, Carole," he rasped in a voice that shook, "don't do that, sweetheart, or this is all going to be over way too soon."

Enflamed by the passionate promise in the arms that bound her to him like bands of steel, Carole felt her strength melting into a central pool where the touch of their bodies seemed to have a life of its own. Lifting her head, she gazed into his eyes through a haze of desire and whispered, "Donnelly."

Donnelly lifted her into his arms. He crossed the living room in giant steps and began to climb the stairs two at a time. "Which way is your bedroom?" he asked as he climbed.

Carole lifted her hand from the straining muscles of his chest and pointed vaguely toward the front of the house. "That way."

At the top of the staircase, he turned left and entered a room that was as black as the storm-tossed, starless night. "Where's the bed?" he asked, impatiently scanning the dark interior.

"Center of the room to your right," Carole answered dreamily, proud of her efficient response as only someone who had drunk a bottle of champagne on an empty stomach could be.

Cautiously advancing toward the bed, Donnelly found the edge and followed it to the wall. Still holding Carole, he swept aside the pillows and pulled back the covers, then lowered her slowly across the sheet and stretched out beside her. "Changed your mind yet?" he asked quietly.

With a deep sigh, Carole undid the two top buttons on his shirt and ran her palm across the smooth, hard-muscled contours of his chest. Rising onto her elbow, she pressed her lips against the pulse point in the hollow of his throat, then trailed slow, hot kisses down the center of his chest.

"I'll take that as a no," Donnelly said in a voice that sounded strangled.

Unfastening the next two buttons, Carole fanned her kisses in a line from the center valley of his chest up to the broad plateau beside it, then back into the valley and across to the other plateau. Her flattened palm caressed the curve of his ribs, smoothing the edge of his shirt back and away.

With a slow moan, Donnelly shivered and caught her hand in his. "Men have been known to die from feeling this good.... Carole." He called out her name in a hoarse protest as Carole slipped her hand from his and drew her fingers back across his ribs to the hollow of his stomach. As her nails raked gently over his skin, the muscles of his stomach rippled in an undulating spasm beneath her touch. With a teeth-chattering groan, Donnelly caught her hand again and held it still.

Donnelly, impatient for the sweet revenge of Carole's own low, passion-racked moans for mercy, rolled her onto her back. His mouth sank into hers, reaching deep and hard as he kissed her. Alive with awakened needs that had been ignored for too long, Carole clung to him, pressing harder still, relentlessly demanding what he was only too eager to give.

In the darkness that made their love a thing of sound and touch, Donnelly's fingertips stroked Carole's shoulder, found the slender strap and followed it to the camisole that bared the beginning swells of her breasts. "How do you get out of this thing?" he asked with tender amusement.

Carole led his hand to a zipper that began under her arm and went down the side. While Donnelly gently tugged the zipper loose, she slipped his shirt out of his pants and down his shoulders to the bulge of his biceps, where it caught and held. Sitting up, Donnelly whipped off his shirt and tossed it to the floor, then unlaced his shoes and left them beside it.

Carole's hand touched his shoulder and slid down his arm. When she came to his hand, she laid her camisole in his palm, and he added it to the pile beside the bed. With two soft swishes, her sandals slid off her feet and onto the floor.

Stretching out beside her again, Donnelly brushed his lips across Carole's. For the first time, he could feel her bare breasts against his chest, and like a great cat poised within range of its prey, he grew strangely patient.

Gently his mouth nibbled at hers, coaxing the beginning tremors of a more urgent need, as his hands stroked the silky smoothness of her shoulders. The weight of his body pressed into hers, shifting and probing in a silent dance as ancient as time itself.

Carole lifted her arms, then slid her fingers through the thick, soft hair at Donnelly's temples. Cupping her hands to his head, she pressed her lips hungrily into his and opened herself to him.

Donnelly moved his hand from her shoulder and stroked down the side of her breast to cup its base in the palm of his hand. As his mouth left hers and moved lower to draw gently at the tender, waiting peak of her breast, he heard at last the trembling moan of surrender he had been seeking.

With the same slowly taunting pleasure she had given him, he fueled the flames inside her until they licked with a thousand tiny tongues of need. Arching her back, Carole held Donnelly's head in her hands and pressed herself nearer to him, demanding with a passion that put an end to his patience.

Donnelly slid his hands across her rib cage. He cupped Carole's back in his hands and lifted her against him as his lips left her breast and moved down the hollow of her stomach. Holding her with one hand, he found the button at the back of her pants and freed it, then slid open the zipper. Reaching inside the flap of silk, he found flesh—warm, soft, resiliently muscled— bare flesh.

As the wealth of his discovery struck him like a jolt of lightning, he rested his face against the gently pulsing hollow of her stomach and released his breath in a moaning, "Oh, my God." While his hands tightly cupped the firm, silken mounds he had bared, Donnelly closed his mind to what lay beyond, to the impatient, throbbing urges of his own body, and struggled to slow the runaway pace of his heart.

Gently, Carole stroked the tensed muscles of his back, soothing the fevered heat of his skin with the cool whisper of her voice. "Donnelly." Her hand squeezed the rounded bulge of muscles at his shoulder and slid down his arm. "Don't stop now."

Donnelly raised himself on one elbow and helped Carole to strip away the slacks that were now her only clothing; he held himself still at her side while she found his belt and unfastened it. Feeling her way in the dark with a patience that for Donnelly was a sweet torture, she unbuttoned his pants. As her hand tugged at the zipper and followed it down, the back of her fingers brushed him.

Sucking in his breath, Donnelly stiffened and felt his mind and blood rush to that one aching point of his body. Hardly daring to move, his whole body pulsed with the waiting as Carole slowly peeled his trousers away and slid the form-fitting underwear down over his rigid thighs and onto the floor.

In no hurry, she let her hand trail back up his leg, enjoying the feel of his sculpted muscles against her palm. As her fingertips slid over the top of his thigh and into the tender hollow of his lower stomach, Donnelly swallowed a groan and grabbed her hand.

"You're making it very hard for me to be patient," he warned in a voice tight with strain.

Beneath her, Carole could feel in his tension what Donnelly's restraint cost him. Hidden by the darkness, she smiled with secret pleasure at the strength that trembled at her touch. Yearning to feel that control unleashed, she leaned over him.

As real as if it were happening now, she remembered the electric jolt that had gone through them both when the tops of her breasts had first touched him that day by the paddock. Eager again for that tender ripple of pleasure, she slowly lowered herself until she could feel the fevered heat of Donnelly's skin against her breasts, the pounding of his heart beneath hers.

The only sounds left to the night were the sorrowful wail of a lonely wind and the shallow rasp of their impassioned breathing. Leaning nearer still, Carole touched his swollen lower lip with the tip of her tongue. Lightly at first, then lingering to feel his mouth part restlessly, Carole stroked her tongue slowly across the surface, then traced the outer curve toward the arching bow of his upper lip.

With an inarticulate growl, Donnelly clutched her shoulders in his powerful hands and lifted her up and away from him. As he held her torso above him, his mouth found her breast and drew it in with the thirst she had aroused and left unslaked. Without releasing her, he rolled to the side, lowering Carole onto her back, and he stretched himself over her.

Hungrily, his lips left her breast and moved to her mouth. Beneath him, Carole strained against him impatiently as her hand slid down his back and pressed Donnelly's tensed body closer. His mouth still covered hers as he asked, "Carole?" Her name was a sigh and a plea.

"Now," she whispered in a voice that shook with the need he had called forth. "Please."

Dawn was an ugly gray. Half-formed, it seemed content to lurk on the horizon, in no hurry to release the waiting day.

Through tired, scratchy eyes, Carole watched the slow rise and fall of Donnelly's bare chest just beneath her cheek and wished the murky predawn could linger forever.

"Do you know what time it is?" Donnelly asked quietly.

Her hand tightened on his waist. "Don't look."

"Do you have any idea what we did with my watch?"

In spite of her sadness, Carole felt an embarrassed giggle rise up. "No," she said, trying not to smile. "But the clock's on the table behind me."

"Oh." As he turned his head toward the clock, Donnelly paused to kiss the top of Carole's rumpled hair. "Oh," he said again with a groan.

"Is it late?" Carole asked, wishing again that she could suspend time and stay with him just a little longer. She wasn't ready to let Donnelly go. She wasn't ready to spend weeks pretending that she didn't really miss him.

"It wouldn't be late," he said with a sigh, "if I didn't have meetings this morning before the plane leaves."

"Did you sleep?" Carole remembered the quiet time, as the storm moved on and she lay awake listening to the rhythm of Donnelly's heartbeat beneath her ear. The feel of his body against hers had been too precious to surrender, and she had fought the contented drowsiness that would have robbed her of their last hours together.

His arms tightened against her back as his hand stroked the rising curve of her hip. "No. You didn't either, did you?"

Rubbing her cheek against his chest, she closed her eyes and breathed in the scent of him, imprinting it in her mind for all the lonely nights to come. "No."

"If they gave an award for best example of bad timing, I think we'd win it hands down." Donnelly drew in a heavy breath and held Carole's head tightly against his chest. "Lord, I don't want to go."

"And there's nothing we can do."

"Not unless you want to quit your job and hide in a suitcase for the next two months."

"You'd let me out at night?" Beneath her ear Carole could hear the hard pounding of his heart, and she knew Donnelly was fighting the same hopeless grief that threatened to overwhelm her.

"Every night, all night," he promised tenderly.

"It's tempting."

With a laugh, Donnelly wrapped both arms around her and held her with a possessive fierceness. "Yeah, it is, isn't it?" He brushed Carole's hair back with his cheek, then kissed her forehead. "You think you can get some sleep after I'm gone?"

"What time is it?"

"A little after five."

Carole shook her head. "It wouldn't be worth it. I'll probably just go for a run and get into the office early. What time do your meetings start?"

"Sevenish. I've got to go by my apartment and pack first. Carole?"

Without raising her head to look, Carole could hear the frown in his voice and felt her heart quicken with apprehension. "Yes?"

"I don't quite know how to say this," he began hesitantly. "But you scared the hell out of me last night. And if you hadn't come down when you did, I was about to kick your door in."

"Donnelly," Carole protested, twisting onto her elbow to look at him.

"Look, sweetheart, I heard you yell. I heard something hit the wall. Okay, so it was your phone this time. But I didn't know that, and it could have been *you*."

In the dim light that filtered through the windows, she saw Donnelly's concern cut dark grooves across his face. "What do you want?" Carole asked, puzzled by his growing intensity.

"A key. I may never have to use it, but just in case, I want a key to your door."

"Well, that's no problem. I can give you the extra I had made for Sloan."

"You don't mind?"

"No." Carole smiled, warming to the idea. "It might come in handy. You know, since your schedule's going to be so hectic, and I sometimes work long hours. If you get back into town and I'm not home yet, you could just let yourself in."

The lines on Donnelly's face tightened again. "You haven't done this before, have you?"

"What?" Carole asked, feeling her heart pound with a beginning anger.

"Given a man the key to your house."

"I thought my life was an open book." Her voice was deceptively quiet as her jaw tightened around her words. "Everyone knows I haven't dated anyone since Andrew. The term 'virgin divorcée' was, I believe, one of the more popular quotes."

"No one knows about me, either," Donnelly answered. The hand that held her arm tightened as the tension inside him increased. "That doesn't mean I'm not here."

"It doesn't mean you're staying, either," Carole snapped, losing control of her temper. "And if you *ever* get inside my house again, you'll have to break the door down to do it."

"Do you really expect me to believe you haven't seen any other man since you divorced Andrew?"

"If I had, would it matter?" Carole shouted, refusing to protest her innocence. She could have seen other men; she should have seen other men; and she'd be damned if she would go crawling to Donnelly for a pat on the head because she hadn't seen any other men.

Donnelly glared at her, his chest heaving and his lips parted for a word that remained unspoken. Then his fingers released his uncomfortable grip on her arm and his eyes closed. Slowly he lifted his hand to cover his face and Carole heard what sounded like a muffled laugh.

"What am I doing?" he asked between his parted fingers.

"From here, you appeared to be doing a whale of a job at being obnoxiously jealous," she answered, still not ready to forgive him. "And you still haven't answered my question."

With a sigh, Donnelly lowered his hand and looked at her with a face that seemed unable to settle into one expression. Softly he repeated her question as his eyes grew serious. "Would it matter if you had been with other men? No. No, it wouldn't matter at all. And I don't know what the hell I was doing just now." His fingers curled under her chin and lifted it until her lips were just beneath his. "Being in love is new to me, Carole. I've never done it before, and I'm sorry if I hurt you."

"All of my life men have tried to dominate me," Carole said quietly. "First my father and then Andrew. And for most of my life they succeeded. It's taken me a long time to learn to live my own life. And as much as I want to make you happy, Donnelly, I can't ever go back to the way I was. I just won't do it."

Carole, giving in to her need to please for one final time, and as irritated with herself as she was with him because she was doing it, set her chin defiantly and answered Donnelly's original question. "There hasn't been another man between Andrew and you—and don't ever ask me to justify myself to you again."

"You have every right to be angry," Donnelly answered apologetically.

"I know," she snapped, still resentful of the growing power he had over her feelings. "There are times when you make me want to hide behind you, and I don't like it."

"I *want* to protect you, Carole. It makes me feel big and strong—" he paused for a beat "—and useful."

"Well, you're going to have to stop it, because it makes me feel weak and useless." In his eyes, Carole could see a great deal of seriousness mixed with his teasing. He was a man used to ruling. It came easily to him, and it wouldn't be easy for him to let it go.

"Never." Donnelly frowned gently. "Carole, do you really think that King is fighting to get you into my campaign, and that Andrew is so determined to get you back, because they see you as weak or useless? And just because I want to protect you, that doesn't mean I don't think you can take care of yourself. It just means I want to help because I love you."

Still not convinced, Carole said, "I'll think about it."

"Damn," Donnelly said, laughing, "I feel like I'm negotiating with King, Jr. Why couldn't you have grown up to be more like your mother? She's sweet."

Carole found herself smiling with him. "I've often wondered that myself. It's terrible, isn't it?" Dipping her head, she let the argument go and kissed the smooth surface of his chest. "Do you want any breakfast?"

Reluctantly, Donnelly slid away from her, and lifted his shirt from the floor as he sat on the side of the bed. "I'd love it," he said, slipping the shirt on, "but I'm already late." He stepped into his underwear, then pulled it up as he stood.

He buttoned his shirt while he walked to the foot of the bed. Carole watched the taut play of Donnelly's thighs as he moved, memorizing the sight of him in the few minutes they had left. At the end of the bed, he bent and retrieved the pale pink robe from the floor and handed it to Carole.

"Nice," he said. "Does it go with what you wore last night?"

Carole nodded as she took it from him and slipped her arms into the sleeves. She wrapped the loose coat around her, then held it closed while she threw back the covers and stood. "I wasn't quite through dressing when you got here."

While Carole went into the closet and replaced the coat with a short white kimono, Donnelly pulled on his pants and tucked in his shirt. "Is that why you only had on one earring?" he called through the half-closed closet door.

"You noticed that?" Carole asked, tying the kimono's belt. She closed the door behind her and stepped back into the bedroom.

From the edge of the bed where he sat lacing his shoes, Donnelly grinned up at her. "It was kind of cute." His eyes roamed the length of her bare legs appreciatively. "So is that. It's a cruel thing to do to a man who's on his way out of town, but it's really cute."

Carole smiled and walked toward him, and she put her arms around his shoulders as he stood. "Two weeks is a long time," she whispered huskily. "I didn't want you to forget me."

Donnelly's hands circled her waist, pulling her to him, then slid lower on her hips. "Slim chance of that," he answered softly. His gaze lingered on her face with a sweet sadness. Then his mouth lowered to capture hers in a kiss that was slow, deep and as filled with longing as the knowledge of their parting could make it.

When breathlessness and the impatient progress of the clock finally forced them apart, Donnelly left his arm around Carole's waist while he led her from the room and down the stairs in silence.

At the front door he stopped, wrapping Carole in his arms as he stared over her head into the gray mist that blocked out the rising of the sun. "Do you have any idea how hard it is for me to leave you?" Gently, he brushed his cheek against her hair. "I'll call. And if you need me, you can always reach me through my headquarters here. Your father would probably be overjoyed to get hold of me for you."

Carole nodded silently, burying her face in the starched front of his shirt. Her throat ached with the tears she refused to shed. It would be like this every time he left, and the more she cared for him, the worse the pain would be, until finally she wouldn't be able to stand to let him go. And then what would happen to them?

Donnelly held her to him so tightly she couldn't breathe, and his voice was filled with the same torment she felt as he whispered, "I love you, Carole."

The silence was filled with his waiting, and Carole burrowed deeper against his chest, clinging with what little strength she had left. If she said it, everything inside her would break, and he would still leave. He had to go, and she had to let him.

Finally Donnelly took her shoulders in his hands and stepped away. His voice was heavy with disappointment. "I'll see you."

Numbly, Carole nodded, unable to lift her eyes as he released her and walked away. When the pounding grief inside her lessened and she finally looked up, he was gone, swallowed by the mist that lingered like a ghostly reminder of their stolen night.

With a sigh that was thick with unshed tears, Carole turned away and climbed the stairs to her bathroom. After tossing aside the kimono, she pinned up her hair and showered hurriedly, refusing to allow herself time to think. Beads of moisture clung to her skin as she dried herself halfway and dressed for running.

Outside, the night's rain had barely touched the intense heat that seemed to be a dying summer's revenge. She dressed lightly, knowing the humidity would be suffocating by the time she finished her run.

Over a gray tank top and matching jogging shorts, she pulled on another, pink tank top, then scrunched pink leg warmers around her calves and ankles to combat early-morning stiffness. She paused long enough for a quick set of stretches in front of her dresser before pulling on a braided sweatband, then left the house for the familiar serenity of the river.

Slowly she stretched out, holding back on her usual pace while her tired, stiff muscles began to warm and loosen. Closing her mind to concrete thoughts, she concentrated on the rhythm of her body, seeking the discipline that would allow her to get through the day and all the long, lonely nights that lay beyond.

Two miles out, and two miles back. At the midpoint, Carole turned automatically and picked up her pace. Blindly she ran, lost inside the silence of her mind, pushing a body that wanted only to lie down and rest. To the side of her, the river was unseen, running its own parallel course with unhurried precision. Other runners were vague shapes forming out of the fog and disappearing into it again, with only the muffled pounding of their feet on wet earth to mark their passage.

Like a familiar companion, her breathing kept her company. Three beats in, four beats out, it fueled the muscles that began to burn with a fatigue that stood like a barrier at the three-mile mark. Beyond the barrier was peace and Carole ran for it, driving through the pain to a place where her body could run all day, to where her mind could float on a plane where anything was possible.

Colors began to come alive as dawn bled across the eastern sky like a ripening rose. Deep pink softened to an apricot glow as the rising sun reflected against the mist that floated from the river's surface to drift across the land.

Dew glistened in the emerald grass on either side of the dirt trail where Carole jogged. Ahead of her, like a figure forming through the veils of a dream, a man stood at the side of the path, watching her approach. He wore a dark suit, with the jacket dangling from his shoulder, held by his index finger under the collar.

Drawing nearer, Carole could see that Donnelly had changed to a fresh suit and had shaved. She slowed her pace, knowing she would otherwise have to stop too quickly or else go past him. Her hard-won peace of mind fled and her heartbeat sped with the joy of seeing him, but she knew he shouldn't be there.

Regardless of why he had come, they both had lives to lead that had nothing to do with each other, and this was not where he should be. Not in public, with the sun quickly burning away the fog that might have protected them.

Slowing to a walk, Carole watched Donnelly's expression as she covered the last yards that separated them. There was no happiness in his eyes, and as she gasped for breath, Carole felt tension painfully stiffen her tired muscles.

The swishing of morning traffic on wet pavement was only a few yards away on Riverside Drive. Glancing nervously behind her while she came to a halt, Carole saw no other runners near. When she turned back to Donnelly's tense face, she tried to smile with the genuine happiness she couldn't help feeling when he was with her, but it didn't work.

"You don't look especially happy to see me," he said.

"I'm always happy to see you," Carole answered quietly. Behind Donnelly she could see a runner approaching. "I'm just not too thrilled to see you *here*."

Donnelly shifted uncomfortably and closed the distance between them by half a foot. He balled his restless hand into a fist and held it stiffly at his side as the runner passed them. "I went by your house, but you weren't there and I didn't have time to wait." He stared down at her, refusing to follow Carole's darting eyes toward the growing number of cars and joggers in the vicinity.

"Did you forget something?" Carole could feel the effort Donnelly was making to keep from touching her. In spite of her common sense, she couldn't help wishing he would give in to the urge.

"Maybe." Donnelly draped his jacket over his arm and shoved his hands into his pockets. "Or maybe I just had to see you again before I left."

"We can't really afford to do things like this, Donnelly," Carole said reasonably. She could see the anger in his eyes as she spoke, and hated saying the words as much as he hated hearing them. But there was too much at risk to take chances on a whim, and one of them had to remember the danger of their position.

His hands were out of his pockets and halfway to her before Donnelly stopped himself and went rigid with frustration. "We left something unfinished," he said in a voice that snapped. "And I decided I wanted to finish it. Today. Now."

Slowly Donnelly's hand reached across the distance to touch her elbow, then slid up her arm. "Damn it, Carole," he said softly, "tell me you love me."

It took all of Carole's strength to stay where she was as she looked into the hurt in Donnelly's eyes. Gently, her fingertips touched his hand and curled over it, "Oh, Donnelly, yes."

He took a step toward her and Carole held up her hand to stop him. "I love you," she said, "but that only makes it harder on both of us." She pulled his hand away from her arm and took a step backward. "We still have to pretend when we're in public, and you still shouldn't be here."

"I don't know how much longer I can go on playing this game, Carole." The happiness that had flared briefly in his eyes dwindled, and his face again settled into a pinched look of dissatisfaction.

"For now, it's the only game we've got." Carole hated the cold sound of her voice, but the truth could be a cold thing. In the afterglow of love, not much else looked very important. Right now, the wrong word from the right person and Donnelly might lose what he had spent a good portion of his life working toward.

"Two months, Donnelly," she said softly, her eyes pleading with him to understand and accept what they couldn't change, "and it will all be over. Maybe you'll win, and maybe you won't. But if you let your feelings for me cost you the election, you'll never forgive yourself, or me."

Donnelly's fingers stiffened, clenched and stiffened again. "And if the election costs me you?" His gaze bored into her with a frowning intensity. "How easy do you think that would be to live with, Carole?"

"I'm not going anywhere," she answered with the closest she could come to a promise.

"But I am, and you won't be coming with me." Slowly his hands extended and caught her just above the elbows. He drew her closer as he spoke. "And two months can be a lifetime."

For an instant Carole was caught by his hypnotic gaze. The world softened, grew fuzzy and melted away. He touched her and they became the only two people on earth. Nothing else mattered. Then, from somewhere deep inside her, discipline rose up and in a frail voice said, "No."

As if amplified, the sound of the traffic whizzed by so close she could feel the rush of air. Running feet thudded at her back, and Carole pulled away. Reluctantly Donnelly released her.

"You're going to be late," she said in the same small voice.

"Someday, Carole, you're going to love me enough that you won't care about things that don't matter." Looking as angry and hurt as he had earlier that morning, Donnelly turned and once again walked away.

This time there was no mist to swallow him up or to hide the sorrow in her longing gaze. Carole watched Donnelly's straight-shouldered walk all the way to his car, and as he drove away, she wondered what would happen to them if that day never came.

Chapter Nine

The day was beautiful, the kind of mid-September day that promised an autumn of crisp, sweatered mornings and golden, shirt-sleeved afternoons. After two miserable weeks spent smiling his way through inedible dinners in small, dusty towns across southern Oklahoma, making after-dinner speeches until he hated the sound of his own voice, the night Donnelly had just spent in Carole's arms was the best sleep he had had since before the August primary.

He had one precious day in Tulsa. Then tomorrow he would be back on the road, smiling, shaking hands and choking down another endless diet of chicken and round green pellets that might once have been sweet peas, with days that were too long and nights that were too short, and exhaustion the only thing that could make him forget the loneliness that never went away.

The ache in his loins burned like a low flame as Donnelly remembered awakening to the soft brush of Carole's lips on his cheek and the rich scent of her perfume wrapping around him like an embrace. The sun was bright, and she'd been dressed for the office already. "Sleep," Carole had whispered, and pressed into his hand the spare key they had both forgotten before his last trip. "I'll see you tonight."

With a reluctant smile, he had relaxed into the soft cushion of her bed and was asleep again before the whispery rustle of her footsteps disappeared. By the time he had awakened again, the sun was almost directly overhead and Donnelly had already missed his first two appointments of the day, one of which was with King Stockton at the Stockton ranch outside of town.

Hurriedly readjusting his schedule for the rest of the day, Donnelly had showered and pulled back on the jeans and plaid western shirt he had worn to Carole's the night before. Not bothering to shave or switch cars, he had left for Black Gold Farms and what he hoped would be a lunch he could recognize as food.

Making a slurring turn from blacktop to gravel, Donnelly heard rocks batter the low-slung underside of the old MG and slowed to a saner speed. Something inside him told him he should worry about his late arrival and the borderline scruffiness of his appearance. But when he tried, Donnelly remembered instead the feel of Carole's smooth cheek rubbing gently against the stubble of his own cheek, and the pleased smile in her rusty brown eyes as she drew away.

Donnelly lifted a hand to his chin and rubbed at the pale blond growth, smiling as the memory of Carole, her scent, her textures, returned, as real as if she were with him. One more night and he would be gone again. With a month and a half left before the election, he didn't know when he would be able to get back.

Wind whipped his dark-blond hair across his forehead. Leaving one hand on the steering wheel of the lightweight sports car, he reached into the glove compartment with the other to draw out a small, square box. While the rain-rutted road fought with him for control of the car, Donnelly flipped open the box and gazed once again at the ring he had been carrying with him for almost two weeks.

The pear-shaped diamond, just over one and a half carats, was set on a narrow gold band. As much as he had ever wanted anything, Donnelly wanted to see the ring on Carole's finger. He wanted to take away the power of Andrew's threats by ending the secrecy of his stolen nights with Carole. He wanted her with him wherever he went, today, tomorrow and through all the tomorrows that would follow.

He wanted all the things every man wants when he falls in love with the one woman he's spent his life waiting for—marriage, a home, a family, sons and daughters, and *their* sons and daughters. But every time he said "I love you," he watched Carole blossom with happiness and then almost instantly shrink inside herself again, as if it would all be taken from her if she began to really believe in it.

In front of him, the two-story, white-pillared ranch house of Black Gold Farms rose up from the flat, green-and-brown landscape. Somewhere inside that house, within the complex and enduring bond between King and Amelia Stockton, lay the answers to at least some of Carole's resistance. And Donnelly was determined to find those answers.

Before he had brought the car to a complete stop in front of the flagstone porch, the entry's double door swung open to reveal an impatiently glaring King Stockton. Donnelly, smiling with the good humor that continued to bubble up from the geyser of happiness his night with Carole had uncapped, unfolded his length from the low seat and stepped out.

His boot heels crunched on the gravel drive as he rounded the car and looked up at King with a grin that made Donnelly appear inappropriately pleased with himself. Aware that he should at least try to *seem* contrite, he found himself chuckling instead as he held out his hand to King.

"Sorry I'm late," Donnelly said with an irrepressibly widening smile. "I overslept."

With a puzzled scowl, King took the hand Donnelly offered him and cautiously sniffed the air for the scent of alcohol. "You look like hell," he answered.

"That depends on your point of view," came Amelia's soft voice as she joined them and extended her hand in greeting to Donnelly. "I'm sure a lot of women voters would approve of such a charmingly rumpled look."

On impulse, Donnelly leaned forward and kissed her cheek as she smiled up at him mischievously. Something about the small, ultrafeminine woman reminded him of the underside of softness that Carole kept so jealously guarded from the sight of others. Carole's brows were a little straighter, her eyes a little wider, her nose a little bolder, but she was her mother's daughter when the blurred edges of passion turned her softly yielding and tender in his arms.

"It's been too long, Amelia," Donnelly said warmly, grateful to this woman who had given life to the woman he loved. "How have you been?"

"A little wilted lately. I'll be glad when this summer's over and I can stop hiding inside. I thank goodness for the few lovely days like today." She led Donnelly toward the back of the house, leaving King to close the door and follow behind. "I hope you're hungry. Martha's outdone herself on lunch, and we have coffee in the study. You do drink coffee, don't you?"

"Yes, I do, thank you." In the study, Donnelly dropped into a deep leather chair with its back to the door and took the cup of coffee Amelia handed him. She sat on the couch next to him and poured fresh cups for herself and King, who entered quietly and took the chair in front of the fireplace.

Facing Donnelly across the coffee table, King watched him drink half a cup of the rich black brew, then said, "You look like you had a rough night."

"I've had a rough two weeks," Donnelly answered gruffly as he held out his cup for Amelia to refill it. With a crooked smile he added, "But I had a *wonderful* night."

Amelia's laugh was a short, throaty ripple before she turned aside King's next barb with an innocent, "A real night's sleep must be heaven after so many nights on the road. Where do you go next, Donnelly?"

"West and north, I think," he said, relishing with careful sips the taste of the hot, fresh coffee. "Actually, my assistants take care of things like where we are and where we're supposed to go next. I just stand up and speak in the direction they point me. When you do two, sometimes three, different speaking engagements a day, it all becomes a blur."

"Couldn't someone help?" Amelia asked sympathetically. "Do you have to do it all alone?"

Donnelly winced, wondering for a moment if she was deliberately setting him up. His eyes darted to King, who was watching her in surprised amusement, and Donnelly realized her concern was genuine. King looked at Donnelly and grinned slowly, acknowledging the opening his wife had innocently given him, even as his continued silence indicated that he would let it pass.

"If I were married," Donnelly said, finally answering her question as carefully as possible, "I imagine my wife would be campaigning with me. My father flies in from Washington when he can, and I have friends who speak on my behalf. But ultimately, I'm the candidate, and that's not something anyone else can do for me. So no matter who else shares in the speaking duties, my job isn't going to be any easier than it is right now."

"I'm sorry Carole couldn't be here," King said quietly, with what, in another man, might have been nothing more than a father's pride in his daughter. "I had really hoped to get the two of you together while you were in town today."

"I don't think it would have made much difference," Donnelly answered. With surprising ease, he pretended she was nothing more than the distant stranger he had once been so determined to avoid. Last night as they had whispered in the dark, holding off sleep for as long as they could, Carole had told him how hard her father had fought to get her to attend this meeting. "She's never made her feelings on the matter secret," Donnelly continued, "and neither have I."

"Hmm," King grunted.

Donnelly glanced at Amelia, who seemed to realize what she had started and smiled back at him apologetically.

"Have you been following the polls?" King asked. With the unhurried patience of a fighter who knows he can go the distance, King returned to the real reason he had asked Donnelly to meet with him.

"We expected to be behind at this point," Donnelly said patiently. "But we're gaining steadily."

Steepling his fingers in front of him, King relaxed into his chair. Though his suit pants didn't give him the same casual air as Donnelly's jeans, he copied the younger man's relaxed posture of an ankle overlying the opposite knee. "Not steadily enough, I don't think. We have six weeks left, and what worries me is that you've never been ahead in the polls."

"What would you suggest?" Donnelly asked. Deceptively quiet, he felt his nerves singing.

What would it have been like, he wondered, to have spent his life countering King's dogged battle instincts? The man never gave up. He just feinted to the side and came back at you from a different direction. And this was what Carole had lived her life with.

That she had survived at all was a tribute to a spirit as stubbornly tenacious as her father's. But it also proved that she could never be forced into anything she had the slightest hesitation about. Life had boomeranged on her too many times for her to tempt fate. Sadly, Donnelly thought about the diamond and knew that it would be leaving with him when he flew out again the next morning. Someday Carole would be his, truly and totally. But today would not be the day.

"I think you know what I would suggest," King answered through the tug of Donnelly's thoughts. "The time for niceties is long passed. If you're going to defeat Andrew Mathison, you're going to have to hurt him. You're going to have to go in hard and fast, and keep hitting him until he's on his knees. Or he's going to bury you come November.''

"And how is this going to be accomplished? Or should I ask? Could it start with 'Carole' and end with 'Stockton'?" Donnelly mocked.

"You need her." King leaned forward, muscles taut with the silent aggression of a panther crouched for the kill.

Donnelly's jaw went rigid, and his eyes glazed with an anger that burned through him with the liquid speed of lava. "Over my dead body," he said softly.

"Gentlemen," Amelia interrupted. She stood and they rose with her, automatically deferring to the quality in Amelia that demanded the remembrance of manners. "Surely lunch is served." She smiled and ushered them from the room, ending the argument before it could escalate.

In the dining room, the table was a visual delight that cooled the lingering sizzle of Donnelly's temper. Three places were set at the end of the table in a cozy, family-style arrangement. A fresh spinach salad was already in place at each seat. On a warming tray in the center of the table, a mouth-wateringly tender roast was sliced paper thin and surrounded by chunks of vegetables simmering in the beef's natural juices.

"I hope you don't mind the informality," Amelia said. Leaving the head of the table for King, she took the seat to his right and motioned Donnelly into the chair across from her. "I thought, after so many weeks of eating out, you might prefer something a little more relaxed."

"It's perfect," Donnelly answered, helping himself to the coffee that was beside the roast. After filling Amelia's cup and then King's, he replaced the pot. "I don't remember the last time I had a decent meal, or a chance to really relax."

From the first time he had met Amelia Stockton, Donnelly had sensed a bond. In her eyes he had seen understanding and empathy, as if they shared an unspoken secret. And whatever its source, the feeling was there still, the same quiet alliance of mutual support.

"If you two promise to behave," Amelia said, her soothing glance including first King and then Donnelly, "I'll let you talk now."

"No shouting allowed?" King asked with a frown that didn't hide his amusement.

"I'm sure Donnelly knows a lot of other places he can go if he wants indigestion with his meal," Amelia said sweetly.

"All right," King began mildly, turning to Donnelly. "I believe we left off with your dead body."

Amelia sighed and once more offered Donnelly an apology with her eyes as she began to eat her salad. Beneath her sympathy, Donnelly could sense more than a little amusement. After a lifetime of dueling with her husband, she enjoyed seeing a fresh sparring partner go a few rounds.

Beneath the good-natured sparks that lit the couple's eyes as they communicated in silent understanding, Donnelly realized they were a family of fighters. For King the battle was like breath. He relished it, fed on it, while Amelia was quiet, bending with the wind, then snapping back with the resilience of a survivor.

Somewhere between the two was Carole. He had seen her flare with the explosive temper of her father, and persevere with the gentle strength of her mother. And like them, she was not used to losing.

"Look," Donnelly asked, "have you asked your daughter about this?"

"She'd come around if you would," King answered.

Donnelly remembered the recorder he had connected to Carole's phone the night before. He remembered her relieved smile that still hadn't wiped away the look of strain that never quite left her face.

Silently studying King's determined expression, Donnelly thought of all the secrets the Stocktons guarded. Sloan Prescott, the illegitimate son no one knew about. Andrew Mathison, an accident of marriage anyone would be glad to forget ever had happened. And the phone calls Carole never mentioned that held bad memories like a guillotine over her head.

"Let's be realistic, King. You're risking a lot if you bring Carole into this. There's a potential for disaster there that, quite frankly, I'm hesitant to introduce into my campaign." Knowing he was massaging one of the few sore spots in King's hide, Donnelly spoke softly. Twirling circles on the white tablecloth with the handle of his fork, he watched the other man's expression for signs of an explosion.

"You saw the interview she gave the night of the primaries, didn't you?" Frowning, King asked the question evenly, almost as if he hadn't heard Donnelly or had chosen to ignore what couldn't be changed.

"Yes." Donnelly laid down his fork and waited, forgetting about the last decent meal he would have for a long time.

"That reporter wasn't kidding, and she wasn't exaggerating by much. There's something about a young, beautiful woman that glamorizes a candidate. Carole wouldn't have to say a word, just stand there.'' King leaned forward and his voice dropped almost to a whisper. ''Just stand there beside you, Donnelly. And in the next poll, I can guarantee you'd be ahead. And there's nothing Mathison could say that wouldn't backfire on him.''

Donnelly lifted his gaze from the crusading flame in King's eyes and looked at Amelia. ''You're her mother. What do you think?''

''It's hard to say. I can remember a time when Carole truly loved politics. She enjoyed every minute of campaigning, and I can still see that spark in her sometimes, even now.'' Amelia's words were thoughtful, and Donnelly knew that she had already answered the question in her own mind many times.

''But the one thing I understand, and that I've never been able to convince King of, is how dangerous Andrew can be,'' she continued, her voice dropping to a quiet urgency. ''He's an utterly ruthless man who can put a charming and convincing face on his most outrageous lies. Sometimes I almost think that he might be a little insane.'' As if her statement had surprised even her, Amelia smiled self-consciously and shrugged. Her eyes searched Donnelly's for understanding. ''Anyway, I know that he scares me, and that he scares Carole. And I know that if he doesn't scare you, he should, because he's capable of absolutely anything.''

''Oh, Amelia, good grief.'' King laid his silverware on his plate with a loud clatter and glared at his wife in exasperation.

Patting King's clenched fist, Amelia smiled again, then looked across the table to Donnelly. ''My husband feels that my interpretation is melodramatic. I don't. I never liked Andrew and he knew it. So after the engagement was announced, he never bothered with trying to fool me again.''

In her mother's explanation, Donnelly could hear all the things Carole had left unsaid, and it hurt him to know how much she had tried to shelter him from the whole truth.

Softly, with a pain that was obvious, Amelia continued. ''It broke my heart to see Carole marry him, but there was nothing I could do to stop it. Andrew knew how I felt, and he enjoyed it. He would smile when no one was watching, as if we shared a dirty secret. I think he's the only person I've ever known that I truly despise.'' She shuddered, and Donnelly wished he could wrap his arms around her and hold her until the pain left them both.

The cold anger he had felt the night he'd found Carole hysterical after one of Mathison's phone calls returned. Sooner or later, he knew, he would have to do something, regardless of the consequences. He wasn't the kind of man who could stand by indefinitely while someone he loved was being hurt, no matter how much Carole wanted him to.

''All of that only makes it more important that we make sure he's defeated,'' King said emphatically.

''And, of course, he's right,'' Amelia said tiredly, with a nod toward King. ''The other side of this coin is that if Andrew is as bad as I think he is, how can we not do everything possible to bring him down?''

Fleetingly, Donnelly remembered the ring and how fervently he wished Carole could leave with him the next day—but not if it meant she would be a pawn in someone else's chess game.

''As long as there is the slightest chance we can defeat Mathison without her, I don't want Carole involved,'' Donnelly said firmly. Inside his chest there was a cold spot, as if he had just shoved Carole away from him and shut the door between them. He had one more night to make up for all the empty nights to come, and he knew it would never be enough.

"What you don't understand, son, is that there isn't the slightest chance. Without her, you've lost already. And with or without your permission, if I can, I'm going to get her out there.''

"You can't do that." Even to himself, Donnelly's words sounded like an empty threat.

King smiled in a cold grimace of triumph. "You wouldn't be the first candidate who got support he didn't want. No, sir." He shook his head slowly, keeping his voice low. "There's nothing you could do, short of publicly denouncing her. And you're not that big a fool."

"You'll never get her to agree.'' Donnelly's words continued to sound strangely hollow, and he felt as if he were fighting himself as well as King. There was nothing he wanted more than to have Carole with him, any way he could get her. All of the high, proud principles he had sworn to uphold meant nothing when faced with the raging desire that just the thought of her could arouse. He didn't even have the strength left to be ashamed of himself.

"We'll see," King said. His smile had all the warmth of a coiled rattler. "We'll see. Care for some more coffee?''

Carole pushed a button and watched calculations stream across the screen in front of her. Preliminary figures for the end of the third quarter showed their costs running five percent above the quarterly budget.

Catching her lower lip between her teeth as she entered new data, Carole compared the breakdowns on a monthly basis and groaned to see that the figures for July and August were on target.

It wasn't hard to tell that her mind hadn't been on business for the past month. All of the overage had come in September, and when King saw the sharp rise in the third-quarter numbers there'd be hell to pay. With a scowl, Carole pushed another button to store the computations, then withdrew the minidisk and filed it in her briefcase.

Sighing, she turned off the personal computer and shoved her chair away from the desk. Outside the window of her home office, daylight lingered despite the late hour. In less than a month, the clocks would be turned back and night would become night once again. After that it would be only a few weeks until the election.

Hardly realizing what she did, Carole allowed her fingertips to stroke the phone, and she wondered which small town would shelter Donnelly that night. The two weeks that had passed since his last, brief visit were the longest, loneliest days of her life. His voice, soft and sweet, in the dark hours just before midnight was the lifeline that carried her from one day to the next. She had never known such happiness or such bittersweet longing, and with every day that passed the deception they lived became harder.

With her hand still resting on the receiver, the phone began to ring. Steeling herself to patience, Carole waited. On the third ring the recorder would activate and she could lift the receiver. Since Donnelly had installed the device, she had erased miles of useless tape waiting for the one call that hadn't come.

Slowly lifting the receiver, Carole took a deep breath. With her free hand she covered the button that shut off the recorder. "Hello."

"Hello, sweetheart. I've missed you."

The words were right, but the voice was all wrong. Where there should have been happiness, Carole felt the cold, hard fist of dread close around her heart and begin to squeeze. She took her hand away from the button and watched the tape uncoil from one spool to the other, recording her long, reluctant silence.

"Is that all the greeting I get? Didn't you miss me, too, just a little?"

"After our last conversation I wasn't sure if you'd be calling again," Carole answered, trying to feel brave but thinking instead how foolish she had been to agree to this.

"How long's it been?" Andrew asked. "A month? And the election's just a little more than a month away. Have you been keeping up with the polls?"

"I know you're still leading." He sounded calm, almost pleasant, and Carole struggled to keep her near-panic from showing in her voice.

"You've been a good girl. I just wanted you to know it hasn't gone unnoticed." He chuckled, enjoying a private joke. "I bet old King is just beside himself. Has he been after you? You can tell me. I know he has."

"What do you mean?" As soon as she said it, Carole knew she had made a mistake. Playing dumb with Andrew had never worked. He knew she knew better, and it only angered him.

"You know exactly what I mean, Carole. It saddens me that you would still try to lie to me. I thought we had gotten past that in our last conversation. Obviously I didn't make my point as clearly as I thought I had."

"Why do you even bother to ask, Andrew?" Carole dropped any pretense of coyness. "You know exactly how King feels and what he must be doing."

"And yet you resist. That must be very hard for you, Carole," Andrew said with real sympathy. "I'm having a reception here Saturday. I'd like it if you could come. I'd send my plane for you."

Stunned, Carole said nothing for a long moment. Finally she asked, "Are you serious?"

"Very. It would put an end to King's pressure and all of that distasteful press speculation. I miss you, Carole." His voice lowered seductively. "I can't tell you how much I miss you."

Carole felt trapped, betrayed. So far Andrew had said nothing that would sound threatening or abusive to anyone who didn't know him as well as she did. On the contrary, he sounded like a sad and lonely man who still carried a torch for his ex-wife and was willing to settle for whatever small scraps of affection he could get.

He couldn't possibly know about the tape, and yet everything he said was calculated to win sympathy from any strangers who might overhear. Whatever the reasons for his suddenly saintly act, she couldn't let him get away with it.

"Please, Andrew," Carole said, putting away her patience, "don't waste our time with phony sentiment. I've done what you asked. I've stayed out of the election. Even at the risk of letting you win, I haven't taken sides since the primaries. The last time we talked you said that would be enough."

"What are you talking about? I told you to stay away from Wakefield's campaign. I never said that would be enough. I never said I'd stop trying to get you back."

"You said a lot more than that." The blood began to pound in her temples as Carole felt his caution dropping away. "I don't like being threatened, Andrew. My father desperately wants me to become involved in this campaign, and the only reason I don't is that I'm afraid of what you'll do. You hinted at some very unpleasant things in your last phone call."

"And I meant them all," Andrew said in a tone that was coldly precise. "I'll do what I have to do. I want you, Carole. I was serious about that. I want you any way I can have you—willing or unwilling. And if I have to destroy both you and Donnelly Wakefield to win this election and get you back, I'll do it."

"There's nothing you can do. If I'm willing to come out in the open, to face the press's questions, you've lost the election."

"Don't be so sure of that. You're a two-for-one deal, sweetheart. You go to the highest bidder. Get King Stockton behind you, and you get his daughter as an extra bonus. I know because I was the first one to buy you."

Like the sting of a wasp, Andrew's voice darted through the telephone line, stabbing with hard, stunning jolts of pain. He laughed, exultant at the silence his attack had drawn. "It could sound very ugly, Carole. It would embarrass you and your family for me to say that, and it could destroy Donnelly. I'd hate to do it," he said sarcastically, "but if you made me, I would."

"No, you wouldn't. You couldn't say anything that tasteless without hurting yourself as much as you would Donnelly." Inside, Carole still reeled at the awful depths his mind could sink to, but she had it on tape this time. And that tape would leave Andrew with no place to hide.

"'I don't have to say anything, Carole," he answered smoothly. "I have people who do these things for me. In fact, if it ever happened, I'd spring to your defense immediately."

His voice filled with emotion as he rehearsed the words. "Ours was a love match, and I'm sure the Carole I was married to would never sell herself to the highest bidder." He chuckled with a nasty enjoyment. "Just because you divorced *me* when I fell out of favor with King doesn't have to mean he's using you to buy Donnelly. Surely no gubernatorial candidate would be lecherous enough to make a deal just to get a woman, not even a woman as desirable as Carole Stockton."

He had gone too far. Carole felt her skin crawl at the sound of his deep, satisfied sigh in her ear. "You're vermin," she hissed.

"But I'm clever vermin, my dear. Don't try to play at my games, Carole. I'm too good at it. And if you're smart you won't make me prove it to you."

"'Someday, Andrew, you're going to go too far." Trembling with an anger that had her on the edge of tears, Carole's voice was no more than a whisper. "And I promise you, I'll be there to watch you fall."

"Have I ever told you, Carole, that I find your anger very erotic? I dream of your angry little hiss and I miss you unbearably."

Revulsion rippled down her spine, and without answering Carole replaced the receiver. She tried to block his last words out of her mind as she put a fresh tape in the machine. With shaking hands that made her movements clumsy, she slipped the tape that held the conversation into her purse.

For weeks her father had begged her to become involved in the campaign, and because of Andrew's threats and Donnelly's reluctance she had refused. Donnelly continued to trail in the polls. The margin was narrow, but it was holding steady, and if things went on as they were, he would lose.

Carole turned in the swivel chair to stare over the low wall of the alcove and out the ceiling-high living room window at the muddy blue sky outside. King was right. She couldn't let Andrew win. Whatever it took, and whatever it cost her, she had to at least try to stop him.

Donnelly wouldn't like it, but the next time he called she would warn him and then she would tell King. She had been patient and reasonable long enough, and she had taken all the abuse from Andrew she intended to take.

When the phone rang again, Carole jumped and whirled to stare at it as if it were a snake. Then, on the third ring, as the recorder clicked into motion, she took another deep breath and lifted the receiver. "Hello."

"Surprised?" Donnelly's tender voice sounded very pleased. "I'm early tonight."

So relieved she could have melted from the happiness, Carole smiled widely. "Sweetheart, hi."

"Is it my imagination, or are you upset about something? You sound a little tense."

Briefly Carole thought about lying to him. She wanted to forget about Andrew's call, and telling Donnelly about it would only make it more real. But by now she had waited too long, and her silence was telling.

"Andrew called, didn't he?" Donnelly asked quietly. "Just now?"

Anger tightened his words and Carole knew there was no way to avoid talking about it. Without thinking, she nodded.

"Play the tape for me," Donnelly said. He didn't need her answer to be able to see the scene as clearly as if he were there. After a month of conducting a romance by telephone, he knew every nuance of Carole's voice and of her silences. He could see the tiny frown lines between her eyes, her lips pressed tightly in stubborn resistance.

"No." No one else knew the kind of things Andrew could say when there was no one else to hear. And once Donnelly heard the tape, she would have to live with the uncomfortable memory showing in his eyes every time Andrew was mentioned.

"I'll have to hear it someday," Donnelly argued gently.

"Not now, please," Carole said in a whisper. "I don't want to hear it again."

"Did he say anything we can use?"

"It wasn't very nice."

"Just a little bit longer, Carole." He ached to hold her in his arms and soothe the hurt that left her sounding battered and withdrawn. The walls he had worked so hard to bring down were up again. "Just a little bit longer, and it'll all be over."

Carole drew in a deep breath then let it out again as she changed her mind about what she'd been about to say. "Donnelly, I need to see you." She couldn't tell him over the phone. There was no way he was going to want her joining his campaign, now of all times, and she wasn't up to another argument with a faceless voice. "How far away are you going to be tomorrow night?"

"Are you serious? Please don't be teasing me. You have no idea how badly I want to see you."

Shy suddenly with the infectious excitement of Donnelly's reaction, Carole said, "You wouldn't mind, then?"

"Mind?" Donnelly's voice slid upward into a boyish register she had never heard in him before. The deep, controlled tones of the public speaker were gone, replaced by words that crackled with happy excitement. "I'd love it. You're really serious? I don't believe it."

Carole laughed. "I'm really serious. But you've got to tell me where to come."

For a minute all sound from Donnelly's end of the line ceased. Then he said slowly, "I don't know. But I can find out. Can I call you at your office tomorrow and tell you? Is it tomorrow night? I'll see you tomorrow?"

"The office is fine, and, yes, it's tomorrow." Carole smiled, and teased in as serious a voice as she could manage. "Unless, of course, you'd rather wait."

Not fooled, Donnelly chuckled. "No way. You show the slightest hesitation, and you'll find me on your doorstep sometime tomorrow night. There are times in every man's life when obstacles cease to matter."

"I think it may be a little hard to sleep tonight," Carole said softly. "I've missed you more than I would have believed I could."

Donnelly sighed. "One more month." His voice was a deep purr. "There's so much I want to say to you, Carole. This is all so unfair to you. You deserve a real romance. I can't even send you flowers or take you to dinner. And now, tomorrow."

There was no happiness left in his tone. A gravelly tiredness dragged at his words, and, too late, Carole remembered that hers was the easy part of their romance. She only had to sit and wait, while Donnelly lived out of a suitcase, never knowing where he would be the next day, hardly knowing where he was at the moment. His life was a series of crises, some political, some personal, and all of them handled quietly and alone.

"I love you, Donnelly. It might not be as good as it could be, but what we have is better than what I had before you. I know it's not easy on you, though, and I'm sorry."

"I'm not worried about myself, Carole. To be with you, I'd take anything I could get, any way I could get it. But..." He paused and let his breath out in another heavy sigh. "The best I can offer you right now is a roadside motel. Clean, private and old. I'm not sure how far love's going to go when you're faced with the reality of it."

"Well..." Carole pondered a childhood memory, an oasis of faded pink tourist cabins seen from the back seat of a passing automobile. Clean, private and old. "As long as it's not called the Dew Drop Inn, I think I can handle it," she said slowly.

"This may be entertaining in more ways than one," Donnelly answered. A touch of humor crept into his tone.

"Travel is a broadening experience," Carole agreed with a smile, while she privately hoped that it wouldn't be as bad as her imagination told her it could be.

"Sweetheart?"

"Uh-huh?"

"You won't be sorry."

Chapter Ten

Carole pulled onto the gravel shoulder of the two-lane road. In the fading light she lifted the crumpled piece of paper from the seat beside her and studied the last of the scribbled directions. Ahead, in the bend of the road, was a cluster of buildings that should be the motel.

Now that she was almost there, her heart pounded with a combination of fear and anticipation. She had been late getting away from the office, and the drive had taken a little more than two hours. Afraid that Donnelly had been waiting, and even more afraid that he hadn't gotten there yet, Carole pulled back onto the road.

As she started into the curve, the obscuring trees slid past her and the Christmas-red neon sign of the Flamingo Court came into full view. Like one-room houses, twelve tiny pink-and-green cottages were strung out to the right of a slightly larger building. In front of the building, a one-story-high, faded pink flamingo perched on one leg, dangling a flashing Office sign from its beak.

Carole suppressed a twinge of apprehension as she inspected the three cars parked at random along the front the cottages. At the far right, in front of the cabin farthest from the office, she found Donnelly's dark sedan slanted at an angle that left just enough room for her Mercedes convertible to pull in beside it.

She drove in through the exit, and had hardly come to a stop with her car tucked into the protective pocket Donnelly had left her, when the cottage door opened and he stepped out. Weak with relief, Carole watched the quick, light steps of his approach. Before she could do more than slide her keys from the ignition, he reached the car and pulled open the door.

Carole turned to speak, then forgot what she was going to say as Donnelly leaned in to kiss her gently on the lips. The scent of his cologne and a strong sense of masculine competency invaded the cool silence of the car while his hand deftly reached across her to unfasten Carole's seat belt, then slid down her arm to take the keys from her hand.

"Did you have any trouble getting here?" he asked, moving his kiss to her jaw, ear and neck as he spoke.

"I only got lost once," Carole murmured, weaker still, and from more than relief. "I took a wrong turn and had to backtrack." Her fingers curled through the hair at the nape of his neck. It was damp, and he smelled warm and fresh from the shower.

"I was afraid of that. Did you bring luggage?" He took her hand in his and helped her from the car.

Gravel crunched under her shoes as Carole clung to the reassurance of his hand and pointed to the rear of her car. "An overnight bag. In the trunk. Have you been waiting long?"

Reluctantly Donnelly let go of her. "A while. Why don't you wait inside?" When Carole looked at the open door of the cabin and then back at him without moving, he chuckled and gave her a nudge. "Go on in. You may be surprised."

The secret pleasure behind his smile made Carole curious, and with a last hesitant look she turned and went toward the open door and the dark interior beyond. Slipping inside, she heard the softly compelling music at the same time her gaze was drawn to the candles that lit the tiny room like twin sets of stars on a moonless night. On the dresser two tall, slender candles flanked a plastic ice bucket filled with a bottle of champagne. On a table at the back of the room, two more candles glowed on either side of a crystal vase filled with red roses and baby's breath.

In the background, an unbelievably deep voice moaned velvety words of love and longing. Straining her eyes against the dark, Carole saw the cassette player on the floor in the corner beyond the bed. The singer's voice was familiar, a vintage memory that was from another time and yet was timeless.

"You like?" Donnelly asked quietly from behind her.

Turning, Carole felt the tears burn down the back of her throat. With less than a day's notice, he had taken what could have been a rocky reunion and turned it into magic. She would never forget this night, or the love Donnelly had lavished on such small and special touches.

"It's wonderful. If you're near enough next week, we'll have to do it again."

"I was hoping you'd say that."

In one unbroken motion he lowered her traveling case to the floor and drew her into his arms. "I can't believe you're here," he said, brushing her hair with his lips. "If you hear I'm suffering from exhaustion, don't believe it. I had to pretend to be sick to get away early tonight. It'll probably be in all the papers tomorrow."

"Donnelly." Carole drew her head back to stare up at him in concern. "You can't afford publicity like that right now."

He shrugged and gave her a guilty, little-boy grin. "What can I say?" He shook his head and kissed the end of her nose. "If you only knew, sweetheart."

With a sigh, Donnelly took her hand and led Carole to the side of the bed. He shook the pillows free of the covers and piled them against the headboard. Then he stretched out and pulled Carole down into the crook of his arm. "Like the music?" he asked quietly.

Carole nodded and watched the candles' flickering reflection in the dresser mirror. The singer's gravelly sighs extolled the pain-pleasure pricks of love with a steamy realism that brought butterflies to her stomach.

"Barry White. It's his old stuff." Donnelly's voice was a deep murmur just above Carole's ear. "I used to listen to it back in the lonely, frustrated days of my youth. Then I was longing for something I'd never had." His hand cupped her chin and tilted her face until the lips that had brushed her hair were less than a whisper from hers. "Now I'm longing for something I can't get enough of."

Carole wanted to let him know how much he meant to her, how much she wanted and missed him when they were apart. She touched his cheek, moist and smooth from a fresh shave, and felt her heart swell with an aching tenderness. Donnelly deserved so much more than she had given him. He deserved the kind of woman who was free to give him the same unrestricted love and devotion that came so naturally from him.

"You're awfully quiet." He kissed her gently, a quick kiss that was meant as a preliminary and nothing more. But his lips returned again and again, staying longer, demanding with an ardor that paid no heed to the cautious whispers of his mind.

Rolling to half cover her body with his, Donnelly slipped his arm beneath Carole and pulled her lower on the bed. His leg slid over hers, and like a horse with the bit between its teeth, his body gave a shudder and raced ahead of the gentle pace he had planned.

In no mood to talk, Carole felt the sudden hard pounding of Donnelly heart, the taut quiver of his muscles straining against his self-control, and the liquid heat of her response was instant. Her tongue slid into his open hungry mouth as her lips battled his with devouring greed.

Over the deep groans and sultry throb of the music came their own heated gasps. The sudden flaring of their passion shook them both with its force. The hard pressure of Donnelly's body against hers ignited Carole with an impatient need that shouted down inhibitions.

With a smooth flick, she slipped her feet from the leather flats she had worn and kicked the shoes over the side of the bed. In the same motion, she shifted her position as Donnelly's leg pressed between her thighs and his hand slid her flared skirt higher on her bare legs.

Drunk with the desire that had grown wild during long weeks without him, Carole tugged the front of Donnelly's shirt free and unfastened the buckle on his belt while his fingers pulled the loose fabric of her satin tap pants to one side and began to stroke the center of fire that drove them both past sanity.

His mouth drew at hers with a shuddering sigh as Carole slowly worked open the reluctant zipper of his trousers. Her hand trembled and her heart tripped to a double-time beat as her fingers slid beneath the elastic of his low-cut briefs. The only sounds were the soft moaning of their breaths, and music that was so far away it might have been a dream.

His lips were still locked with hers in a kiss neither would ever wish to end, as Donnelly slid deeper into the vee of her thighs, past the soft brush of satin and flesh, into the moist, dark fires that were life and death, beginning and end, and everything he had ever wanted in the still, quiet hours of his soul.

For a long moment they lay motionless, lost in the feel of each other, savoring a union as total as a man and woman can achieve, where heart, mind and body are welded in one sweet instant of beginning. Then slowly, like a blind man cautiously feeling his way through an empty room, Donnelly began to move—one shallow stroke outward, then back; a long, reluctant retreat with a tantalizingly slow return. Deeper still, then shallow; a lazy, swirling withdrawal followed by a swift, steady plunge; tasting all the flavors of a desire that built to a peak of stunning height, then hovered like a bird gliding on an updraft, far above the earth in an effortless flight that soared higher still, on and on without end.

Carole's breath was ragged as she clung to Donnelly and rode the currents of passion that locked them together. The world spun in a concert of powerful need and exertion that fanned their emotional heat with a physical one. Inside her, the burning sang and flamed higher as Donnelly's kiss hardened and his body twisted against hers, pressing closer.

Her scream was short and sharp, like something wild set free. A spiral of pleasure sliced through her, gripping with long, hard fingers that gradually loosened and skittered away on soft, tickling fingertips. Beneath her hands, Donnelly's muscles were rigid, and tiny quivers rang along the surface of his skin. With taut control, he moved against her in long, steady surges, ending in a final thrust that drew the breath from him in an uneven moan.

Patiently he stroked the last breath of flame within her until he felt Carole's body go soft and yielding in his arms; then his movements grew slowly more shallow and irregular, until finally they ceased altogether and he lay quietly locked within her warm embrace.

Donnelly pulled Carole to him with crushing tightness and rolled onto his side and held her against his chest. He let out his breath in a long sigh, then said, "Damn."

Beneath her cheek, his shirt was wet with the sweat that coated both of them. Her skirt was a twisted mess around her waist. His unfastened belt buckle bit into the flesh below her hipbone, and Carole glowed with the happy exhaustion of a hedonist. Twisting in his arms, she reached between them and pulled the buckle into the hollow between their waists. "I'm speechless," she said with a smile.

"It *was* a bit sudden."

Carole turned her head and stared into turquoise eyes that looked more proud than repentant. "At least you took off your jacket," she said in a teasing voice that was still husky with the currents that had slowed but not ceased.

Donnelly touched her lower lip with his fingertip. Any trace of makeup was gone. Her skin was dewy and flushed a delicate shell pink. Her eyes glittered like dark stars in a pale sky. "A lucky coincidence." He kissed her, and as her mouth opened to him with an innocent warmth, the same dizzy madness came flooding back.

Like a flash fire galloping across the plains, the heat of her touch passed through his skin and into the pit of his stomach. Donnelly felt his arms involuntarily tighten around her as his body came to instant attention. In a losing struggle for patience, he broke off the kiss and pulled his head back to look at her.

"Do you have to leave tomorrow? We can do *something*. Somehow we can keep it quiet." Slowly, he let his head dip forward until his forehead was touching hers. Donnelly's heart pounded in his ears and his head roared with the shout of emotions that had been ignored for too long. "No election is worth what we're going through, Carole. I love you."

Hurting with the desperation in Donnelly's voice and with her own longing for the same things he wanted, Carole placed her fingertips against his mouth. "Shh," she whispered. "You feel that way now, but if you let your feelings for me ruin your chance for election, you'd never forgive yourself—or me."

White-hot longing seared him, made worse by the knowledge that she was right and that there would be this one night and no more until their desire again built to a peak that made them willing to risk anything for a few private hours together. "Carole, Carole," Donnelly murmured, holding her so tightly their bodies might have been one solid, taut unit.

Her fevered lips moved over his throat, leaving a trail of soft, hot kisses. When she reached his waiting mouth, their hopeless longing gave the kiss a wild, sad passion. There was no room to breathe, to move, to think. The world shrank to a small universe bounded by candlelight, throbbing music and the heated touch of two lovers who had no tomorrow.

Knowing there would be no slow, gentle seduction this time either, Donnelly slid Carole beneath him and felt her legs part to welcome him. "If this is all we have," he whispered through the freight-train roar in his ears, "we'll make it a night to remember."

Cold chills chased over Carole's skin at his words, and she shivered uncontrollably while his hand tugged her underwear down her thighs and past her knees. Covering her body with his, Donnelly held her against his chest as he entered her, and the heat of a volcano seemed to explode inside her.

"Remember me tomorrow," he whispered with each thrust. "Think of me at night." His voice groaned with the almost mindless desire that drove them both. "Miss me."

The candles burned low and then guttered. The tape reversed automatically and the music went on and on. And they never slept at all.

The weather was glorious, with a warmth that seemed to glow rather than burn, and the air had the dusty taste of autumn. Leaves were a picture-postcard blend of green, red, gold and burnt orange, with a few brown ones already collecting in gutters and crunching beneath hurrying feet. It was less than a month until the election, and a week since Carole had gone to meet Donnelly.

Butterflies of anticipation collided inside her stomach as Carole drove her car into the garage and then went back across the driveway to enter through the front door. In their conversation the previous evening she and Donnelly had discussed meeting again before the week was out, before his campaign moved on to the center of the state and a head-to-head confrontation in what was a Mathison stronghold. Tonight they were to confirm their arrangements, and Carole found herself growing as nervous as a bride on her wedding night.

Pausing to check her empty mailbox, she saw through the glass door that a large brown mailing envelope was face down on the floor of the foyer. The corner that had been used to guide it under the door remained outside, and kneeling, Carole caught the wedge of envelope and pulled it back out. She unlocked the door and began to climb the stairs as she turned the envelope over and saw there was no address on it.

Curiosity was strong, but combined with it was a reluctance Carole couldn't define. After laying the envelope unopened on the coffee table, she climbed the stairs to her bedroom, changed out of her office clothes and took a quick shower instead of her usual long after-work soak in a bubble bath.

As she turned off the water and opened the glass door to step out of the warm, steamy comfort of the shower stall, she heard the telephone ringing. She slipped into a long terry-cloth robe and pulled off her shower cap, then crossed the hall to her desk and lifted the receiver with a heart-pounding apprehension that had become almost expected. No matter how hard she tried, her first hellos were breathless and strained. Only when she was able to turn off the recorder could she relax.

"Hello."

"Carole? This is Diane Michaelson. Am I catching you at a bad time?"

"Uh, no," Carole answered slowly as her wariness changed to a new target. Something in Diane's voice held the same breathless tension as her own. "I just got in. I was changing clothes."

"I know this is going to sound strange," Diane said, "but if you don't have other plans, I'd like to stop by for a few minutes this evening."

"Oh?" Carole frowned, silently agreeing that it did sound strange. But what was even stranger was the hesitancy in Diane's voice. There was no hint of the super reporter Carole had grown accustomed to. Instead, Diane sounded concerned and a little uncertain, and for some reason she couldn't put her finger on, Carole found that it worried her. When Diane Michealson began to sound compassionate, something was terribly wrong.

"Strictly off the record," Diane added when Carole didn't answer immediately.

"I'll be here," Carole said finally. "When should I expect you?"

"In about an hour." Diane sounded relieved, then grew hesitant. "Carole, have you received a plain brown envelope?"

Wishing she were imagining the conversation, Carole saw the turning reels of the recorder and realized she had forgotten to turn if off. "Yes."

"Have you opened it?"

"No." Carole's stomach was knotted like a fist, and her words seemed to die once they touched the air.

"You might want to," Diane said gently. "I'll see you in an hour."

She hung up then, and Carole found herself staring at the blank wall, listening to a dial tone. Her fingers clutched the telephone so tightly that it hurt when she unbent them to replace the receiver. Automatically, she rewound the tape and erased the conversation, then went down to the kitchen to fix tea.

With a cup of hot tea in front of her, Carole wrapped her robe tighter and sat down on the couch. The unmarked envelope stared back at her from the coffee table. Cradling her tea in both hands, she blew on its surface and watched the envelope through the steam that rose over the top of the cup.

Still holding the cup in her right hand, she reached out with her left and turned the envelope over. With her thumb and index finger, she bent up the two prongs that held the flap closed. She took a sip of her tea, then slipped her thumbnail under the edge of the sealed flap and worked it loose.

With the flap finally open, she took a long drink of tea and set the cup in its saucer. Her nervous stomach rolled as the hot, sweet liquid trickled down. Carole reached out to lift the envelope with a hand that trembled. Without removing the contents, she could see the top edge of a black-and-white glossy.

She turned the envelope upside down, and the photographs came tumbling out onto the couch beside her. Faceup, on top, was a grainy blowup obviously taken from across the highway from the motel. In the top left corner was the Flamingo Court sign. In the lower right corner the tail end of Carole's car was tucked cozily close to Donnelly's.

She turned over the next picture and found a close-up of the back of the two cars, showing the license plates in unmistakable detail. The third picture had been taken as she and Donnelly were leaving, later than they had planned and earlier than they wanted. On the top of the car was Carole's overnight case. Beside it was the vase of roses, a sentimental remembrance that still sat on her bedroom dresser. Withered and blackened with age, the roses brought back memories that were too fresh and sweet to discard.

In the picture, a tall blond man held a slender blond woman pressed against the car door in a passionate embrace that sizzled even in the reduced clarity of the blowup. They could have been any man, any woman. But they weren't. Carole knew it, and whoever took the picture knew it, too. So did Diane Michaelson, and in less than an hour she would be arriving to talk about it.

Long years of exposure to the intrigues her father and husband had manipulated had taught Carole one important lesson: Never jump to conclusions. Just in case Diane was not the one behind the pictures, just in case there was still a way to salvage the situation, Carole stacked the pictures neatly and replaced them in the envelope, then slid it into a drawer at the base of the coffee table.

Locking her jaw against the nervous chattering of her teeth, Carole went upstairs to change clothes and to try to regain her composure before Diane arrived. Chills climbed the stepladder of her spine, then danced across her shoulders and down her arms as she huddled in her terry-cloth robe and studied her winter clothes.

After stepping into a pair of slim white flannel slacks, she pulled a heavy, fanny-hugging white sweater on over them. To this she added a pair of white calfskin loafers with two-inch stacked heels. As she withdrew from the closet and started toward the jewelry box on her dresser, Carole's nervous shivers began to calm. Then the phone rang again.

Two quick steps brought Carole across the room, where she took a pearl rope from the bottom drawer of her jewelry box and dropped it over her head. As she hurried to the phone, she knotted the pearls in front to partially cover the deep vee of her sweater neck.

Without having to check the mirror, she knew she looked as cool and dignified as she could without being too obvious. Carole Stockton, the legendary ice maiden. She might not be able to convince Diane that pictures lie, but she might be able to persuade her not to go public with the story.

Lifting the receiver on the run, she questioned, "Yes?" As she waited for a reply, she saw that Diane was due in less than fifteen minutes.

Donnelly laughed. "Is somebody chasing you?"

Carole tried to put a smile in her voice as she shut off the recorder, then rewound and erased the tape. "Not exactly." She picked up the phone and went to sit on the settee in the corner. "You're early," she said, relaxing against the cushions.

"I couldn't wait. Are we still on for tomorrow?"

"Tomorrow?" As if somebody had dumped ice water over her, the chills returned, and Carole found herself back where she had been a month earlier.

From the carefree eagerness in his voice, it was obvious Donnelly had not received a brown envelope. So far, she alone was the target, and Donnelly was only a victim who was still unaware he had been caught in the cross fire.

At this point, she had nothing but questions to share with him, not answers. Someone was stalking one or both of them, and until she could tell him everything, Carole decided that she wouldn't tell Donnelly anything.

"Yoo-hoo, Carole, where'd you go?" The teasing patience in his voice held an undercurrent of tension.

"I'm here," Carole answered, wondering how she could tell him that she couldn't meet him. Whoever had found them the last time could do it again. And until she discovered who was behind the pictures, she couldn't afford to lead them to Donnelly again.

"I don't know how I'm going to live till tomorrow night." His voice was warm and soft, as smooth as melting butter. "I dreamed about you last night."

Though knowing she shouldn't give in to the seduction of his words, Carole couldn't help herself. She missed him so badly it hurt to breathe. "What did you dream?"

"I'll show you tomorrow." There was no tension left in his voice, just promise, hot and ripe and knee-weakening.

Carole's stomach did a slow somersault, and if Donnelly had walked through her door at that moment with a battery of photographers following him, she wouldn't have cared. It took all her strength to swallow her own bitter disappointment and say, "Something's come up at the office, sweetheart. I think we're going to have to call tomorrow off."

"How about tonight?" The buttery warmth was gone from his voice.

"Same project." Carole found it hard to get the words out around the hard knot in her chest. "I'm going to be busy all night."

"How about the night after?" Donnelly pressed, beginning to sound tight-jawed with controlled anger.

"Maybe. I'll try." Unreleased tears swam inside her, stuck there, burning behind her eyes and choking off her words. "I'm sorry, honey."

"You don't sound very sorry, Carole. You sound determined. Is it something you want to talk about?"

"There's nothing, really."

"I thought by now, at least, we'd gotten past the point where you'd lie to me." Donnelly was irritated and making no attempt to hide it. He released his breath in a heavy sigh. "Why don't we continue this tomorrow night? Maybe by then you'll have it sorted out a little better."

"Donnelly," Carole said in a soft plea for understanding. Downstairs the quiet chime of the doorbell interrupted her, too low for Donnelly to hear but loud enough to chase away her thoughts.

"Good night, baby. Don't take too long."

"Donnelly, I love you." The dial tone cut into her words, and Carole knew he hadn't heard her. As she stood to replace the receiver, she could feel his anger and disappointment go with her, and it was the disappointment that hurt most. He had trusted her to be honest with him. She hadn't been, and he'd known it, and it wouldn't matter to him that she had done it for his own good. Donnelly was an honorable man, and honorable men lived by rules that didn't leave a lot of room for human error.

The doorbell rang again, echoing through the house with a long, hollow sound. As she slowly descended the stairs, Carole tried to collect her thoughts, but they had a confused life of their own. Sadness was a deep, dark well inside of her, and the sound of Donnelly's last words left one more bitter taste in an already miserable evening.

They had defied the odds by giving in to a love that wouldn't leave them alone. They had convinced themselves they could make it work, and now Carole had begun to wonder if it wouldn't be that very love that would tear them apart in the end. It was her love for

Donnelly that made her protect him instinctively when she felt they were being threatened. And it was his love for her that made him so fiercely resent that same instinct.

Turning the last corner, Carole saw Diane Michaelson standing in the fading light outside her door. She wore a tailored navy suit, and tucked under her arm was a white clutch purse and a large, plain brown envelope. Her expression held the same nervous concern that Carole had heard in her voice earlier.

With a long, deep breath, Carole mentally squared her shoulders. If Diane wasn't responsible for the pictures, that left only Andrew, and Diane didn't seem any happier with the situation than Carole felt. There was still a chance to keep Donnelly out of it, and while there was a hope left she would fight for it.

"Diane," she said with a smile as she pulled the door open, "come in."

"It was good of you to let me come," Diane answered. She waited while Carole closed the door; then the two of them climbed the stairs together.

Entering the dining room, Carole asked, "Can I get you something to drink?"

"A double vodka martini would be great," Diane said wistfully, "but I still have to work tonight."

"How about a small glass of wine?"

"That would be heaven."

"Why don't you go on into the living room while I get it." Carole went to the kitchen while Diane turned toward the living room. Her voice drifted after Carole, sounding strained but sincere as she lifted it to cover the distance.

"Your house is really lovely. Did you decorate it yourself?"

"Yes," Carole called as she poured the wine. "I had just gotten that couch for my apartment in Washington, so I brought it with me when I came back here." Coming into the living room, she finished as she handed Diane her wine. "I had trouble finding a condo with a living room big enough to handle it."

Diane sipped the wine and sighed. The envelope was under her purse on the corner of the coffee table. "This place surprises me, somehow." With a reporter's eye for detail, her gaze roamed the room. "It has the sophistication I had expected, but at the same time there's something very personal about it. There is a feeling of warmth and openness that I can't quite put my finger on."

Carole molded her palms to the wineglass and leaned back against the couch, a slash of white on a background of dark, mossy green. "Is there anything else I can get you?" she asked quietly.

Diane took another sip of wine and looked briefly at Carole. "I guess I should get to the point, shouldn't I?" Slipping the envelope from under her purse, she slid it down the coffee table to where Carole sat at a right angle to her. "This was delivered to my office this morning by a party or parties unknown."

Carole set down her wineglass and opened the flap. The surprise she showed when she pulled out the pictures wasn't feigned. They were different pictures, taken at a different time. Staring hard, she recognized the pink satin camisole top and pants she had worn the night of the primary. She stood just inside the open doorway, facing the camera under the bright light of the foyer. A tall blond man in a dark suit was in front of her with his back to the camera. There was a look of rigid anger in his stance, and his fingers dug deeply into her shoul-

ders. There was no way of positively identifying either
the man or his intentions.

The second picture shattered any rising hope the first
one might have encouraged. It was no longer night, and
the morning had a half-lit, misty look. Again, Carole
saw herself standing in the open doorway, wearing a
belted white kimono that stopped just short of de-
cency, and looking as if she were about to cry. On the
porch, facing the camera and obviously on his way out,
was Donnelly still wearing the same dark suit and
looking as angry as he had seemed in the first picture.

Carole slid the offending photo behind the other one,
returned them both to the envelope and laid it back on
the coffee table. She lifted her wineglass with both
hands to minimize her trembling then took a sip and felt
the wine coat the desert dryness of her throat.

"Why did you bring these to me?" Carole asked in a
voice devoid of inflection.

"Because I have the disturbing feeling that someone
is trying to use me," Diane answered with the no
nonsense precision Carole had come to expect. "And I
don't like to be manipulated."

Carole took a deep breath and relaxed against the
back of the couch. Swirling the wine in her glass, she
watched pinpoints of light dance inside it. "Where do
we go from here?" she asked quietly.

"I want to know who did this." Diane set her wine
glass on the coffee table and leaned forward with her
elbows braced against her knees. Her dark eyes searched
Carole's face. "I want to know what he hopes to gain
I want to know how you feel about it."

"For something that's off the record, this is beginning to sound amazingly like an interview." Carole took
a slow sip of wine as she watched Diane's reaction.

"This may come as a shock to you, Ms. Stockton, but I believe as strongly in the duties of the press as I do in the importance of its freedom. Those pictures tell quite a story, and if anybody else got a little brown envelope today, I'm losing a scoop just by being here. But I don't want just a story. I want the truth."

"And what are you going to do when you know?" Carole recognized the sincerity in Diane's voice and wondered how much to tell her. No one would believe the truth about Andrew, and the only proof she had was illegally obtained.

And after her last conversation with Donnelly, she wasn't really sure anymore what her relationship was with him. There was no doubt that they loved each other, but how long would love be enough when everything else was tearing them apart?

"When I have the truth, then I'll decide what to do with this," Diane said, answering Carole's question as she lifted the envelope of pictures from the coffee table and held it in the air, then set it down again next to her wineglass. "So..." She lifted her wine and settled against the back of the sofa with an air of quiet expectancy. "Are you going to level with me?"

"If you were going to venture a guess as to who's responsible for those pictures, who would it be?" Carole asked cautiously.

Diane took a sip of wine. "If it were Donnelly Wakefield looking for publicity, I think it would have been more tastefully done. This is not a good time to be revealing the private passions of any candidate, so I would say it comes from the other camp."

"With the knowledge and permission of Governor Mathison, or without it?" Carole asked, watching Diane's dark, intelligent eyes begin to glow with new thoughts.

"It could have been anyone. And there's no way to prove otherwise, is there?" she answered, scrutinizing Carole's reaction as closely as Carole had watched hers.

Carole shook her head and said softly, "None at all."

"But you're sure that Mathison ordered it."

"If you're not responsible for these pictures, he's the only one left."

"Talk about dirty politics," Diane said quietly as her thoughts drew her into herself. Frowning, she sipped her wine and stared at the envelope on the coffee table. "Were your pictures the same?" she asked finally.

"They're in the drawer at your feet," Carole said. Without making a conscious decision, she had decided to trust the other woman. She had to take the first step back into the sunlight sometime. It was her desire for secrecy that had given Andrew the wedge he needed. As Carole watched Diane take out the envelope and study the pictures, she felt only relief.

When Diane returned the pictures to their envelope, she picked up her own set from the coffee table and shut both of them away in Carole's hiding place. "This thing between you and Donnelly is pretty serious, isn't it?" Without needing Carole's acknowledgment, she continued, "Does he know about these pictures?"

Carole shook her head. "He's got enough to worry about right now without adding that."

"What I don't understand is what Mathison would have to gain from this. Using his ex-wife to smear his opponent has got to sound as sleazy to the voting public as it does to me, and he's too smart a politician not to realize that. So what's he doing?"

Carole took a deep breath, then a big gulp of the wine she had been nursing along. "He's warning me. It's a sample of what could happen if I continue to see Donnelly."

"Why include me?" Diane leaned forward again, tensing as she began to catch the scent of a story that might be too big to be believed. "How could he know I wouldn't go with just the pictures and no story?"

Carole shrugged. "Either way, he would win. If you come to me, I realize how far he's willing to go. And if you hadn't come to me, you would never have believed he was actually the one behind it, so he's still safe."

"But I did come to you," Diane argued. "And now I'm starting to believe you. So what I want to know next is, what can we do?"

"Wait," Carole said with the patient smile of someone who sees the end in sight. "Now that he's made his first mistake, there'll be others. And we'll be waiting."

Chapter Eleven

Carole lay awake, staring into the dark void that blurred the shapes of the room, listening to the night sounds that drifted through the open windows. The air was cool and fresh, damp with the hint of moistness that precedes fall's first killing frost.

There were only two weeks left before the election, and the two parties had begun to push for a debate that neither candidate wanted. Andrew hadn't made another move in the week since Carole had received the photographs. And Donnelly had hung up on her in disgust three days ago. He hadn't called again since.

Forcing her eyes closed, Carole rolled over and buried her face in her pillow. Two weeks. Just two weeks left. Donnelly was hurt and angered by her refusal to meet him again, but if they could just last until the election, she could make him understand. Diane had agreed to sit on the story for as long as she could, and it was weeks since Carole had talked to Andrew. There had been only the pictures. The pictures.

Carole's stomach turned over, and she curled into a tight knot under the bulky comforter. Andrew knew; he had known since the primary, since the first night she and Donnelly had spent together. And all this time he had been toying with her.

The phone rang, and instead of her usual dread, Carole felt only relief as she rolled over and saw that it was a quarter till twelve, the hour Donnelly usually reached his hotel room. She threw back the covers, and found her way to the phone in the office alcove as quickly as if it had been noon instead of midnight.

"Yes?" she asked, catching herself just as she was about to say Donnelly's name.

"My, but you sound happy to hear from me," Andrew said. "Or could it be that you were expecting someone else?" When Carole didn't answer, he continued in a voice that flowed as smoothly as oil, "Did you get my little present?"

"So, it *was* you!" A cool draft curled around her, and Carole found herself beginning to shiver beneath the cotton ruffles of her baby-doll pajamas.

"Oh, yes," Andrew agreed quickly. "I see that Diane Michaelson came to you with her set. I was a little disappointed in her for that."

"Life's full of little disappointments," Carole said sarcastically. Now that he had called, she found that she wasn't afraid of Andrew any longer, or of anything he could do to her. Next to the misery she felt at being estranged from Donnelly, Andrew seemed no more than a minor irritant. She was hurt not because he had called, but because Donnelly hadn't.

"I'm even more disappointed in you, Carole. It seems this flirtation with Wakefield is more serious than I had thought. I can't allow it, you know. I've warned you before."

Not for the first time, Carole thought she heard a note in Andrew's voice that was just beyond reason, over the line into a realm where he created his own reality. "And what were you planning to do about it?" she asked cautiously.

"There's a party at the capitol Saturday night," he said. "I thought we might announce our engagement."

"What?" Carole was too stunned to be outraged.

"I'll send a plane for you, of course. And you should have plenty of time to get a really knockout dress. Why don't you go to Dallas and pick up several things, just in case you want to stay over? You can charge them to me."

He sounded happy, pleased with himself and his plans, and sure that Carole would be just as pleased. He was the Andrew she had first married, a man who was generous, commanding and self-assured. And for just an instant Carole was almost sorry for the Andrew who might once have been a decent man, before the fear and loneliness and greed had twisted him into something no one could ever love.

"Andrew," she said slowly, "you know I can't do that."

"But you have to, Carole," he answered calmly. "Because if you don't, I'll send those pictures to every newspaper and television station in the state. I'll ruin your reputation and Donnelly's credibility. He'll not only lose this election, he'll lose any chance he has to ever hold a political office. And you'll lose *him*, Carole, because no man would ever forgive you for that."

"You won't do any of that, Andrew," Carole said evenly, "and if you try, you're the one who'll be ruined."

"What have you done, Carole?" Andrew was instantly tense, recognizing that her tone held more than an idle bluff.

For a moment Carole debated. Then she flipped the rewind switch on the recorder and ran the tape back for the space of a few seconds. Hitting the playback switch, she held the phone to the recorder and listened to her voice: " ... the one who'll be ruined." Andrew's gruff reply followed: "What have you done, Carole?"

Leaving the tape to pick up recording where it had left off, she returned the receiver to her ear. "That's what I've done, Andrew. You send out those pictures, and I'll send out that tape."

"It seems I've underestimated you," Andrew said. His voice sounded strained but composed. "Or perhaps it was King who arranged this. Either way, I'm doubly disappointed in you, Carole. A man's arrangements with his wife should be kept private."

"Former wife," Carole corrected. "And I wouldn't call those pictures very private."

"I warned you what would happen if you took a lover," Andrew snapped. "You took your chances and lost."

"I haven't lost yet. And as long as I have this tape, I don't think I will. I'm giving you one last chance to conduct this campaign fairly, Andrew. I suggest you take it."

Without waiting for his reply, Carole hung up. Her mind was spinning with fatigue and the strain of controlling her emotions. Rage and frustration had replaced the dread Andrew had once inspired. He had become a nuisance, and win or lose, Carole knew that in two more weeks any control Andrew ever had over her life would all be over.

Regardless of what happened with Donnelly, she knew that the past truly had become the past, and it would never again have the power to hurt her.

Sloan pulled into the driveway behind her and was out of his pickup before Carole brought her car to a full halt inside the garage. As she opened the car door and got out, Sloan called, "I'll go in the front way and bring your mail up. And I expect to smell cooking by the time I get to the head of the stairs."

"Fat chance," Carole said, rounding the back of her car just in time to see Sloan stop with one foot on the front porch.

"Carole," he said in a whisper. Without turning, he gestured to her with his hand. "Come here."

"What is it?" Carole asked, starting toward him.

"Shh." Sloan glided up the last step onto the porch. Turning toward her on the balls of his feet, he held his finger to his lips and motioned her forward again. When Carole reached the base of the porch, he pointed to the door, which stood ajar by several inches.

"Oh my God," Carole groaned. The tape. All day long she had been trying to remember what she had done with it the night before. Now, as clearly as if she were living it again, she saw herself hanging up the phone and returning to the cozy warmth of her bed, leaving the tape to silently record the hushed sounds of the night until it ran out and shut itself off. It was still there. Maybe.

"I don't want to jump to any conclusions here," Sloan whispered, "but my first guess is that you've been robbed."

"Oh my God," Carole said again. "And Daddy's coming to dinner." What if it wasn't robbery? If the only thing missing was the tape? How could she ever explain it?

"Could you hold it down a little?" Sloan hissed. "This door is open. They may still be in there."

Silently cursing herself for a fool, Carole darted past Sloan and through the door. She should have realized Andrew might do something like this. If they were still inside, there might be a chance to stop them before they got away with the tape.

In the foyer, Sloan grabbed her wrist and jerked Carole behind him. "What the hell do you think you're doing?" he demanded. "Get to a phone and call the police. I'll stay here."

"No," Carole answered in the same angry whisper he had used. "No police." While he glared at her suspiciously, she slipped past him onto the first step and tugged at the arm that held her back. "Come on."

"Okay," he snapped impatiently, and climbed past her. "Just in case, get ready to run. If anything happens, I want you down these stairs and out of the house before I can blink." He stopped and glared at her. "And if they shoot me, you *will* call the police. Okay?"

Carole couldn't help smiling as she shoved him up the stairs ahead of her. "Okay."

At the top of the staircase, they emerged on tiptoe to a house that was in perfect order except for papers scattered on the kitchen and living room floors. Leaving Sloan behind, Carole darted up the stairs to the next floor two at a time. Without breaking stride, she crossed the landing to the alcove and came to a sagging halt. The telephone was unplugged. The recorder was gone. And the tape that was in the machine, along with all of her blanks, was gone.

The one tape that was in her safety-deposit box, the one Andrew didn't know about, was all that was left. She'd done the two things Donnelly had told her never to do, and because of it, Andrew's confession about the pictures was gone. *Nice going, Carole,* she congratulated herself as she trudged back down the stairs to the living room. *You just made the all-star stupid team.*

The litter on the living room floor had been picked up, and Sloan sat on the sofa in the middle of a paper storm. On the coffee table in front of him was a lineup of eight-by-ten photos. He lifted one and studied Carole with cold eyes. When he spoke, he managed to do it without unclenching his jaw.

"What the hell is this?"

"A blackmail attempt," Carole answered coolly, and sat at the end of the sofa farthest from him.

"I warned that son-of-a—" Sloan slammed the picture down, bit off his words and hurled himself from the couch to stalk to the glass door overlooking the balcony. For a long minute he stood there, ramrod stiff, then whirled back to face Carole. "How long have you been seeing him? How long did it take him to break the promise he made to me?"

"Wait a minute," Carole said, growing indignant at Sloan's reaction. "Who I see is my business. And no one—including you—would have had any idea what was going on if Andrew hadn't been having Donnelly followed."

"How long?" Sloan asked again.

"Since the night of the primary," Carole snapped back at him.

"Damn!" Sloan whirled and braced himself spread-eagled against the fireplace. "My best friend and my sister, sneaking around behind my back," he fumed. Still talking to the wall, he shouted, "For two months!"

"It wasn't *your* back we were avoiding," Carole said calmly.

Sloan turned to face her and crossed his arms on his chest. "Does Dad know?"

"No one knows. Except for Andrew and his crew of photographers. And last week Diane Michaelson, and now you."

"Diane Michaelson?" Sloan shouted. His arms sprang open in supplication, and Carole jumped in alarm.

"Would you please stop yelling?" she begged, and suddenly she realized that she would have to tell Donnelly everything she had been holding back. She had given Andrew a chance to call a truce, and this had been his answer. Anything Donnelly decided to do at this point, she would have to accept.

"How did Diane Michaelson get into this?" Sloan's voice sounded hoarse in his attempt to control the shout that kept rising up in him.

"Get into what?" King asked from the dining room. Taking a few steps into the living room, he frowned into Carole's startled eyes. "Did you know your door's open?"

"I didn't hear you come in," Carole said, fervently wishing Donnelly were there. After months of insisting on secrecy, she could see no way to avoid confessing everything, and she couldn't help thinking of it as a betrayal of Donnelly.

"No wonder," King answered, turning his frown to Sloan. "What are you yelling about?"

Sloan scowled at Carole, who shrugged and curled deeper into the corner of the couch. From beneath lowered lashes she watched Sloan scoop up the pictures and hand them to King. Without a word, King took the photos to the tall window across the room and stood with his back to his children while he studied the pictures.

When he finally turned back to face them, there was a frown on his brow and a smile twitching at the corners of his mouth. "Well, I'll be damned, girl. You sure had us fooled, didn't you?" Walking back across the room, he dropped the pictures onto the coffee table. "Who did this?"

"Mathison," Sloan answered.

"Hmm," King said, looking from his son to his daughter. "How long have you been seeing him?"

"Since the primary," Sloan answered for her again.

"What's Diane Michaelson got to do with this?" King asked Carole, then slid his eyes toward Sloan.

"I haven't the slightest idea," Sloan said with a shrug.

King smiled. "Good." He threaded his way between the coffee table and Carole's knees and sat beside her on the couch. "Now, what's going on here, baby? It looks like you've been busy."

Carole heaved a deep sigh and took the big, work-muscled hand her father offered her. Holding tightly to his gentle strength, she began at the beginning and talked her way through to the present.

When she finished, King patted her hand, then withdrew his hand and leaned back as he looked across the

offee table to Sloan. "Well, this is all just interesting
s hell," he said quietly, "but what do we do now?"

"I don't think we should do anything until I've talked
o Donnelly," Carole said.

"Do you know how to get hold of him?" King asked.

She shook her head and stared at her hands clasped
n her lap. Now that she had confessed everything, she
ould no longer remember why the secrecy had been so
mportant. Sloan had calmed down, and King wasn't
eacting at all the way she had thought he would.

"Donnelly's so upset with me right now, he hasn't
alled in three days." She looked at her father with the
ind of trusting entreaty she hadn't felt since child-
ood. "He said once that you could find him for me if
needed him."

King's eyes glazed with a film of tears that wouldn't
all. "You really love him, don't you, honey?" He
rapped his arms around her and pulled Carole to him
n a long, loving embrace. "Don't worry, baby, we'll
ind him for you," he murmured soothingly, then re-
eased her and started toward the phone on the dining
oom wall.

King had barely disappeared around the corner when
e retraced his steps into the living room. "And here he
."

"Donnelly," Sloan said in surprise as Donnelly ap-
eared behind King.

"I think I'll go close that door before we run out of
oom in here," King said.

Carole turned toward Donnelly, but before her gaze
ot as far as his face, she saw the brown envelope he
eld in his hand and her happy relief died. When her
yes finally staggered up to his, she found Donnelly

scowling at the photos King tossed onto the coffee ta ble.

Without a word, he dropped his envelope into her la and walked to stand beside Sloan in front of the fire place, his stiff back turned to her. With a heart like rock, Carole slipped the photographs out of the enve lope. The first one was of her disappearing into th motel room as Donnelly lifted her overnight case from the trunk of her car; the second showed them exiting th motel room arm in arm in what was obviously the ligh of dawn the following morning. The second one was b far the clearest shot of their faces that she had seen yet and it left no doubt as to exactly who they were or wha they were doing.

Before Carole could put the pictures away, King re turned to reach over her shoulder and take them fror her. After a quick glance, he tossed them onto the cof fee table on top of the others.

"Different shots, same location," he said to Don nelly. "How many more variations can we expect?"

"That's about it," Donnelly said. "We haven't reall had a chance to see that much of each other."

"Anything is too much," Sloan said in a belligeren undertone. "I warned you what could happen."

"Don't start it, Sloan," Donnelly growled. "I'm no in the mood." The muscles at the side of his jav twitched as he finally turned to look Carole in the eyes "Can I see you upstairs? Alone?"

In spite of his anger, Carole heard the softening i Donnelly's tone when his words were addressed to her In a silent sigh of relief, she let out the breath she ha been holding, nodded and stood. She took slow step toward the stairs, then waited for Donnelly to draw eve with her.

His hand cupped her elbow and held her close to him as they began to climb. At the first landing, he asked, "How much do they know?" His head nodded in the direction of the living room.

"Everything."

"Which is more than I know."

Carole could feel his tensed anger in every movement he made and in every word he forced out between gritted teeth. At the head of the stairs, he glanced into the alcove and saw the empty spot where the recorder had been. "They were pretty bold, coming in through the front door. How did Andrew find out about the tapes?"

"Tape," Carole corrected as the hand at her elbow guided her into the bedroom. "Just the one from last night. And how did *you* know?"

"I saw the marks on the door." He kicked the bedroom door closed with his foot and led Carole to the bed. "How did he find out?" he asked again.

"I told him."

Donnelly muffled a curse, stood and paced to the wall, then turned and came back to the bed. "Why?" he asked, standing over her.

Carole tried not to smile as the absurdity of their situation struck her. "It seemed like a good idea at the time," she said with a shrug.

Donnelly sat down again and took both of her hands in his. "I assume you got your pictures last week when you canceled out on me with that miserably inadequate excuse."

When Carole nodded, he grunted in disgust and asked, "Are we the only ones who've gotten pictures?"

Carole sighed and rubbed her temples that were be ginning to twinge with the warning of a headache "Diane Michaelson got a set the same day I did."

Donnelly threw back his head and groaned, "Hol mackerel," as he stood and paced to the wall again This time he leaned his back against it and shoved h hands into his front pant pockets. "And why haven't w been the objects of a week-long exposé series?"

His voice sounded tired, and for the first time Ca ole noticed the dark circles under his eyes. "She's su picious of things that are too easy," she explaine slowly. "Diane came to me first, and after I took gamble and leveled with her, she decided to sit on th story until something new developed."

"Would you call this a development?" Donnell asked.

"I know this is all my fault," Carole said, miserab and contrite and ready to do anything that would wir the trapped look off Donnelly's face. "You told n never to let him know about the tapes and never to leav one here, and I did both."

Donnelly pushed himself away from the wall an stared at the ceiling with his legs spread wide for ba ance. "Well," he said, drawing the words out slowly he thought, "he had the pictures and you had the tap And as long as he knew, you had a standoff. So, I ca see why you told him." He lowered his gaze to Caro and frowned. "But I don't understand why you left th tape here."

"I was more worried about not hearing from yc than I was about anything he could do." Carole slid h eyes away from Donnelly to the floor. "And I just fo got to take it out."

In a quick, silent movement, Donnelly was beside her, lifting her face until he could look into her eyes. "I'd call that real progress," he said with a smile. He pulled her into his arms, held her head against his pounding heart and stroked her hair while his voice dropped to a murmur. "I think I have a solution. If you'll agree, we can give Diane Michaelson a development that'll leave Andrew with nowhere to turn. Then we can get rid of all these people and..."

He turned Carole's face toward him and kissed her with sudden passion. When his lips finally slipped away from hers, Carole asked in a shaky, whispery voice, "You're not mad at me?"

"I'm mad *about* you, not *at* you." Donnelly caught her face between his palms and kissed her again hard, then said, "Leave your eyes closed."

With her eyes closed, Carole heard the rustle of his clothing and felt her heart pound in anticipation. In a dim, insignificant corner of her mind, she remembered that her father and Sloan were waiting for them downstairs, but it didn't matter.

Now, after the worst possible things she could imagine had actually happened, the only thing that mattered was Donnelly. As long as he still loved her, as long as he was with her, she didn't need or want anything else. And if that was love, then she had never loved before.

After taking her hands in his, Donnelly laid something into the cradle of her palms, then held her hands cupped together in his.

"Open your eyes," he said softly.

Carole did as he said and found herself looking into the shining happiness in his eyes. Then she lowered her gaze to her open hands and a tiny box that held a large, glittering diamond in its velvet interior.

Donnelly slipped the diamond out of its nest, turned her left hand over and slipped the ring onto her finger. "Carole Stockton, I'd be the happiest man in the world if you'd keep this ring and say you'll marry me." Before she could answer, he said, "I'm not hurrying you. I'll wait as long as you want. I just want to know that someday..."

His voice broke off and he waited, frowning, for her to speak.

As she stared at the ring, Carole couldn't help wondering where he had gotten it and how long he'd had it. Was this the solution he had talked about? Why hadn't he said he loved her? Why didn't he want to marry right away? Afraid to read more into the proposal than he had intended, she asked quietly, "When would we announce it?"

"Damn it, Carole!" Like an explosion, Donnelly was off the bed and several paces across the room before he stopped and turned back to face her. "Will you please, for just a minute, stop being logical?" He dropped to his knees at her feet and grasped her arms in his hands. "I love you. I want to marry you," he practically shouted. "This is not a business deal."

"Oh." Carole sighed, cupping her palms against his cheeks and beaming with a smile so wide it hurt. "I wasn't sure. Yes," she said with relief. "Yes, I'd love to marry you."

From just outside the closed door came King's happy whoop, followed almost immediately by a knock.

"Yes?" Donnelly said, rising from his knees to sit beside Carole on the bed.

The door opened and King stood in the doorway. "I don't mean to interrupt, but I just had an idea."

Donnelly slipped his arm around Carole's shoulders and held her in the protective pocket of his side. "If it concerns us, I'll do the thinking, thank you." He stood and brought Carole with him, ducking his head to speak to her. "If it's okay with you, sweetheart, I suggest we call Diane Michaelson and offer her an exclusive in time for the ten o'clock news."

"That was my idea," King said, stepping back as they reached the doorway.

"Congratulations," Donnelly answered. "And what do you think we should do after that?"

"Make sure Andrew sees the announcement," King said, a step behind them on the staircase.

Donnelly nodded, talking to King over his shoulder. "If you don't mind, I'll let you make that phone call. I'm afraid of what I'd say, and Carole's had too many conversations with him already."

King's lips spread away from his teeth in a feral grin. "It would be my pleasure."

When they reached the base of the staircase, the sizzle and aroma of cooking greeted them with a soothing domesticity. From the kitchen, Sloan called, "Steaks okay with everybody? I, personally, am starving."

"Great man in a crisis," Donnelly said with a smile as he squeezed Carole's shoulder and let go. "You want to call Diane while I help Sloan with the salad?"

"Anything in particular I should say?" Carole asked, walking with him across the dining room.

"You handled it fine before. I'll leave it up to you."

With a kiss on her cheek, Donnelly went into the kitchen to help Sloan, and King stayed with Carole in the dining room. The heft of the diamond on her finger was a strange but reassuring weight as Carole dialed Diane's number and waited to be connected.

"Diane," she said when the connection was finally made. "How would you like an exclusive?"

"What's happened?" Diane asked, feeling excitement tingle as the happiness in Carole's voice reached her.

"Something we'd like to get on the ten o'clock news tonight if you can get here in time."

"It's six-thirty now. If the story's good enough, I can drop everything and be there and set up by seven-thirty. So now, give. What's going on? You sound so happy as a . . . Wait, you're not. You couldn't be."

"Of course I could," Carole said with a slow smile. "And the story's all yours."

"You and what's-his-name are getting you-know-what?" Diane asked, laughing as she confirmed her suspicions without revealing the secret. "That's wonderful. I'm really happy for you. And Carole," she said, dropping her voice to a whisper, "thank you. I really appreciate your calling me about this."

"I owed you one. See you in an hour?"

"I can't wait. Will you both be there?"

"Yes."

"This is going to be great. Bye now."

"Steaks are ready," Sloan said, coming out of the kitchen to set the table as Carole hung up. "How long have we got?"

"About an hour," Carole said.

King took the phone from her hand and dialed, as she leaned against the wall and took a deep, steadying breath. Donnelly came out of the kitchen and stood next to her.

"It's King Stockton," King said into the phone. "He'll talk to me." There was silence, then his teeth gleamed behind a wide, nasty grin. "Andrew. So nice to hear your voice. It's been too long."

Carole slipped her arm around Donnelly's waist and leaned her head on his chest. His hand caressed her arm, warming her with a feeling of safety that didn't need words.

"Definitely," King continued after a listening silence. "I'm calling to make sure you don't miss something you're going to be very interested in.... No, I'm not going to tell you what it is. That would destroy all the suspense, and I know how you love suspense.... It doesn't matter where I'm calling from, Andrew. But if you're wondering if I've talked to Carole, yes, I have. And I don't like what she had to tell me.... Now, there's no need to talk like that, Andrew. You're just getting yourself all upset. My daughter's never going to remarry you, because you're a disgusting little worm, and she's too good a woman to be remarried to the same disgusting little worm she's already had to divorce once.... Now, don't hang up yet, boy. I haven't had a chance to tell you why I called."

While Andrew talked, King leaned down to accept the kiss Carole bestowed on his cheek. Over the top of her head he winked at Donnelly, who was smiling gleefully at the end of the conversation he could hear. "Now, now, now. Just calm down," King said to Andrew, then paused to sniff at the seared brown steak Sloan waved under his nose on the way to the table. "If you'll just shut up, I'll be through and gone. My dinner's getting cold. Now, the thing is, I want you to watch Diane Michaelson tonight at ten. And after you see the story she's going to do, I want you to think about it real hard. And then what I want you to do is to forget you ever knew my daughter. If someone says the name Carole Stockton to you, I want you to get amnesia."

King's good-old-boy facade was gone. His face was hard and his voice was harder, and he was talking with very slow and deliberate clarity, with no room for interruption. "One more phone call, one more trick, one more attempt to slur my daughter's name or reputation, and every filthy little detail of your life is going to be splashed across every newspaper and TV screen in the state. Try me, Andrew, and politically and personally you're going to be dead meat. Now, is there any point I've left unclear...? No? Good. Have a good night." King hung up and looked at Donnelly. "Can you think of anything I left out?"

Donnelly shook his head and drew Carole in front of him toward the table. "Seems sufficient to me."

"The only thing that might have been better is a good, hard right-cross administered emphatically to his jaw," Sloan said.

"Now is not the time," Donnelly answered. As he pulled out Carole's chair and seated her, his eyes caught Sloan's across the table, and together they smiled in timeless and immediate understanding.

Chapter Twelve

Damn it!" King slammed the newspaper down onto Carole's dining table. "Can you believe this?" he shouted. "With the election tomorrow, he does this!"

Donnelly picked up the paper and studied it. "In your experienced and professional opinion," he asked King calmly, "how bad do you think this is?"

Carole took the paper from Donnelly and looked it over. The pictures were the same as the ones she had seen half an hour earlier on the cover of another small rural newspaper. They were variations of the ones Andrew had mailed originally, yet in some subtle way they were worse.

The picture showing Donnelly grabbing her by the shoulders in the lighted foyer had a suggested violence to it that was unpleasant in the grainy blowup, blurred by the pulp paper. In an accompanying, smaller photograph, the short kimono Carole wore managed to look less Dior than bordello, and certainly like nothing that belonged in the governor's mansion.

"The story suggests that the esteemed candidate and his society fiancée were amusing themselves in a tawdry affair and only decided to dignify it with an engagement when they were discovered by the press," King said.

"Diane Michaelson, specifically," Donnelly added. "Do you think she had anything to do with this?"

"No," Carole interrupted. "She's the one who brought this over." She touched the second paper, folded in half on the dining table. "She's furious. If you read this carefully, it makes her look like she was covering up for us."

"Which she was," King said. He held up his hand to stop the angry answer Carole was forming. "I know she was just being a responsible journalist, but without that tape Andrew stole, there's no way to substantiate a defense."

"There's no time even if we could," Donnelly said. He tore the cover page off the paper, angrily wadded it into a ball and tossed it into the corner, barely missing King's head.

Carole looked at her father as he glared at Donnelly. "We could lose, couldn't we?" she asked softly.

"The engagement put you ahead in the polls. I hate to beat a dead horse, but if Donnelly had agreed to let you campaign with him then, he'd be in a lot more solid position right now. As it is, some people will believe the story, and some people won't." King shrugged. "I think we had it won, and I think Andrew knew that. We should have realized he might do something like this out of desperation. But . . ."

Donnelly heaved a sigh and caught one of Carole's pale blond curls in the crook of his finger, smiling at her as she turned to look at him. "Either way, I've won the thing that's most important to me."

Carole tried to accept the reassurance he offered, but it didn't stop the feeling of failure that picked her up and slammed her down again like a piece of driftwood caught in a wave. "But in spite of everything we tried, I still may have cost you the election."

Donnelly's hand raked through her hair, then cupped the back of her head and shook gently. "If I win, it's partly because of you. If I lose, it's partly because of Andrew. But win or lose, it's mostly because of me. Either the people of this state want me or they don't." He held her head steady as he looked into her eyes, banishing the guilt that lingered there. "We're going to accept their decision and go on with our lives, and be grateful that we've got each other."

Just as Donnelly's lips began to lower toward hers, King cleared his throat with exaggerated force. When Donnelly stopped and looked at him, King asked, "What about the press?"

"I don't see any reason to dignify this with a reply," Donnelly said, unconsciously tightening the arm that had lowered to encircle Carole's shoulders.

King looked heavenward and then back again. "Well, that's consistent. But she's my daughter, and there are a few things I'd like to say."

"Do you really think that would help anything?" Donnelly asked quietly.

"My ulcer."

"You don't have an ulcer," Carole said with an indulgent smile. Donnelly was right. She didn't really care anymore what happened the next day, so long as she and Donnelly were still together when it was finished.

"We'll see about that when this election's over," King answered. Looking to Donnelly again, he asked, "What are you going to do now?"

"Take the phone off the hook, turn out the lights and get a good night's sleep." Donnelly stood, pulling Carole to her feet behind him. "You'll take care of everything for us tonight, won't you?" he asked, taking King by the shoulder and gently guiding him toward the stairs.

"You're the only man I've ever met who *might* be more stubborn than I am," King grumbled. With one foot on the steps leading down to the front door, he turned back and took Carole's hand in his. "Are you as happy as you look, baby?"

Carole's smile widened and she squeezed his hand. "Yes."

King nodded, grinned and started down the stairs. His soft chuckles drifted back as he disappeared from sight. When the sound of the closing door shut them away in the privacy of their sanctuary, Donnelly's chuckles joined the echoes of King's.

"What's with you two?" Carole asked, frowning up at the dreamy look of amusement on his face.

"Remember who spent two thankless years trying to get us together?"

"Oh," Carole said slowly, remembering all the times she had avoided her father's attempts to put her in Donnelly's proximity.

Donnelly reached behind Carole's back and turned off the light, then slipped his arm around her waist and turned her toward the stairs to the bedroom. "Win or lose tomorrow, I think your father has what he really wanted, too."

Cody Wakefield nervously held the taxi door while Donnelly exited the back seat. Sloan leaned into the passenger window and handed the driver a bill. "Wait here," he said. "We won't be long."

At Donnelly's shoulder as they headed toward the hotel door, Cody asked, "Are you sure you want to do this?"

Waiting for Sloan to enter first, Donnelly said, "Definitely. But are you sure you want to be here? You may get your picture in the paper."

"Just in case he calls the police, I may be able to help," Cody answered.

A younger, slimmer version of his older brother, Cody didn't look any happier with the situation than he felt. The polls had closed, and the Mathison previctory party had spilled over into the Oklahoma City hotel lobby. With Sloan running interference and Cody bringing up the rear, they guarded Donnelly's passage through the throng as well as they could, but with each step more heads turned and the whispers grew louder.

"The natives are getting restless," Sloan said over his shoulder to Donnelly. "Do you know where we're supposed to be going?"

"To the elevators and down a floor."

"This is not one of your brighter ideas, Donnelly," Cody said in an undertone. "And if that taxi isn't waiting outside when we leave, we could be in big trouble."

"You don't even know what I'm doing here, Cody," Donnelly said with a laugh. His brother's disapproving accompaniment was both a comfort and a nuisance, but even if Cody was his brother, Donnelly had better sense than to tell an officer of the law that he was planning to punch his opponent's lights out.

"And I'd appreciate it if you would keep it that way," Cody answered.

In the elevator, Sloan smiled confidingly. "It's just a conference, Cody. And we're just here to see that Donnelly isn't accosted or disturbed."

"And I'm the pope," Cody answered.

Stepping aside for Cody to exit first as the elevator doors opened again, Sloan said, "Your Eminence."

"Heads up, you two," Donnelly said, suddenly becoming serious. "This is where it gets tricky."

Across the room, Carole saw Liann Wakefield, Cody's wife, and Barbara Wakefield, mother of the Wakefield boys, scanning the room with perplexed expressions. Standing next to her, King grumbled, "Where could they be?"

At his side, Amelia looked at Carole with an innocence that bordered on the saintly, and Carole knew her mother shared her suspicions. It was almost two hours since she had seen Donnelly leave by a side door. Almost simultaneously, Sloan and Cody had also disappeared. They could be doing anything, and yet...

A few yards away, the picture on the giant television screen stuttered, darkened and brightened again with a new image. A newscaster whose face was familiar but whose name Carole couldn't remember spoke in controlled excitement while the camera zeroed in on a closed set of double doors flanked on either side by Sloan and Cody, who stared straight ahead with no-nonsense expressions.

"I'll be damned," King said, smacking his open palm with his fist. "They didn't take *me*."

"I think you were left behind to guard the castle, dear," Amelia said soothingly.

"Surely they're just talking," Carole said.

"Of course," Amelia agreed, making it clear that they both knew better. Touching King's arm, she said, "Don't you think we should hear what he's saying?"

As they moved closer to the television, the doors in the center of the screen opened and Donnelly came out, combing the fingers of one hand through the hair that had fallen across his brow while he tenderly flexed the knuckles of his other hand. Like a well-practiced drill team, Sloan and Cody fell into step, fore and aft, and the sea of people parted in a wedge that shoved the reporter in the opposite direction from the departing trio.

Hurrying toward the open set of doors, with the cameraman in pursuit, the frustrated newscaster was cut off by a spokesman who emerged from the dark room and pulled the doors closed behind him.

"Can you give us a statement?" the journalist asked. Shoving the microphone into the spokesman's face and moving closer to share the mike, he continued, "Can you tell us what Donnelly Wakefield and Governor Mathison spoke about? Were the pictures that mysteriously appeared in newspapers all over the state yesterday mentioned? Before the door closed behind Governor Mathison, I thought I glimpsed signs of what might have been a scuffle. Can you comment on that?"

Finally he stopped and the other man began. "I was not privy to the discussion; however, I'm sure you're aware that Mr. Wakefield is marrying Governor Mathison's ex-wife. It was my understanding that the conversation was of a personal rather than a political nature." The man cleared his throat, and in spite of his cool manner, he appeared to be perspiring. "To the best of my knowledge, the meeting was an amicable one, prearranged and agreed to by the governor." He began to move away. "If you have any further questions, I'm sure Governor Mathison will be happy to answer them later. Now, if you'll excuse me."

Clearly skeptical, the reporter faced the camera. "There we have the statement from Governor Mathison's spokesman. As we are able to throughout the evening, we will attempt to bring you further information on this unprecedented and still-unexplained meeting between the two candidates, who are at this moment deadlocked in the race for the governor's seat as the returns continue to roll in."

"Ooh, it's gonna hit the fan now," King said. Before the picture had shifted again to the election returns, he took Carole's arm and prepared to lead her from the room. He took a key from his pocket and handed it to Amelia. "Get Liann and Barbara and put them away in the Wakefield suite. I'll take Carole to ours and make sure no calls are put through to either room." He kissed Amelia on the cheek and gave her a smile of thanks. "Then you come join us."

Giving his hand a squeeze as she took the key from him, Amelia looked at Carole. "You're not upset with him, are you?" she asked, obviously referring to Donnelly.

"I don't know," Carole said, remembering how many times she had told him to hold on to his temper until after the election. An hour after the polls closed wasn't what she had meant.

Amelia smiled gently and touched her daughter's cheek. "Don't be."

With his arm around her, King guided Carole through the crowd to the elevators and up to the private suite they had taken for the long night. Once there, he handed her a small glass of white wine. "Drink this," he said with a tender smile that curved crookedly up one side of his face. "I doubt that you got much sleep last night. Why don't you go lie down? I'll wake you when Donnelly gets back."

Giving him back the empty glass, Carole nodded, then went into the bedroom. Its only light, a small lamp on the dresser, gave off a weak, pink glow. Stretching out on the bed, she barely had time to close her eyes before she was asleep.

Slowly, like a dream, she became aware of the fragrance of Donnelly's cologne and the soft brush of his lips on her cheek. Opening her eyes enough to know that he was real, she touched the hand that gently caressed her shoulder. "I can't believe you did that," she accused in a sleepy, sulky voice as she remembered the images that had faded in and out while she slept.

"Mad at me?" Donnelly asked, turning his hand to catch hers in his grip.

"How did you get in to see him?" Carole asked, coming awake, and a smile began to tug at the corners of her mouth.

"I'm an important man." He kissed the back of her hand. "We're running neck and neck in the returns. Tomorrow I may be the governor elect. Everyone was very cooperative. Even Andrew."

Carole drew her mouth down into a straight, serious line. "Did you really hit him?"

Donnelly grinned. "Twice. He's got a little cut on his lip that probably won't show, but by tomorrow he's going to have a beauty of a shiner."

"That was a very immature act," she said sternly.

"I know. Aren't you going to thank me?"

"Did Andrew hit you?"

Donnelly shook his head. "He's not very good at tha
kind of thing. After I flattened him, I almost felt guilty
but that only lasted a minute and then I was incredibl
happy. Aren't you going to thank me?"

"Have you talked to the press yet?"

"I told them it was a personal matter and that An
drew and I parted in perfect understanding." An edg
of seriousness crept into Donnelly's good humor. "H
understands perfectly that this is nothing compared t
what I will do if he ever, to my knowledge, even think
about you again."

Carole smiled softly and wrapped her hands aroun
the back of Donnelly's neck, pulling his face closer t
hers. "Thank you."

"You're welcome." Covering her lips with his, h
thought of the coming night and all the nights tha
would follow. The wait was over.

A quiet knock at the door reminded them that the
were not alone, and reluctantly they released the kis
that had only begun.

"Yes?" Donnelly called.

King opened the door and leaned in. "The guest yo
requested has arrived, and everybody else has bee
rounded up."

"Thank you." King withdrew and closed the doo
behind him as Donnelly dismissed him and turned bac
to Carole. "I have something to tell you. To ask you
actually."

Carole frowned, sensing the hesitant tension that wa
building in Donnelly. "What?"

"It's late. Almost eleven. And Andrew and I are still running within a percentage point or two of each other. We're swapping the lead every fifteen minutes. Your father thinks—and for once I agree with him—that we won't know anything until morning, when all the votes are in and counted."

"Yes?" Carole said, knowing that he still hadn't said what he intended to say.

"Right now. Tonight. Before we know." He took a deep breath and pushed the words out as he exhaled. "I want you to marry me. Now. When we get the word in the morning, I want it to be as man and wife." He grinned, and stroked her cheek with his fingertip. "God, that sounds nice. Man and wife. Oh, Carole." He caught her face between his hands and covered her lips with small, light kisses that grew deeper and longer as his hands slid beneath her and pulled her against him. "We'll wait if you want to," he whispered between kisses, "but I'm so tired of waiting."

"But how?" she asked. "It's so late, and I—" She broke off, stroking her fingers across the simple, cream-colored satin dress Donnelly had helped her choose for the election-night celebrations.

For the first time, she noticed that he had changed into a pearl-gray suit that was elegant and understated. Slowly it dawned on her that this was not the impulsive decision Donnelly would have her believe.

"But I'm all wrinkled," she protested weakly as he began to smile.

"It's just our parents, and Sloan, Cody and Liann. No one else will see you but the minister, and he's the same one who married my parents." Donnelly play-fully nudged the end of her nose with the tip of his finger. "And I don't think he can see too well anymore. So, who's going to care?"

A reluctant grin began to struggle with her stern expression. "How long have you been planning this?"

"Since that Sunday I came back to your house after Sloan left."

Carole gave in to the smile, realizing, as she felt the happiness and contentment grow stronger inside her that she liked the idea. She'd already had one huge wedding, with all the extras, and a marriage that was a miserable disaster. Donnelly, she knew, was a man who was more concerned with substance than with ceremony. With him, the exchange of vows would be simple and sincere, and the years after would be filled with all the extras love could provide.

"You reminded me of a kitten who'd been stepped on one too many times," he said in a voice that was misty with remembrance. He scooped her into his arms and tenderly lifted her against his chest. "There was a part of you that was warm and sweet, and desperately wanted to be loved. And another part of you hid the fear and hurt behind sharp claws and angry hisses when anyone came too near." His breath fanned her hair as he spoke. "I was so afraid I'd never get past the defenses you kept throwing up, that I'd lose you forever."

Carole slid her hand under his jacket and spread her palm flat over the hard muscles of his chest. Beneath her hand she felt the strong beat of his heart. "Why didn't you give up on me?" The heat of her breath curled against his neck and came back to her. "I was scared you'd lose patience and just stop trying."

Donnelly laughed softly. "I might have if I hadn't known your parents and found out that Sloan was your rother. After that, I decided that you were just as well-intentioned, independent and bullheaded as the rest of hem, and that if I just hung in there, you'd come round eventually."

"I wouldn't describe it quite that way," Carole said. `aking her hand out of his jacket, she sat straighter and rowned into his laughing turquoise eyes. "Before you et so romantic that I change my mind, maybe we'd etter get this over with."

Donnelly stood and pulled her up beside him, holding her tightly in his arms. "Smile for me," he whispered. "I won't marry someone who's pouting."

Carole tried to fight the smile that began to quiver on er lips. Looking at him through downcast lashes, she aid, "I'm not pouting."

He hooked his index finger under her chin and tilted er face upward. "Carole, are you ready to marry me?"

In his eyes, desire and uncertainty begged for an anwer, and the love that grew stronger inside Carole every ay blossomed a little larger. "Yes."

Sometime during the night the rain had begun. As the ight of dawn bled weakly across the horizon, the lownpour had faded to a drizzle. Standing at the floor-o-ceiling window of the hotel bedroom, Carole stared ut at the early morning traffic. Headlights reflected on he black sheen of the streets below.

"Restless?"

At the sound of Donnelly's voice, she turned and saw im outlined against the pale sheets. His expression was ost in the shadows of the room.

"A little, I guess," Carole answered, letting the sheer rapery fall closed. "I almost wish we didn't have to ind out. I wish we could have a little more time to ourselves. To honeymoon, to get to know each other, maybe even quarrel without worrying about a whole state finding out.''

''I may not win,'' Donnelly said softly. ''And even if I do, it'll be months before I take office.''

He threw back the covers and swung his legs over the side of the bed. The thick carpet silenced the weight of his footsteps as he crossed the room to where Carole stood by the window. He slipped his arm around her waist and pulled her to him, and through the thin cotton of her robe Carole felt the warmth of his bare chest against her back.

''Are you sorry?'' he asked as he laid his cheek against her hair. ''Did I rush you too much?''

Carole arched her neck backward to rest her head on his shoulder and she covered his hands with hers. As he dipped his head to take the kiss she invited, she whispered, ''No.''

His mouth pressed gently against hers, and the memories his touch aroused turned Carole soft and weak inside. They had had so little time together, and it made each night a time of special and incomparable meaning. Each touch was something new and unexplored; each kiss, a gift to be savored and unwrapped with slow and loving attention.

Gently Donnelly turned Carole in his arms until she faced him. His hands loosened the belt that held her robe together, while his lips covered hers with a deepening intensity. The tip of his tongue circled hers, then darted into the interior with short, quick strokes and withdrew again. His hands slid beneath the robe and guided it away from her shoulders until her bare body was pressed, hot and yielding, against his.

Carole's heart pounded wildly inside her, and she leaned against the strength of his arms. Outside their room, the city was coming to life, and soon the world would again intrude on the time their love was allowed. But for now, Donnelly was hers alone in the remaining minutes that were no longer night and not yet day.

When the phone rang, Carole felt Donnelly's heart leap. His arms tightened around her as he stiffened and held his breath through the second ring.

"Answer it, Donnelly," Carole urged through the painful grip of his arms. His hesitance told her more clearly than any words could have how much he wanted to be governor and how deeply the wound would go if he had lost.

The phone rang on as he slowly released the arms that seemed to be frozen around her. He took a step toward the phone, then stopped. "I never asked you if you could be happy as the governor's wife," he said quietly. "This is a hell of a time to get around to it."

"As long as the governor is you," Carole said. "Now answer the phone."

In two long strides he was across the room and had the phone off its cradle. "Yes," he growled, twisting his body to face the telephone and the wall behind it.

After the first word, Carole could hear nothing but vague mumbles. A few sentences into the conversation, Donnelly grew silent, listening. Then he folded his long-limbed body into a sitting position on the side of the bed and hung up the phone.

Carole picked up her robe from the floor and slipped her arms into it. "Who was it?" she asked finally.

"Your father." Donnelly lifted his head and watched her walk toward the bed.

"And?" she prompted, then grew silent while she waited for an answer. In the half light she thought she saw him smile.

"He just read me Andrew's telegram of concession. It's all over."

Lost between the dread of winning and the equal dread of losing, Carole remained motionless. In a few short months they would walk into the governor's mansion hand in hand, and for four years it would be their home. It was more than just a job, and it would change both of their lives forever. She would need all the strength and love Donnelly had to give her, and she knew he would need the same from her.

"It won't be easy, Carole, for either of us." Donnelly held out his hand, and Carole moved slowly forward to take it. He spread his legs and guided her inside the opening to sit on his thigh. With one arm around her waist, he touched her chin with his fingertip and smiled. "But I can guarantee you, it'll never be dull, either."

The morning sounds outside seemed far away. In the purplish darkness of the room, Donnelly's intimate nearness made everything else seem unimportant. "What do we do now?" she asked, hoping that her father would continue to guard their privacy for a little longer.

Donnelly's hand stroked her arm, while the hand that held her waist pulled her closer, reminding them both of the bare flesh on flesh where her thighs made contact with his. "We have a press conference at ten this morning. Until then..." His hand again slid the short robe away from her shoulders and a lazy smile spread across his face. "I suggest we return to the activities that were..." The robe fell to the floor, and Donnelly's lips covered hers in a series of soft, short pecks. "... interrupted by your father's phone call."

He lifted her in his arms, turned and laid her on the bed, then he stretched out beside her. He kissed the satiny skin of her shoulder, wound his fingers through her loose curls and whispered against the fragrant warmth of her neck, "Are you happy?"

Carole touched his cheek with her fingertips, tracing the curve of his face from his brow to his jaw, and smiled with a contentment she felt only with Donnelly. "More than I've ever been in my life. More than I ever dreamed I could be."

Outside, the weak flame of dawn faded. Thunder rumbled, and rain tapped softly against the windowpanes. Donnelly's arms gathered her to him with a protective impatience, and as the fires inside her began to flare, Carole felt the sweet languor of time settle over her.

Today, tomorrow and through the tomorrows yet to come, she would cherish him and stand by him, just as he had cherished her through all the days that lay behind them.

"Thank you," she whispered, kissing the soft wave that lay across his forehead.

"For what?"

How could she say it? Carole wondered. For loving her? For not giving up, and for not letting her give up? For making her learn to live again?

"For being you," she said finally.

The Silhouette Cameo Tote Bag Now available for just $6.99

Handsomely designed in blue and bright pink, its stylish good looks make the Cameo Tote Bag an attractive accessory. The Cameo Tote Bag is big and roomy (13″ square), with reinforced handles and a snap-shut top. You can buy the Cameo Tote Bag for $6.99, plus $1.50 for postage and handling.

Send your name and address with check or money order for $6.99 (plus $1.50 postage and handling), a total of $8.49 to:

Silhouette Books
120 Brighton Road
P.O. Box 5084
Clifton, NJ 07015-5084
ATTN: Tote Bag

The Silhouette Cameo Tote Bag can be purchased pre-paid only. No charges will be accepted. Please allow 4 to 6 weeks for delivery.

N.Y. State Residents Please Add Sales Tax

Offer not available in Canada.

COMING NEXT MONTH

SOMETHING ABOUT SUMMER—Linda Shaw
State Prosecutor Summer MacLean didn't know what to do when she
found herself handcuffed to a suspect determined to prove he was
innocent . . . and who happened to look like her late husband.

EQUAL SHARES—Sondra Stanford
When Shannon Edwards inherited fifty-one percent of a troubled
business, she went to check it out. She expected a problem, but not the
sexiest man alive . . . her partner.

ALMOST FOREVER—Linda Howard
Max Conroy was buying out the company where Claire worked, and used
her to get the vital information. What he didn't figure on was falling in
love.

MATCHED PAIR—Carole Halston
The handsome gambler and the glamorous sophisticate met across the
blackjack table, and it was passion at first sight. Neither realized they were
living a fantasy that could keep them apart.

SILVER THAW—Natalie Bishop
Mallory owned prize Christmas trees, but had no one to market them. The
only man willing to help her was the man who had once sworn he
loved her.

EMERALD LOVE, SAPPHIRE DREAMS—Monica Barrie
Pres Wyman had been the school nerd. But when Megan Teal hired him to
help her salvage a sunken galleon, she found the erstwhile nerd had
become a living Adonis.

AVAILABLE THIS MONTH:

MISTY MORNINGS, MAGIC NIGHTS
Ada Steward

SWEET PROMISE
Ginna Gray

SUMMER'S STORM
Patti Beckman

WHITE LACE AND PROMISES
Debbie Macomber

SULLIVAN vs. SULLIVAN
Jillian Blake

RAGGED RAINBOWS
Linda Lael Miller

FOUR UNIQUE SERIES
FOR EVERY WOMAN YOU ARE . . .

Silhouette Romance

Heartwarming romances that will make you laugh and cry as they bring you all the wonder and magic of falling in love.

6 titles per month

Silhouette Special Edition

Expanded romances written with emotion and heightened romantic tension to ensure powerful stories. A rare blend of passion and dramatic realism.

6 titles per month

Silhouette Desire

Believable, sensuous, compelling—and above all, romantic—these stories deliver the promise of love, the guarantee of satisfaction.

6 titles per month

Silhouette Intimate Moments

Love stories that entice; longer, more sensuous romances filled with adventure, suspense, glamour and melodrama.

4 titles per month

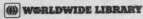